BLACK ROD

BLACK ROD

Bertie Denham

BELLEW PUBLISHING
LONDON

This edition first published in Great Britain 1997

Bellew Publishing Company Limited
8 Balham Hill, London SW 12 9EA

Copyright © Bertie Denham

ISBN 185725 115 6

Typeset by Antony Gray
Printed and bound in Great Britain by
Hartnolls Ltd, Bodmin, Cornwall

TO

General Sir Edward Jones, KCB, CBE
1995–
Admiral Sir Richard Thomas, KCB, KCVO, OBE
1992–95
Air Chief Marshal Sir John Gingell, GBE, KCB, KCVO
1985–92
Lt-General Sir David House, GCB, KCVO, CBE, MC
1978–85

AND TO THE MEMORY OF

Admiral Sir Frank Twiss, KCB, KCVO, DSC
1970–78
Air Vice Marshal Sir George Mills, GCB, DFC
1963–70
General Sir Brian Horrocks, KCB, KBE, DSO, MC
1949–63

Gentlemen Ushers of the Black Rod,
none of whom bear any resemblance to any
Black Rod mentioned in this book.

The author would like to thank the following for their very kind help and specialist advice in relation to the writing of this book, whilst at the same time absolving them from the slightest responsibility for any inaccuracies that may have resulted from his own misapplication of the facts that they have supplied.

Sir Crispin Agnew of Lochnaw, Bart, QC, *Rothesay Herald of Arms*

Richard Bird Esq., *the Cabinet Office Secretariat*

Sir Clifford Boulton, GCB, *former Clerk of the House of Commons*

Dr Patrick Barden, BVSC, PhD, *Heraldic Flag Painter*

David Butler Esq., CBE, *Nuffield College, Oxford*

Alastair Campbell of Airds, *Unicorn Puirsuivant*

Jim Corbett Esq.

Patience Corbett

Captain J. B. Coutts,
a former president of the Highland Cattle Society

The Right Hon. the Duke of Devonshire, KG, MC

The Rt Hon. the Earl Ferrers

Air Chief Marshal Sir John Gingell, GBE, KCB, KCVO

The Lord Glenarthur

The Earl of Halsbury, FRS

Christian, Lady Hesketh

The Lord Kimball

Dr Sarah-Jane Kitching

The Lord King of Wartaby

The Earl Lloyd George of Dwyfor

The Lord Lucas of Chilworth
David Marx Esq., *John Rigby & Co.*
J. S. McCall Esq.
The Rt Hon. the Lord Mackay of Clashfern, *Lord Chancellor*
Murdo Maclean Esq.
The Lady Maclean
Angus Nicol Esq.
The Duke of Norfolk, KG, GCVO, CB, CBE, MC, *Earl Marshal*
Sir Martin Reid, KBE, CMG
Mrs Maureen Robb
The Lady Saltoun of Abernethy
Douglas Slater Esq.
The Viscount Slim, OBE
The Lord Strathcona and Mount Royal
N. O. Taube Esq.
Walter Wallace Esq., CVO, CBE, DSC
Sir Michael Wheeler-Booth, KCB, *Clerk of the Parliaments*
The Lord Williams of Elvel, CBE
Richard Wilkin Esq., CVO, MBE
Bob Worcester Esq. of Mori
Dr Ron Zeegan, OBE

PRINCIPAL CHARACTERS

Derek, 3rd Viscount Thyrde, *Deputy Chief Whip, House of Lords*

Thomas, Earl of Lavenham, *Chief Whip, House of Lords*

Air Chief Marshal Sir Alastair MacRodrick, *Gentleman Usher of the Black Rod*

Roger Truefitt, *Head of the West Indian and Atlantic Department FCO*

The Rt Hon. Geoffrey Robertson, MP, *former Labour Solicitor-General for Scotland*

Geordie Maclean, *a Scottish farmer*

Rodrick MacRodrick of MacRodrick, *Chief of the Clan MacRodrick*

Dougal MacRodrick, *Rodrick's head stalker*

Malcolm MacRodrick, *Rodrick's younger brother and heir presumptive*

Roddy and Rannie MacRodrick, *Malcolm's sons*

The Rt. Hon. Charles Fortescue MP, *Prime Minister*

The Rt Hon. Albert Wainwright MP, *Leader of Her Majesty's Opposition*

The Rt. Hon. Percival Strickland MP, *Foreign and Commonwealth Secretary*

Jack Singleton MP, *Parliamentary Under Secretary of State, FCO*

The Hon. Julian Mallicent, *Derek's son*

The Rt Hon. (Tony) the Lord Dysart, *Lord President of the Council*

The Honourable Zechariah Hall, *first minister of Larna*

Dr Septimus Baker, *leader of the Larnacan opposition*

John J. MacRodrick JUNIOR, *president of the American Clan Society*

The Rt Hon. Henry Chanter MP, *Government Chief Whip, Commons*

Gwilym Thomas, *Private Secretary to the Leader and Chief Whip, House of Lords*

John Antrobus, *Clerk to Private Bills, House of Lords*

Simon Shaw, *a stockbroker*

Tug Wilson MP, *a Labour back-bench member*

Lieutenant George Richards, USAF, *air attaché to the US Embassy*

Catriona Campbell

Dougalina MacRodrick, *Rodrick's housekeeper*

The Dowager Viscountess Thyrde, *Derek's mother*

Sally Nichols, *Julian's nanny*

Penny Seymour, *a government whip's secretary*

Monique Fourier, *a nightclub hostess*

Amanda, *a whippet*

Seamus Ruadh the tenth of Kilpatrick, *a Highland bull*

Bridget, *a show smooth collie*

THE FAMILY

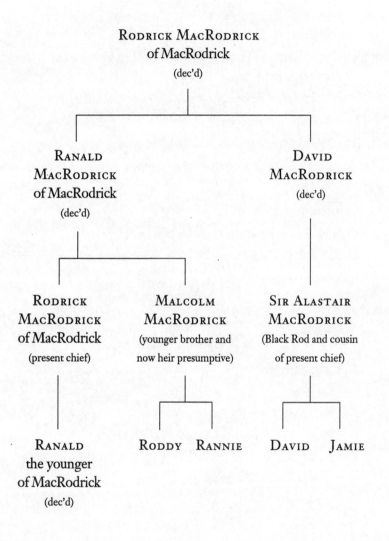

RODRICK MACRODRICK
of MacRodrick
(dec'd)

RANALD
MACRODRICK
of MacRodrick
(dec'd)

DAVID
MACRODRICK
(dec'd)

RODRICK
MACRODRICK
of MacRodrick
(present chief)

MALCOLM
MACRODRICK
(younger brother and
now heir presumptive)

SIR ALASTAIR
MACRODRICK
(Black Rod and cousin
of present chief)

RANALD
the younger
of MacRodrick
(dec'd)

RODDY   RANNIE

DAVID   JAMIE

EXTRACTS FROM THE *DAILY TELEGRAPH*

Tuesday, 6 October

**Viscount Thyrde and
Miss J. Elton**
The engagement is announced
between Derek, son of the late
Viscount Thyrde and
Viscountess Thyrde, of Shipton,
Northamptonshire, and Julia,
only daughter of Sir John Elton,
Bart, and the late Lady Elton, of
Burston Manor, Gloucestershire.

Wednesday, 9 December

THYRDE – ELTON – On
Tuesday, December 8, at
St Margaret's Westminster,
Derek, son of the late Viscount
Thyrde and Viscountess
Thyrde, to Julia, only daughter
of Sir John and the late Lady
Elton, of Burston Manor,
Gloucestershire.

Tuesday, 21 September

THYRDE.—On Sunday, September 19,
at Queen Charlotte's, to JULIA, wife of
DEREK, Viscount Thyrde, a son.

Thursday, 30 September

THYRDE.—On Wednesday, September
29, suddenly at Thyrde,
Northamptonshire, JULIA, beloved
wife of Derek.

CHAPTER ONE

I wondered whether I ought to have added 'and beloved mother of Julian'. But then I thought probably not. At ten days old, the poor little beast hadn't had much time to belove anyone.

And, in any case, my decision to call him that had barely been arrived at. Julia and I had always meant to christen him 'Derek', so that he could be 'Derry' after my father. But, in the circumstances, 'Julian' had seemed to be the only name.

She had seemed so well, so happy, when I had left London on the day that it happened. The telephone call had come at around lunchtime. *Post-partum haemorrhage*, sudden severe blood-loss, followed by collapse – and death two hours later – they were terribly sorry but there had been nothing anyone could do.

And so I had become a widower, for the second time and still in my mid-forties, this time it is true with a son and heir to show for it. My immediate superiors had wanted me to go away for a while, take a holiday. But I couldn't think of anywhere I wanted to go, anything I wanted to do.

These were the thoughts that were with me as I was walking down one of the corridors of the House of Lords, some two weeks later, but the red leather upholstery and red carpets of the southern end of the Palace of Westminster, hushed and dimly lit, have a curiously comforting effect about them – almost one of analgesia. Portraits on the walls of peers long gone, but whose names and sometimes even faces and characteristics, live on in the House of the present, give a sense of continuity and permanence, something to cling to. And I think that it must have been this that had decided me instinctively to carry on working, in an environment possessing the quality of at least numbing slightly the grief and troubles of the world outside.

'Ah, Derek, just the man I was looking for.'

I looked up to see Tom Lavenham coming towards me. Chief Whip of the House of Lords, slim, grey haired, commanding, he was the statesman earl to every inch of his six foot three.

I had been his deputy for something over a year.

'Hello, Tom,' I said.

He put a hand on my shoulder.

'Look, if we asked you to leave home for a while, how soon do you think you could manage to get away?'

I shook my head. 'I've already told you, I'd rather stay on.' A sudden thought struck me. 'Unless, of course, it would make it easier for the rest of you?'

'No, it's nothing like that, I promise you. We really have got a job in mind for you.'

'Well, in that case . . .' I thought for a moment, the funeral over, everything fixed up pretty well for Julian down in Northamptonshire, ' . . . almost immediately, I suppose.'

'Good. Well, it's like this, a rather difficult problem has arisen over . . .'

Tom Lavenham stopped abruptly and we both turned. I could have sworn that I hadn't heard a sound, but at exactly the same moment we had each become aware of the presence of a third party. The compact, rather sinister, figure of Black Rod, in archaic tail-coat, knee breeches and silk stockings, all black, with a sword in a black scabbard and silver-buckled black shoes, was padding silently by.

'Better go to my room, I think.' He took my arm and we walked off down the corridor together. And then he added, 'I hate that man.'

'Why do you hate that man?'

'Oh, I don't know, he gives me the willies. Always creeping up on one,' Tom said.

A few months before, Air Chief Marshal Sir Alastair MacRodrick, GCB, CBE, AFC, had been appointed to the office of Gentleman Usher of the Black Rod, to give him his proper style and title – an office he was only the third Scotsman to hold throughout the six centuries of its existence. Not many of their lordships, even among those who had served in the Air Force with him, admitted to knowing him well. Soon after his arrival, there had been a light-hearted attempt to invest him with the nickname, 'Black Rod-*rick*', but, as soon as it became apparent that he was not only not amused but also genuinely upset by it, it had been tacitly dropped.

He was austere of face and distant of manner, but the aspect that caused most concern was the highly disconcerting way in which he seemed to materialise almost out of nowhere whenever two or more people chanced to get into conversation in a corridor – as Tom and I had just experienced to our cost.

'So, what is this job you've got for me?'

Tom had poured out a drink for each of us. We were in his room on the West-Front Corridor, settled in two armchairs on either side of the window which looked out on to Old Palace Yard. It was a cold, wet, murky late morning outside.

'Well, you know we've got the Independence of Larna Bill coming up next session. Pretty soon, in fact. It's due to have its first reading in the Commons immediately after the opening of Parliament in a fortnight's time.'

'Vaguely,' I said. 'I'm never quite sure where Larna is.'

'In the West Indies, south of Jamaica. Well, a fairly major snag has just arisen. Everybody's always assumed that the ruling party would romp home in the elections after independence and now it seems there's quite a chance the other fellows'll get in.'

'And that wouldn't suit us?'

'Hardly. They'd almost certainly take Larna out of the Commonwealth. The key to the whole thing, apparently, is the foremost landowner on the island, whose family has always had tremendous influence out there, and he's the one man who just could sway the result.'

'He being?'

'A Scotsman, Chief of the Clan MacRodrick. Rodrick MacRodrick of MacRodrick, to give him his full style and title. You don't know him, do you?'

'No, I'm afraid not. Any relation to our MacRodrick?'

'Yes, Black Rod's his first cousin – that's why I didn't want to say too much out there. Well, The MacRodrick has always been sound enough, but he's getting on a bit and far from well. In fact, he's not expected to live another twelve months and it could be even less. He had a son, Ranald, who was equally reliable, but Ranald MacRodrick was killed in a motor-smash out in Larna three or four months ago, under slightly suspicious circumstances. The trouble is that the next heir to the clan chiefship is The MacRodrick's younger brother, Malcolm MacRodrick – you know, the Labour MP for one of those Glasgow constituencies.'

'And Malcolm's a baddie?'

Tom nodded.

'He favours the opposition faction, quite open about it, in fact. So much so that, since the son's death, our people have been trying to persuade The MacRodrick to leave his island possessions away from the chiefship but, even though he must want the best for Larna, he won't hear of it. Flatly refuses even to discuss the matter again. That's where you come in.'

'Me? What on earth can I do?'

'Well, since the doors are firmly closed to any further official contact, it's just possible that a totally informal one might work. We want you to scrape up an acquaintance with him, get as close to him as you can, see if you can find out why he's so adamant and, if you should get any sort of opening, give him a bit of a nudge in the right direction.'

'You're not asking much, are you? But why me?'

'Two reasons, Derek. You must admit that you've had a considerable degree of success over problems not so very dissimilar to this one, on more than one occasion. But, perhaps even more important, you're the only member of the government who has the best of all possible reasons for taking a certain amount of time off politics, just at the moment, and who really could be seen to be acting totally unofficially.'

He paused for a moment.

'And you might just find that having a problem like this to solve will help to take your mind off things. Will you do it? Incidentally, this is a personal request from the Prime Minister.'

I got up and looked out of the window at the rain-sodden waste of Old Palace Yard, the water dripping miserably from the statue of Richard Coeur de Lion, mounted and armed, with sword drawn and flourished defiantly, away to the right. What had I got to lose? I turned back to Tom.

'All right,' I said.

'Good. Take just as long as you need but obviously the sooner you can come up with anything the better. I've already fixed for you to have a full briefing at the FCO this afternoon, er . . . just on the offchance that you might have been prepared to accept, of course.'

'Thanks. I suppose I'd better be getting some sort of tropical kit together. What sort of climate are they likely to be having out there?'

Tom Lavenham grinned.

'It's warm winter woollies you'll be needing, young Derek. The MacRodrick's in Scotland. You'll find him up there on the other Larna – his island off the west coast of Argyll.'

* * *

'Just how much do you know about the West Indies?' said Roger Truefitt.

The Head of the West Indian and Atlantic Department of the Foreign and Commonwealth Office, WIAD to friends, was a cheerful, instantly likeable man, a year or two younger than me, with a mop of red hair that he constantly tried to smooth into place. Counsellor by rank, he was totally wrapped up in his job and seemed only too delighted to be given the opportunity to talk about it.

'Not very much. Can we assume "nothing" – and start from there?' I said.

Roger grinned.

'Well, imagine the Caribbean Sea to be in the shape of a very irregular rectangle or possibly oval, the base of which is formed by the north coast of South America and the left-hand side by central America. The top and the right-hand sides are made up by the West Indian Islands themselves. Here, I'll show you.'

We were sitting in the Map Room, one wall of which was lined from end to end with a nest of what looked like broad wooden drawers. Roger Truefitt got to his feet and walked over to them, picking up one of those poles with a hook on the end, of the sort that one uses for opening out-of-reach skylights, on the way. He engaged the business end of the pole in a brass ring on one of the drawers and pulled it outwards and downwards so that the single map that it had contained hung suspended against the fronts of the drawers below it in the nest.

'The larger islands are known as the Greater Antilles and run approximately west to east, Cuba on the left and that middle one . . . ' he used his pole as a pointer, ' . . . is divided into Haiti and the Dominican Republic, with Puerto Rico on the right. Then, the smaller islands, the Lesser Antilles, curve round and southwards until, with Trinidad and Tobago at the bottom, they almost meet the highest north-eastern point of South America. There are two more Greater Antilles islands which could be described as floating free in the northern part of the oval – Jamaica there, some hundred miles south of Cuba, and Larna here, sixty miles below that.'

He came back to the table where I was still sitting and resumed his seat next to mine.

'So, as much as anything could be said to do so, Larna lies in the very centre of the Caribbean Sea. Clear so far?'

'Very much so.'

'All right, then. The dividing-line between the Greater and Lesser Antilles is an important one because, when Columbus discovered the West Indies in 1492, the inhabitants of the former were a simple and friendly people called the Arawaks whereas those of the latter were a far more warlike race whom the Spanish called the Caribs or cannibals, that being one of their less endearing characteristics. When it came to colonising, therefore, they decided to leave the islands of the Lesser Antilles strictly alone. So, by the beginning of the seventeenth century, Spain was in possession of all five islands of the Greater

Antilles: Cuba; Hispaniola, encompassing the present day Haiti and Dominican Republic; Puerto Rico; Sant' Jago, or Jamaica; and Santa Margaretta, now Larna; leaving the whole of the Lesser Antilles to the Caribs – the poor old Arawaks were virtually extinct by then – or anyone else who wanted them. It was then that the other European countries decided to play a more active part, and we, the British, with no little danger, managed to establish colonies in two islands of the Lesser Antilles, St Kitts and Barbados, in 1624.'

Roger paused and looked up at me anxiously, brushing a hand over the red tuffet of his hair as he did so.

'You will let me know if I'm boring you?'

'Far from it,' I said.

'Well, not long after the Civil War, Cromwell conceived the idea that some sort of foreign coup might improve his image at home. So he despatched Admiral Penn and General Venables from Dover, with a task force of two and a half thousand men, to attack the Spanish at Santo Domingo on the southern coast of Hispaniola with a view to establishing the first non-Spanish Colony in the Greater Antilles. The plan was to recruit another four thousand from the existing British West Indian colonies on the way – and that is where the MacRodricks come in.'

He paused again.

'How good is your history?'

'On a par with my geography,' I said.

'Ah, then we'll have to go back a year or two. In the early 1640s, the then chief's younger son Ranald MacRodrick, with a party of his fellow clansmen from their west-coast island, joined the King's Army in Scotland, under the generalship of Montrose. They served with him throughout his initial victories until, in 1646, after the disastrous battle of Philiphaugh, Montrose was ordered by King Charles the First to make peace and, although he himself had to leave the country, his followers, Ranald and his men among them, had been free to go home, in their case back to the original Larna. But in 1650, when Montrose had returned to Scotland, this time on behalf of the exiled King Charles the Second, the MacRodricks were among the few to rejoin him and, after his almost immediate defeat at Carbisdale where Montrose was taken and later hanged, Ranald and his small band of surviving clansmen managed to escape the country. They made their way to France, in the first instance, and their movements from there on are uncertain, but we do know that they fetched up in the Caribbean by the beginning of 1655.'

'In time to be recruited by Penn and Venables?' I said.

'Exactly, but in the event the attack on Santo Domingo turned out to be an utter fiasco. You can't blame the MacRodricks, of course, most of their fellow recruits were pretty rough and they were completely routed by the Spanish, only just managing to get back to their ships in time. But Penn and Venables were far too windy about the prospect of reporting total failure back to Cromwell, so they decided to sail on south to Jamaica where they found only token resistance – and took that instead.'

'So we acquired Jamaica almost by accident?'

'You could say so, Larna too come to that, because Larna was a direct consequence of it. The MacRodricks, like others of the conquering army, were given grants of land to settle on in Jamaica and they did pretty well there too. Five years later, they received news that the Restoration of King Charles the Second had come about and this meant that they were all free to return home to Scotland. But Ranald was a younger son, remember, so this didn't hold out many attractions to him and he applied instead for a warrant from the king to take and colonise the island of Santa Margaretta to the south. The receipt of the application coincided with the time when Montrose was having every kind of posthumous honour heaped upon him and MacRodrick, who had been his staunchest supporter, received his warrant without undue delay.

'And made good use of it?'

Roger nodded.

'On 3 December 1661, they took Santa Margaretta, cut off as it now was by Jamaica from the rest of the Spanish islands, without a shot being fired. The first thing Ranald did was to change its name to "Larna" and the whole thing was a success from the start. Up to then, the principal livelihood of the West Indies had been agriculture – cattle, cereals, a certain amount of tobacco – but the establishment of Larna coincided with the time that sugar became the only crop of any importance in the West Indies and this, involving two things, a large amount of capital expenditure from the top together with intensive labour from below, was ideally suited to the Scottish clan system. Back in the highlands and islands at that time, the chief owned all the clan lands, various parts of which could be *feued out* to his cadets who became leaseholders, paying for the privilege in kind, either with produce or service, but having in return almost total security of tenure; under them again came the *tacksmen* or tenants, who had only limited security, either for their own lifetime or more often for up to three generations; finally, there were the *cotters*, or paid labourers, who nominally had no security at all but whose welfare was, by tradition, the responsibility of those above. It was a system that was understood and accepted by everybody and the loyalty of each man was owed, not only to his superiors, in order of priority ascending right up as far as the chief of the clan, but also to the land itself.'

He looked round at me anxiously.

'Stop me if I'm telling you anything you know already.'

I shook my head.

'Well, some fifteen years later, Ranald MacRodrick had word that his father and elder brother were both dead, that he, Ranald, was now Chief of the Clan MacRodrick and that he should return to Scotland and consolidate himself in that position, immediately. And from that time on, the two Larnas became integrated in the minds of all MacRodricks as equal ranking parts of the clan territory – to the immense advantage of both. It soon became the custom for the eldest son of the chief to spend the majority of his young adulthood in the Caribbean island. There was two-way traffic both of people and ideas and, in years of hardship in one island or the other, cross subsidisation between the two Larnas. At the time of the Highland Clearances, for instance, the MacRodricks were able to operate their own voluntary scheme of emigration and thereby avoided the bitterness that still persists in other parts of Scotland to this day.'

'But how does slavery fit into all this?' I said.

'Ah yes, I was coming to that. In Larna as elsewhere, they soon found it impossible to work the sugar plantations without the use of negro slave labour but here too the advantages of the clan system prevailed. Though slaves in law, they were treated from the first as belonging to the wider clan family, with all the protection that that involved, cotters to begin with and later, some of them, even tacksmen. The actual abolition of slavery was hardly noticed there. And that is why the unrest and discontent prevalent in other Caribbean Islands largely passed Larna by. It became a Crown Colony in 1923 and, until eighteen months ago, seemed happy to remain so. They've always considered themselves fully paid-up members of the Clan MacRodrick – which, indeed, after just about three centuries of interbreeding, to all intents and purposes, they are.'

'So, what went wrong?'

He considered for a moment.

'A change of attitude's at the root of it, I suppose, a feeling that somehow Larna's got left behind in the worldwide move to independence. Another factor's probably the general weakening of clan loyalties back in Scotland itself and that seems to have transmitted itself to their Larna. But, most of all, there's been a slow but steady influx of dissidents from other parts of the Caribbean and these have gradually formed themselves into an opposition party, the People's Progressive Movement or PPM – up to a couple of years ago the Larnacans never bothered themselves with such a thing as a political party at all!'

Roger snorted.

'You can be sure of one thing,' he said, 'if the name of any party includes the word "people's" in it, the very last item in their order of priorities will be what the people actually want.'

'But they've still been gaining ground in Larna?'

'Far too much for my liking. Principally among the young, of course, not that there aren't some pretty good young members of the Larna National Party, too – that's what the people who, thank God, are still running the island now call themselves. Oddly enough, it was the People's Progressive Movement that started pressing for independence first.'

'Why oddly?'

'Usually it's the other way round, the governing party want independence and the opposition are against it. Anyway, the National Party felt that they couldn't be left behind and started asking for it too and, once that happened, we had no alternative but to go along with it. There was a referendum on independence first which, somewhat naturally in the circumstances, was passed overwhelmingly, followed by a constitutional conference in May. But, while the National Party want an independent monarchy within the Commonwealth, with our Queen as Queen of Larna, the PPM are going all out for becoming a republic outside it and these were the only two points that the conference couldn't agree on. They will be decided by a general election after the Independence Bill is passed.'

'What's in it for them – the People's Progressive Movement?'

'Power mainly, that would be an end in itself, as far as the actual politicians are concerned. But we think they've almost certainly got some form of outside backing too and, if that should be the case, the motives of whoever they may be could be far more complicated. The tourist trade and mineral resources, both of them grossly underdeveloped – those are the respectable ones – then there's drugs, of course, money-laundering, off-shore banking and for all of these the geographical position of Larna in relation to the rest of the Caribbean could be a major factor. And the hell of it is that there's an increasing possibility that the PPM might get in.'

'Do they have opinion polls in Larna?'

'Yes, since the constitutional conference in May. The PPM's own paper, the *Voice of the People*, has been commissioning them, but who's paying for them we can only guess. The referendum was on the fourth Thursday in April and the *Voice*, as they like to call it, has published the results every fourth Thursday since June.'

'How have they been going?'

'Let's see.' Roger took a sheet of paper out of his pocket. 'June the twenty-fourth, fifty-seven per cent to thirty-three, in the LNP's favour, of course, with ten per cent "don't knows" – they include the "won't tells" as well as the genuinely undecided. But since then the PPM's been creeping up steadily, July the twenty-second, fifty-three to thirty-six and eleven per cent "don't knows", August the twenty-sixth, fifty to thirty-six and fourteen per cent "don't knows", and the most recent, September the twenty-third, forty-seven to thirty-nine with still fourteen per cent "don't knows". That's a swing of eight per cent over three months and getting too damned close for comfort.'

'Eight per cent?'

'Yes, the swing's worked out by re-allocating the "don't knows", taking the difference and dividing by two. Effectively eight people in a hundred have moved from the LNP to the PPM and I don't like the rise in the "don't knows" over the period either. Our vote is soft, no doubt about it.'

'Ah! I'll take your word for it. And, if the PPM do get in, just how much of a disaster would that be?' I said.

'Well, this will be one of the last of our West Indian islands to get its independence – in the past we seem to have been only too eager to throw them away. And, of the whole lot, Larna has always been regarded as having the best chance of retaining and building on all that was good over three centuries of colonial rule. That is why we're all so desperately anxious that nothing should go wrong this time. And it could be worse than that, infinitely worse. Imagine an island the entire inhabitants of which have been brought up from childhood to revere this country, its traditions and its way of life, allowing itself to be sold off into what could be a totalitarian regime.'

'But . . . if they feel that way, why do they even consider supporting the People's Progressive Movement?'

'God knows. Electorates are like that, I suppose. We can only hope that they come to their senses before it's too late.'

Roger Truefitt stared in silence for a moment or two, gazing at the map of the West Indies, as though it might contain some hitherto concealed source of inspiration which, given time, it would be prepared to disgorge.

'If only The MacRodrick weren't dying,' he said. 'It's just not possible to overestimate the almost mystic loyalty in which the Larnacan holds the clan chief of the day, and always has done. Or if his son hadn't been killed . . . '

'Yes, I heard about that. He was a good chap, I'm told.'

'Young Ranald? The best. An heir to the clan chiefship was always called Rodrick in the old days, but they changed that – alternating it generation by generation with Ranald, in honour of the founder of Larna, and it's come down in direct line, father to eldest son, ever since. That's all gone now, more's the pity.'

'How did it happen?'

'Drove over a precipice on his way home one night. They said it was an accident, but . . . he loved fast cars, drove them superbly, never took risks and knew every inch of the roads on the island. There were no skidmarks and the car was burnt out when they found it.'

'Leaving Rodrick's younger brother, Malcolm as the next heir. What about him?'

'Well, he's made it all too clear that *he* supports the People's Progressive Movement.'

'But what's he like otherwise? What sort of chief would be make?'

Roger Truefitt shook his head and stood up.

'Hard to say, really. Time will tell.'

And it was clear from his whole demeanour that that particular subject was closed as far as he was concerned. 'Do you know Rodrick . . . the present chief?'

'I've never met him,' I said. 'But I hope to. I'm off to Scotland by the sleeper tonight.'

*   *   *

'The drearily wet day had evolved into an equally dreary foggy night and I found my sleeper, Berth One – Coach D, in the second half of the train, dumped a couple of suitcases on the bunk and made my name with the attendant, handing over my tickets and booking early-morning tea and a call for the morning, bearing in mind that I had to change not only trains but also stations at the other end. Then I walked along the corridor to the refreshment car. It was only the length of my own coach up the train.

There was one table untaken, but even that was littered with used glasses, empty vodka miniatures and half-empty tonic tins, all bearing witness to recent occupation. I sat down at one of the two chairs and ordered coffee and malt whisky. When they arrived, the waiter took the unappetising detritus away with him.

I looked around me and most of my fellow revellers seemed to consist of middle-aged men and pretty girls in approximately equal quantities; secretaries? mistresses? both, possibly; but there was one other single chap just across the compartment from me. I caught his eye and looked quickly away again in case he might read into a longer glance an invitation to join me. But the problem was solved almost immediately by a member of one of the larger parties coming over and asking if he might borrow my second chair.

The train started and gathered speed and I gazed aimlessly through the window at the progression of parallel orange lines of streetlights, mistily diffused against the blackness of the night beyond and superimposed at glass level with reflections of movement behind me; a scatter of people passing by my table; brisk pouring and passings over at the bar; one blue-shirted arm waving rhythmically in gesticulation. At the same time, the background of sound effects presented a not dissimilar medley; the dull rumble of the train, changing its tone each time it ran through a suburban station; the muted babble of voices in which individual snatches of conversation stood momentarily out from the rest until they were lost again – ' . . . *well, when it's going through Carlisle, there's this sharp bend and . . .* ' an insistent man's voice, '*Yes, honestlee . . .* ' a shrill female one, ' . . . *got to get it over and done with, I suppose, but . . .* ' indeterminate, that time; and the 'Hur, hur, hur,' of a brayingly repetitious laugh.

I turned to look at their silly cheerful faces and suddenly I felt incredibly lonely. What was I doing here, I thought, the one spectator looking in, as from the outside, on this little arena of artificial jollity, when only three weeks ago I would have been one of them – or, better still, one of two of them? After a few more minutes, I had had enough of it and I drank up and left.

Back outside the door of my sleeper, I stood in the corridor for a while and allowed the comparative peace of normal night railway noises to wash the tension away from me. I began to turn over in my mind the course of action that I would have to embark on in the morning. Somehow I had to stage-manage what would seem like a chance meeting with The MacRodrick or I would get exactly the same sort of rebuff that all the official approaches had received already. And how was I going to begin to do that – let alone develop the acquaintanceship quickly enough and to such a point that the sort of questions I would have to ask him would appear other than a total impertinence? Slowly the vaguest outline of at least a possible line of approach began to present itself.

Tom Lavenham had been right, I suddenly realised: having a problem such as this to solve really did tend to take things off one's mind.

The train slowed down and came to a halt at a station whose name seemed vaguely familiar as the only scheduled stop on the way. It can't have been more than a minute or two, though it seemed much longer; I heard from behind me the outside door into the next coach opening, sounds of suitcases being hurled in, their owner following. Not before time, because the train instantly moved off and had started to gather speed before I heard the door slam shut again.

At that point, suddenly and without any warning, all the lights went out.

The sliding door to my own coach opened and there was a sound of footsteps coming tentatively towards me.

'Is anyone there?' The voice was soft and feminine, with the just discernible lilt of a Scottish accent to it.

I strained through the almost total blackness to catch a glimpse of its owner, but I could see nothing.

'Yes, here,' I said.

'This wouldn't be Coach A by any chance?'

'I'm afraid not, this one's D. The refreshment car comes next and C, B and A should be beyond that. But British Rail don't always put them in the right order.'

'Hell!' There was a pause followed by a low chuckle, more of a gurgle really, throaty but definitely attractive. 'Sorry, but it's just my luck. What with this fog, I barely managed to catch the train.'

'I'd hang on here for a bit, if I were you. The lights can't be long coming on again.'

But the lights remained resolutely off as the train rumbled on. And on.

'Is your sleeper near here?'

'Yes,' I said, 'just behind where I'm standing.'

'Can we sit in it? You don't mind, do you?'

'Of course not. Let's have your cases, then.'

She passed them on to me and I led the way, holding the door of the sleeping compartment open for her behind me. Then she sat down on the bunk and I beside her.

'Ah, that's better. Well, since it seems we're to be marooned here together, what's you name?'

I told her. 'Derek Thyrde, as in first, second and . . . but not spelt like that. What's yours?'

'Catriona, with the accent on the second vowel; it's a name that only a Scot can pronounce really properly; Catriona Campbell,' she said.

I reached out instinctively and a cool dry hand found mine, the fingers slim, the grasp firm.

'Where do you live?'

'I've got a small house in London, but at Thyrde mainly. It's a village in Northamptonshire.'

'Same as your own name, that's smart. It means you're a lord, doesn't it?'

'Yes. My family name's "Mallicent" – Derek Mallicent, third Viscount Thyrde. You can just imagine how, all my time at school, I was never allowed to hear the end of *that*.'

'I'm from Larna,' she said.

'Really?' This was an unexpected bonus. I tried to make my voice sound casual. 'It's one of the places I'm hoping to visit in the next day or two.'

'No, Larna in the West Indies, I mean. It's the first time I've been in this country, actually. What do you do?'

'Er . . . ' explaining the job of a whip in the House of Lords is virtually impossible, 'in a manner of speaking, I'm a politician. And you?'

Again, that throaty gurgle, which somehow I found infinitely endearing. 'I'm a politician too. In a manner of speaking,' she said. 'Are you married?'

It was the sort of question that in the normal course of events I would have instinctively tried to skirt round with a stranger – to save embarrassment to her as much as to me; and shocked expressions of sympathy were the one thing that I dreaded above all others. But here, in the darkness, a straight answer seemed the most natural and easy thing to give.

'I have been. Twice. But not now,' I said.

'Would you like to talk about it?' The tone was gentle, undemanding. Almost without realising what I was doing, I found myself letting it all come out to her, to a girl I had only just met, a girl I had so far never even seen. I told her about Diana, my first wife, killed in the hunting-field several years before. I told her about Julia, how she had been first longstanding girlfriend, then wife, then mother of my child . . . and finally about *her* death.

'Poor old Derek.'

Her hand found my knee and gave it a friendly, sympathetic squeeze. I laid my own hand on it. At that moment, just as suddenly, and equally without warning, the lights came on again.

For a matter of seconds, the unaccustomed glare dazzled me, until my eyes adjusted themselves to it and I was able to focus on my companion.

Catriona Campbell was the most beautiful girl that I had ever seen in my life. She was also black.

CHAPTER TWO

'My now, Massa Derek, what was you 'specking. A nice white gel, p'rhaps?'

It wasn't her colour that I was staring at, it was the whole overwhelming impression she created. The coat and skirt of faded blue-jean material set off her glorious looks to perfection. She had dark silky hair, flawless skin the colour of dark honey fresh from the extractor, glinting grey eyes, high cheekbones, a tip-tilted little nose, a mouth of just the right tantalising fullness and a lithe, long-limbed, high-breasted body.

'Wow!' I said.

But Catriona was still bubbling over with delight at the wonder that I had not been able to prevent from showing on my face.

She put her hand on my sleeve.

'I really am half-Scottish, you know.' Then she looked at her watch. 'Goodness, is that the time? I must go and find my own sleeper.'

I stood up as she did.

'I'll bring your luggage along, then.'

'No, really.'

She put a hand on each of my shoulders and pressed me gently but firmly down on my sleeper again. Then she leant over and gave me a soft but all too brief kiss on the lips.

'See, you, Derek,' she said.

'Yes, but wait, I don't know where you're staying or anything. How can I . . .'

Catriona Campbell turned and gave me a ravishing smile from the doorway, shaking her head slowly from side to side as she did so.

And then she was gone.

Out of my sleeping compartment and, for all I knew, out of my life.

*   *   *

I was woken up by the attendant knocking on the door of my sleeping compartment.

'Finished with your tray yet, sir.'

The train was standing in Glasgow Central Station. I could see that the untouched tea-tray was already on the ledge over my bunk. Catriona . . .

'No. Yes, I mean. Take it away, please, I must have overslept,' I said.

I had meant to be up, dressed and along the corridor by the time we came into Glasgow Central, so that I could intercept her as she got off the train.

I threw on my clothes, seized hold of my suitcases and dashed out on to the platform and along to Coach A, at what was now the rear of the train.

No sign of the attendant, there. No one in any of the sleepers, as I peered in though the windows of each of them. There were one or two people in front of me, wheeling luggage trolleys in the direction of the ticket barrier, but none was Catriona.

There were three possibilities – she could be catching another train, she could be being met or taking a taxi to anywhere else in Glasgow, or outside it for that matter, or else she could be having breakfast somewhere on the station.

I thought quickly. If she were having breakfast there could still be a certain amount of time for me to find her. If she were catching a connection from this station, I could locate all the possible ones and have a look on them before they were likely to go. But, if she were taking a taxi, she would be waiting in a queue for one now, or even away already.

First the taxi queue, then. I left my cases to take their chance by themselves on the platform and sprinted all the way to the rank, dodging round people as I did so. No sign of her there. Then I walked slowly back towards the indicator of train departures, recovering my breath and composure as I did so. Two trains were waiting, not very likely connections either of them for passengers recently arrived from London but I tried both of them – the platforms first and then the train. Nothing. Next I toured the various fast-food refreshment places. All blank. Finally, I went up in the lift to the station hotel. Had a very pretty black girl come up in the last half an hour or so? 'Fraid not, they said. They really seemed rather sorry about it. I went back to the platform my own train had arrived on and found my suitcases waiting safely for me.

It was the first good news of the day.

Off again to the taxi queue and, after a short wait, I took one to Queen Street Station where my own connection to Oban went from. There was one final hope and, although it was a strong one, I had left it until the last because, if it should prove to be the case, there would be absolutely no hurry. Catriona herself might be on her way to the Scottish Larna and she could well be taking the same train.

*   *   *

'She wasn't. Someone got on at the very last minute and, remembering her sudden appearance the night before, I hoped it might be her. As soon as I saw that it was a man, I lost interest. I was dimly aware of him coming along the middle of compartment towards me, mackintosh over arm, brown felt hat on head.

'Hello, Derek. I didn't expect to find you here.'

I glanced up and then immediately sprang to my feet.

'Geoffrey! Come and join me.'

Geoffrey Robertson, Solicitor-General for Scotland in the last Labour government, still an MP and an old friend of mine – he had even taken the trouble to come down to Thyrde for Julia's funeral – one of the people whom I was always delighted to see.

Mid- to late-sixties by appearance, short, thin, sparse grey hair, clean-shaven and bespectacled, he put hat, coat and briefcase on the rack and we both sat down.

'And what might be bringing you up to these parts?' he said.

'I'm taking a bit of time off. How well do you know Larna?'

'Well enough. I ought to, it's in my constituency.' He grinned. 'Unless you mean the one in the West Indies?'

'This one,' I said. 'I thought I'd have a look round some of the islands. But, I'm quite interested in both actually.'

'Ah, well I've never actually been to the Caribbean. But I'm a member of the Commons Select Committee on Foreign Affairs. As you can imagine, they've been discussing Larna *ad nauseam* lately.'

The girl with the refreshment trolley came up to our table and, while coffee was being poured out and paid for, I made an instant decision. There have been many times in the past when, as a whip, I have had to take members of the opposition into my confidence in a way that would have appalled my ministerial colleagues had they know about it. Here was a man who could be of quite exceptional help to me on several counts and one in whom I knew that I could trust absolutely.

'Look, Geoffrey,' I said. 'Can I tell you something that really must not, in any circumstances, go any further?'

His eyebrows rose slightly.

'Certainly. Privy Council terms, if you wish.'

'That'd be splendid . . . although I'm not a Privy Councillor,' I said.

Geoffrey smiled.

'Well, whips' terms, if you prefer it. I'm told that you fellows regard that as even more binding. But for that matter, I've never been a whip.'

He listened in silence as I gave him as full a version as I dared of the mission with which I'd been entrusted.

'Shame about young Ranald,' he said when I had finished, 'he was a first-class lad.'

'So, I've been hearing from everyone,' I said. 'But what about his uncle, Rodrick's younger brother. I tried to sound out my Foreign Office contact about Malcolm but, as soon as I did so, he clammed up completely.'

'Well he would, wouldn't he?'

'How do you mean?'

Geoffrey gave a short laugh.

'Be your age, Derek. There may well be a change of government in the near future and he could find himself working for a party in which Malcolm has a lot of influence – too much for my liking. You of all people know that civil servants must be politically neutral.'

'I see. What do you think about him, then?'

'Malcolm? The trouble is he's too darned plausible. He's managed to convince my party that the People's Progressive Movement represent the best future for the island.'

'But . . . just how sincere do you think he is about it?'

There was a pause for a moment.

Then, 'Let me put it this way. I can't see Malcolm MacRodrick losing out financially if the PPM get in.'

'But why can't The MacRodrick see that?' I said.

'What exactly is it that the government have asked him to do?'

'Well, leave the Caribbean property to someone else.'

'There's your answer, then. They've asked Rodrick to leave a large part of the clan territory away from the next chief of the clan. He wouldn't do that in a hundred years, it would go against the whole philosophy of the clan system. Now, if they'd tried to get him to bypass his younger brother for the actual chiefship and make sure that the succession went to some other member of the family, they might have got somewhere.'

'Is that possible?' I said.

'Oh, yes. It could miss out the direct heir and go straight on to the next generation. To a grandson, for instance.'

'Has Malcolm got a son?'

A mischievous gleam came into Geoffrey's eye.

'Aye, he has a son. Two of 'em, in fact.'

'And . . . what are they like?'

'The lovely Roddy and Rannie? Chips off the old block. Worthy sons of their father,' he said.

'Oh, my God.'

The train was now passing through heather and low hills, every burn tumbling in spate. There was weak sunlight coming in through the window by the table where we were sitting. But there was no heat in it and, from the lowering of the sky, there would be rain later.

'And who's next in line after them?' I said.

'There's a cousin of some sort, Alastair MacRodrick. Hasn't he just been made Gentleman Usher of the Black Rod in your House?'

'Yes,' I said. 'How about him, then?'

'Ah, I'd been hoping you'd be able to tell me that. A bit of a mystery man from all accounts. There's one consolation, though, he couldn't be worse than Malcolm or Roddy.' Geoffrey raised his eyebrows in exaggerated horror. 'Or Rannie. Especially Rannie!' he said.

'And you could bypass all three of them?'

'It's been done. There'd have to be some good reason, of course, and it would need the approval of Lord Lyon.'

'Lord Lyon?'

'The senior Scottish herald, the equivalent of Garter King at Arms in England. Yes, there's a possibility that something along those lines *could* be done in the present instance, though I've no doubt Malcolm would put up a fight. They say he's already been borrowing pretty heavily on his prospects of succession to the chiefship,' he said.

'Do you think it's too late for me to try the chiefship line with The MacRodrick now?'

'It's a different angle, at any rate. Incidentally, how do you plan to approach him? I could give you an introduction, of course, but a cup of tea or a drink would be all you'd be likely to get out of that.'

'I thought of writing and asking his permission to walk round the island for a day or two.'

Geoffrey shook his head.

'I doubt if that'd be much better. He's always been a bit of a recluse, has Rodrick, even more so since his son died and his wife soon after.'

'I didn't know about the wife,' I said.

'Yes, within a matter of weeks, I believe.' He paused. 'His main interest, apart from his two islands that is, has always been his fold of Highland cattle.

How are you on Highlanders yourself?'

'Well, I've always been fascinated by them,' I said. 'I've sometimes thought of getting some to keep down in my park at Thyrde.'

Geoffrey Robertson leant forward.

'Now we're really getting somewhere. The Highland Cattle Society hold their annual show and sale in Oban next Monday and Tuesday and Rodrick's bound to have some entered. If you were to buy a couple of his in-calf heifers there, not only would you be buying first-class beasts but it would also give you the best chance of getting to know him that you could possibly have,' he said.

* * *

The Oban Cattle Mart had managed to achieve for the occasion an atmosphere somewhere between that of agricultural markets the country over and the National Hunt Festival at Cheltenham. Wide-horned, shaggy-coated cattle, red predominantly but some a lot lighter, with the occasional black, dun or brindle amongst them, occupied six-barred pens in ones, twos, threes or fours in the large roofed area behind the actual auction room, champing hay contentedly. They turned their heads from time to time to survey passers-by with a slightly blasé lack of interest in their all-too-honest eyes.

As for the human element, felt hats or cloth caps, with headscarves for the women, oily green waterproof coats and gumboots seemed to be the regulation dress.

'Ah, there you are, Derek.'

Geoffrey Robertson detached himself from a group of farmers and came over to me.

'Look, how serious are you about starting your own fold of Highlanders?'

'Very,' I said.

The idea had been appealing to me more and more, since we had first talked about it in the Glasgow to Oban train.

'Reason I ask is a bit of a snag's come up – there's no heifers here from Larna, in-calf or otherwise. But The MacRodrick's got a bull entered – that's him, over there, with the yellow ticket on him. You'll need to buy some heifers to go with him of course and it'll cost you a lot more money doing it that way round. Not so much as it would have before the BSE scare, of course. And having a really good bull would get your fold off to the best possible start.'

'Not to mention the added effect on Rodrick.'

Geoffrey grinned.

'Aye, he really would be interested in you if he saw you buying his.'

We walked over and had a look at him, a magnificent animal of a rich red colour with a wide spread of perfectly matched horns and a back as straight as a ruler.

I began to have slight misgivings.

'Won't he be terribly expensive?' I said.

'Not necessarily, he only got third prize in the judging and it's the first two that'll attract the money. But Rodrick doesn't miss a thing where Highland cattle are concerned and, if you're going to get anywhere with him, he'll need to be convinced not only that you're serious about it but also that you know what you're doing – or at least that you've taken the trouble to get the right advice. Otherwise, as far as your main object is concerned, the whole exercise will be a waste of time.'

'I see that,' I said. 'How do I set about it?'

'Well, another snag is the bulls are last in the sale tomorrow so you'll have to buy the heifers first and take a chance on not being outbid when the Larna bull comes on. And it's heifers ready for the bull you'll now be needing. Look, I've got a catalogue for you,' he held it out to me, open; 'that'll be class two there. Now, you'll have to buy enough of them to justify having a bull of your own and they'll need to be of good enough quality for a Larna bull, or it will be small compliment to The MacRodrick personally, but not too good for a man starting out from the beginning. And you shouldn't pay too fancy a price for them – the bull neither, for that matter.' He smiled. 'Have you got all that, I think it'll do for a start?'

'Er . . . I think so,' I said. 'Can you advise me on all these points.'

Geoffrey shook his head.

'No, but I'll soon find someone who can.' He turned towards the group of farmers that he'd been with on my arrival. 'Geordie,' he called, 'can you spare a moment?'

One of their number, a broad-shouldered man of about my own age with very fair hair and a cheerful weatherbeaten face walked over towards us.

'Geordie Maclean,' Geoffrey murmured to me, 'reckoned to be one of the best judges of a beast in these parts.'

He introduced us and we shook hands.

'Lord Thyrde's come up here to buy cattle,' he said. 'He doesn't know a lot about Highlanders yet. Can you help him?'

Geordie's face lit up with obvious pleasure.

'I'll be glad to,' he said.

'It's heifers he wants advice over. He's a fancy to buy the Larna bull.'

'Aye, it's a good enough beast. The MacRodrick'll not be best pleased with the placing, I'm thinking, but then it's Colonel Fairfax's farm-manager is this year's judge and the laird and the colonel never did get on.' He turned to me. 'Can you give me an idea as to what you have in mind, then?'

I explained about my plans to start a small fold where I lived in Northamptonshire and that I wanted his advice about the numbers that I ought to aim for and the sort of price that I ought to go up to, bearing in mind the quality of the bull that I was hoping to buy.

Geordie nodded silently and led us through the middeny slush that surrounded the pens. He climbed into some of them, feeling various parts of the anatomy of selected occupants, explaining the good and bad points of each to Geoffrey and myself and checking their breeding for any incompatibility with that of The MacRodrick's bull. After about three-quarters of an hour, we adjourned to the crowded smoke-filled Mart Bar for further discussion, a dram or two and what appeared to be the local delicacy, deservedly so as I discovered, consisting of a high-rimmed, crisp-pastried individual mutton pie.

Between five and eight, it was agreed, was the number of heifers that I should aim for and these, like the Larna fold, should all be attested free from EBL (Enzootic Bovine Leukosis or cattle cancer) and IBR (Infectious Bovine Rhinotrachitis or cattle flu).

When we left him, seven of the lot numbers in my catalogue were ringed as being, in Geordie's opinion, the best possible in view of my particular circumstances, with a further nine starred as being 'such as I couldn't go far wrong with'. In the margin, against each of them, I had written the price that my mentor thought represented their true worth, as well as that which I should in no circumstances exceed. The net result was that, if all went well, I should be able to fill my quota of heifers at an average cost of twelve hundred guineas.

'If you get some of them cheaper, though, you could maybe go a wee bit higher on the others.'

The MacRodrick's bull would be good value at four thousand guineas but in no circumstances should I go beyond five.

*　　*　　*

'There now, look at that, will you?'

The auctioneer gave a couple of admonitory taps with his hammer and some forty or fifty conversations came to an abrupt, if momentary, halt. His clerk, sitting in a white coat beside him, peered obediently forwards. The pervasive but rather pleasant smell of damp tweed was everywhere and smoke from pipe tobacco weaved its way towards the roof.

'Lot thirty-one, Ribn Ruadh, the fifteenth of Foracher – a fine beast if ever I saw one – from Mr Macwilliam's running on the high ground at Foracher. Good square end on her – shall I say a thousand guineas? Nine hundred, then, seven, six? Five, surely? Four, thank you, sir. Four bid, four bid, four bid . . . .

I raised my catalogue.

'And fifty. Four-fifty, four-fifty, five . . . '

The first of Geordie's recommended seven had been led into the ring.

I had reached the Oban Mart early on Geoffrey Robertson's advice and established myself on the hindmost of the four or five tiers, looking down on to the ring, and there he had shortly joined me. The benches had filled up around and below us, as had the space for standing round the rail of the ring. There were those who had come to buy, those who had come to sell, those who had come to watch prices for future sales or purchases, those who had come simply to watch.

We had sat as white-coated cattlemen led the individual beasts around the ring, the owner of each or his factor standing below the rostrum to see fair play and saying the odd word in private to the auctioneer, while the more forthright among them ostentatiously pointed out bids to him that he might have missed. By the time that all twenty-six lots of class one – three-year-old heifers mostly in calf had either been sold or withdrawn as having failed to reach their reserve, and the first lot of class two – two-year-olds ready for the bull – had been brought in, I was just beginning to be able to distinguish the component parts of the auctioneer's patter and to get some sort of idea as to the technique of bidding. Geoffrey Robertson and I had already managed to infiltrate ourselves into a strategic position closer to the ring.

'Five bid . . . and fifty, six bid, six bid, and fifty, seven, seven-fifty, eight, eight-fifty, nine, nine-fifty, ten . . . ten bid, ten bid, ten bid, I'll take twenties now, ten-twenty, forty, sixty, eighty, eleven hundred, eleven bid, eleven bid, eleven bid. All done, now?' The hammer came down on the front of the rostrum. 'Sold to you, sir . . . ' the auctioneer raised his eyebrows in my direction.

I gave the card on which I had written my name and address in advance to one of the Mart employees in the ring, who took it over to the rostrum.

The auctioneer glanced at it.

' . . . Lord Thyrde, Northamptonshire,' he said and passed it on to the clerk beside him who, in turn, scribbled the details down in his book. The Thyrde fold of pedigree Highland cattle had come into being at last.

'Well done, Derek,' said Geoffrey from beside me and I turned to wave my thanks to Geordie on the third layer up, who jerked his thumb up and grinned.

'Lot thirty-two . . .'

Lot thirty-two was one of Geordie's possibles, of a rich red colour that I had particularly admired in her pen the day before. In any case, if I was to be sure of getting the minimum number of heifers that had been prescribed, I would almost certainly be needing one or two of this second category. I decided to have a go at her too.

' . . . seven bid, seven bid, and fifty, eight, eight bid, eight bid, twenties now, and twenty, forty, sixty, eighty. Eight-eighty, eight-eighty, eight-eighty, eight-eighty. All done?'

Again, the hammer.

'Lord Thyrde, Northamptonshire,' said the auctioneer. 'Lot thirty-three . . .'

Lot thirty-three, a splendid looking beast of the same rich colour, had been awarded the first-prize red ticket for two-year-olds, which she wore attached to her head-collar as she was led round the ring. She had been ruthlessly banned by Geordie as being way out of my class. I kept the hand holding my catalogue firmly down by my side and watched covetously as she was knocked down for five thousand guineas.

Lot thirty-four was also on the embargo list, but this time as not being of a quality worthy of the notice of the Larna bull, The MacRodrick and, consequently, of me. The price limped up to five hundred guineas, where the auctioneer glanced down at its owner and then shrugged his shoulders. 'Sorry boys, Hector says "no".'

Lot thirty-five, however, did carry Geordie's seal of approval. This time I let the bidding creep to eight hundred guineas before putting in a bid. I felt I was getting rather proficient at it – at any rate, I was enjoying myself enormously.

'Eight bid, eight bid, and fifty, nine, nine-fifty, ten, ten-fifty, eleven, eleven bid, eleven bid, eleven bid, and fifty, twelve, and fifty, thirteen. Thirteen bid, thirteen bid, thirteen. Against you, Lord Thyrde.'

I shook my head.

Thirteen hundred guineas had been the highest sum that Geordie had recommended I should spend on that particular beast.

By the time that the whole of class two had come under the hammer, I had become the owner of seven two-year-old heifers, four out of the seven recommended ones and three of the nine possibles. The last lot in the class I had most fun of all bidding for, paying two hundred guineas over Geordie's recommended maximum. I was making the best of his ruling that, if I had saved money on some of them, I could perhaps go a bit over on the others and two hundred guineas happened to be the exact sum that I had in hand.

'Time for a dram, I think,' said Geoffrey Robertson. 'The bulls won't be coming on for an hour or so yet.'

We collected Geordie from his seat below us and adjourned to the Mart Bar for celebratory drams and mutton pies.

* * *

The three of us stood by the ringside together, this time.

The bull that had won the second prize came under the hammer first. He was a magnificent dark brindle beast and, as soon as I saw him, I found myself wishing that he was the one I was to bid for. He went for four thousand, three hundred guineas.

Then came the first-prize winner. The bidding was regular but not sensational, paused slightly at four thousand guineas, picked up again and the hammer came down at four thousand nine hundred and fifty.

'He'd not have got that, if it hadn't been for the ticket,' Geordie said.

Next in the catalogue was the Larna bull.

There was a general pricking up of attention, straightening of backs, as the winner of the third prize was led into the ring, an alertness that had not been there for the first two lots in this class. My regrets over the brindled bull vanished – here, standing in the ring with what one could only describe as nobility, was a truly magnificent beast.

Even the auctioneer was silent as though any comment from him was superfluous.

'Ossian the third of Kilpatrick,' he said matter of factly, 'from The MacRodrick's fold on Larna. What am I bid, ladies and gentlemen? Five thousand? Four and a half? Four? Three and a half, surely?'

Geordie tapped me on the shoulder.

'Wait till I give you the word before you come in.'

I nodded.

'Three thousand then,' said the auctioneer. 'At three thousand guineas, thirty bid, thirty-two, two bid, two bid, thirty-two, thirty-four, six, eight, at three thousand eight hundred guineas, then?'

I felt Geordie's second tap on my elbow and raised my catalogue.

'Four thousand. Thank you, sir. At four thousand guineas, forty bid, forty bid, forty-two, forty-two bid, two bid, two bid, I'll take hundreds now, four three.' There were only two of us left in it. 'At four thousand three hundred, at four three, four four, four four bid, at four thousand five hundred guineas.'

There was a long pause and I thought that I had got it.

Then, 'Four six, four seven, eight, nine, five thousand.'

That was to have been my limit. But I couldn't lose it now – not for a hundred guineas.

I raised my catalogue again.

'Five one,' said the auctioneer, followed by the inevitable, 'five two.'

There was a warning tug on my sleeve from Geoffrey. To hell with it, I thought. Just once more.

'Five three. Five thousand three hundred guineas bid. Do I hear five thousand four hundred? Thank you, sir. Five thousand four hundred. Four, four bid. At five thousand four hundred, then.' He looked at me. 'Against you, sir.'

I shook my head with very real regret and the bull was knocked down for five thousand four hundred guineas. The whole thing had been for nothing after all.

'Bad luck,' said Geoffrey, 'but it wouldn't have done for you to go higher.'

Geordie nodded. 'I know that other bidder,' he said, 'he'd have gone on for another few hundred yet.'

*   *   *

'It's a fine well-matched lot of beasts you've got there,' said a voice behind us.

I had paid my account in the Mart office and made arrangements for the transportation of my, now condemned to be spinsters, fold of cattle down to Northamptonshire, and the three of us had gone out to the back in search of them. We had found all seven gathered together in two adjoining pens of their own.

We all turned to see a tall grey-haired man, leaning on a cromach with its horn head carved in the form of a leaping salmon. His browny-green plus-four suit seemed to hang in folds about his gaunt carcass and his hand-knitted woollen stockings terminated in a pair of old-fashioned metal-studded turned-up shepherd's brogues, with a tongue over the lace holes to keep out heather and water. He was clean shaven, with a dew-lapped throat not very far from the colour of his tweeds, and obtrusive eyebrows, but the most formidable part of him was a pair of very piercing blue eyes.

'Good day to you, Geordie. And you, you old Red, are you living yet?' He clapped Geoffrey on the shoulder. 'Introduce me, will you?'

'There's nothing I should like better,' said Geoffrey Robertson. 'This is

Lord Thyrde, who's up from Northamptonshire to buy cattle. Derek, meet Rodrick MacRodrick of MacRodrick.'

'Aye, it's a fine lot of heifers, you've got there. It's a good eye for a beast you'll be having.'

'Not me, I'm afraid,' I said. 'The credit must all go to Geordie, here.'

The blue eyes twinkled and he smiled at my adviser. 'I guessed as much. Well, it's a good eye for a man you have then, and that's maybe better still. But I wanted to thank you for the lift you gave to my bull, back in the mart there.'

'Not at all, sir,' I said. 'I really wanted it.'

'Aye, I wouldn't let him go higher,' said Geordie. 'It was a fair price he fetched, notwithstanding.'

'The market's the best judge, often as not,' said Geoffrey, with a sideways glance at The MacRodrick.

'Harumph!' He cleared his throat noisily. 'Like master, like man, old Fairfax himself isn't fit to judge a class of hamsters. Put the fellow properly in his place today, though, that's why I'm so grateful to Lord Thyrde here.' He looked at me. 'Thyrde? Thyrde? You wouldn't be old Derry Mallicent's son by any chance, would you?'

'Yes, I am,' I said.

'Really? He was at m'tutor's at Eton. Killed in the war, you'd scarcely remember him, I suppose?'

'No, he died before I was born. I was a posthumous child,' I said.

'Harumph!' I was soon to learn that, with The MacRodrick, this particular noise had become an affectation used to cover up any moment of emotion. 'You'll still be wanting a bull, then?'

'Yes, very much,' I said.

'I've one back at home as good as the one you saw today. Geordie's seen him. He'll vouch for him, won't you, Geordie?'

'Aye, Lord Thyrde couldn't go far wrong with him. Well, if you'll excuse me, gentlemen, I have to be on my way.'

While I was saying goodbye to him and thanking him for all his help, I was aware of Geoffrey talking in an undertone to The MacRodrick and, from the latter's muffled 'harumph', I assumed that he was telling him about Julia.

'This bull, now,' he said, as I came back to them, 'I could let you have him for the same as your final bid today. But you'd better see him first to make sure he'll suit you. Come over by the ferry tomorrow – there's another returns to Oban on Friday – you'll be my guest at the castle for a couple of nights.'

CHAPTER THREE

I was standing at the starboard rail of the Caledonian MacBrayne ferry to Larna and Colonsay, the wind in my face, fresh, damp and salty, seagulls wheeling and calling above me and white-topped waves chopping below. One part of my mind was taking in the ever-changing pattern of the south-eastern Mull coastline as it filtered by to the front of me. Another was concentrated on the next stage of my mission which lay ahead.

I had had an almost incredible run of luck so far: the chance meeting with Geoffrey Robertson on the train; his inspired plan about the Highland cattle sale and its apparent failure turning out to be even more fortunate; Rodrick MacRodrick having been a friend of my father's at school and he realising the connection between us; but would it continue? Here I was with a totally unsolicited invitation to be his guest at the castle, but I still had to persuade him to talk to me about his intentions with regard to the Caribbean Larna and, if I got the timing wrong or handled it badly, would he suspect that the whole thing had been the put-up job which indeed it was? On the whole I thought not, if only because the sequence of coincidences was so unlikely, and I had little conscience over deceiving him because what I was trying to do was in the interests of Larna which, if the general opinion of The MacRodrick was accurate, would also be in his own.

At that moment I felt a tap on my shoulder. I turned round and there, standing just behind me, macintoshed, sou'westered and looking every bit as beautiful as I remembered her, was Catriona Campbell, grinning up at me.

'I told you I'd be seeing you,' she said.

'Catriona, how *lovely* to see you. I overslept on the train the other day and found I'd totally missed you by the time I could get dressed. Where on earth did you disappear to?'

'I was staying with some friends from the Caribbean in Glasgow. But what are you doing here?' She paused and then nodded. 'Oh yes, I remember you did say something about hoping to go to Larna.'

'That's right. I was lucky enough to meet The MacRodrick in Oban. I'm staying with him at the castle for a couple of nights.'

'Good, so am I,' she said.

She moved forward and put both gloved hands on the white-painted rail beside me.

'Hold on a moment, will you, I'm about to see for the first time something I've been looking forward to all my life. It's a sight that all Larnacans dream about – we're brought up with pictures of it from the nursery. Those are the hills of Laggan with the island at the point there and as soon as we round that we'll see Castle Rodrick, the first glimpse of our Scottish namesake. It's only then that we know we've come home.'

I stood and watched in silence as we approached and rounded the island, dividing my attention between the view as it slowly emerged from behind the high cliffs to the right and the face of my companion beside me. Perched dramatically on a hilltop across several hundred yards of water from the south-east point of Mull, the gaunt lines of a granite keep were slowly materialising, silhouetted against an angry evening sky – great black lowering clouds among a medley of colours, greys and almost purples, fading to traces of the palest of pale washed blue. And Catriona, a slight smile with a mixture of pride and eagerness on her face, was standing there entranced, lost in a small piece of heaven that was all her own.

The boat turned into the Sound of Larna and, as the castle grew closer, the details became clearer: small vertical slit windows spaced at irregular intervals, castellation topping the massive walls, circular towers with pointed tops to them, tiled roofs and countless chimneys, a square flag of indistinguishable detail undulating gently around its pole at the very top. Then, as the boat turned into a small bay that opened out from the river mouth beyond the castle, a great archway came into view, leading no doubt to an inner courtyard of some sort. Catriona slipped a hand into mine and, almost involuntarily it seemed, stood on tiptoe to give me a kiss . . . but only on the cheek, this time.

'There now, wasn't that wonderful? Now I can die happy,' she said.

*   *   *

The little village of Kilpatrick lay across the river from the castle and, as we came down the gangway on to its quay, I was struck by the extraordinary atmosphere of the island. There was an aura of gothic timelessness and calm about it. We were met by a massive man dressed in a faded coat and plus-four shooting suit of the same tweed that our host had been wearing at the cattle sale, the day before.

'Miss Campbell? Lord Thyrde? I'm Dougal, head stalker to The MacRodrick. I'm to take you up to the castle,' he said.

He loaded our luggage into the back of a waiting Land-Rover and drove us over the river, up a winding drive, through the archway and into the courtyard that did indeed lie within.

'I'll look to your cases later,' he said. 'Follow me just now. The laird will be waiting for you in the drawing-room upstairs.'

The drawing-room, large and rectangular, presented a successful mixture between Georgian and Scottish medieval. The walls had a red and gilt paper of formal design and the windows, which were on two adjoining sides, were deep embrasures formed by round-topped arches leading back through three-quarters of the wall's four-foot thickness to narrow upright glazed slits at the far end. Chintz-covered sofas surrounded the open log-fire and from one of them The MacRodrick rose to his feet and uncoiled himself to his full height. The blue fawn whippet beside him raised its head from between its front paws and eyed us suspiciously.

'Catriona, my dear.' He took both her hands in his and kissed her cheek. 'And Derek, may I call you that? You two have met I see.' He took my hand. 'How good to see you here.'

Then he introduced Catriona and me in turn to the other occupants of the room.

'My cousin Alastair, I think you already know?'

In a light brown tweed country suit, infinitely more informal than the archaic garb in which I was accustomed to see him, he somehow contrived to look only marginally less sinister.

I smiled at him.

'Good evening, Black Rod.'

'My brother, Malcolm?' said Rodrick.

I looked at the dreaded Malcolm MacRodrick with interest.

He was a was a younger stockier version of Rodrick, with a square jowl-less jaw and the same blue eyes, but far less piercing and with no trace that I could see of the latter's twinkle about them. He wore an Old-Etonian tie with a pink carnation in the buttonhole of his mid-grey suit, the classic combination for a former member of that establishment but unusual perhaps in such a dedicated member of the Labour Party. His was a face that was vaguely familiar to me from about the Palace of Westminster, but one that I had never been able to put a name to.

I held out my hand to him. He seemed to study it for a moment as though deciding whether or not to shake it. His tone when he spoke was a lazy drawl.

'Nice to meet you, old boy,' he said.

'And my nephews, Roddy and Rannie.'

They were both in their late 'teens or very early twenties and dark-haired, but there the resemblance ended. Roddy was short and slightly thickset with a confident and ebullient manner and Rannie taller and thinner with a decidedly sulky face.

'Hi,' said Roddy.

'I hate being called Rannie. It's a beast of a name,' Rannie said.

'And finally meet Amanda.'

The whippet got up, raised herself to her full seventeen inches and snaked her head forward to be stroked. The fact that I was clearly trusted by her master was at least something in my favour but, in her eyes, I was still very much on probation – of that there was no doubt at all.

Malcolm issued drinks to all of us on behalf of his brother and, after a short time, while I was temporarily omitted from the various conversations that were taking place, I took my whisky and water over to one of the windows and looked out across the several hundred yards of sea that formed the Sound of Larna to the south coast of Mull.

'It's a grand view, isn't it.'

I glanced round to see that Rodrick had come up beside me, the faithful Amanda at his heel.

'That's Lochbuie straight across from us, with the modern Lochbuie House – its Victorian actually – at the far end and Castle Moy, that's fourteenth century, to the right of it. There's actually a third house between the two, a Georgian one, but you can't see it from here, and between them they cover all the centuries the Maclaines of Lochbuie lived there. Those two hills on the skyline are Benbuie on the left and Craig Ben on the right. The entry to the loch is marked by those two points – Rubhn Dubh or Black Point, that's Smithy Rock to the west of it, and Gull Point with Frank Lockwood's Island to the east; that's where you'd have had the first view of the castle on the way over. The cliffs are nine hundred feet high at that point.'

He turned and looked at me anxiously. 'Sorry to be boring you with so much detail.'

'No, I like it,' I said.

'There's a bit of history to it too. You see that fall of shale between the point and the island?'

'Yes.'

'There's a cave underneath all that called Lord Lovat's. It got blocked by the fall in 1926. The Lovat of the day is said to have escaped from the English redcoats by hiding in it after the '45, then he was rowed across the sound to Larna and laid up here for several days before moving on.'

He stooped and stroked the whippet's head.

'You'll be wanting to see your room, I expect.'

'I'm terribly sorry but I haven't brought a dinner-jacket with me.'

'Don't worry. It'll be just us tonight and tomorrow, so come down as you are. I'll tell the others,' he said.

*   *   *

Which no doubt he had. Rodrick, Black Rod and myself came down dressed in much the same clothes as we had been wearing before dinner. Malcolm and his two sons were uniformly resplendent in dinner jacket, waistcoat and trousers, all in tartan, with a black tie. Roddy just had a bumptious look about him but Rannie was openly smirking when he thought I wasn't looking, his face reverting to a sullen expression as soon as I caught his eye.

We sat at one end of a long refectory table, our host at the head with Catriona on his right, brother Malcolm on the other side of her and Roddy beyond him. I drew Cousin Alastair on my left, with Rannie on his other side.

Crimson velvet curtains were already drawn and great branched candelabra provided the only light. Pictures of former MacRodricks hung dimly on the high walls. The food was delicious and the head stalker Dougal, now in jacket and kilt performing the office of butler, handed it round in silver dishes to be helped on to silver-gilt plates.

I noticed that Rodrick did little more than pick at his food – cutting it up into little bits, taking up the odd forkful and putting it down again – and that, at the end of each course, even the minute amount to which he had helped himself was taken away virtually untouched. He divided his attention between Catriona and myself with equal charm. Alastair on the other hand confined his conversation to House of Lords matters, on which he very flatteringly sought my opinion and advice in a low, rather intense, voice.

The best known duty of Black Rod, is to summon 'the faithful Commons' to the bar of the House of Lords, there to listen to The Queen making her 'Gracious Speech' at the State Opening of Parliament. He marches down the long series of galleries and lobbies that separate the two Houses, to the cry of 'Hats off, strangers', passed on from doorkeeper to doorkeeper. On reaching the House of Commons, he has the door slammed in his face, a historic gesture of independence shown by that House to the Sovereign. He then knocks on the door three times with the butt end of his rod of office and the Commons relent and, led by their Speaker, follow him more or less meekly on his journey back.

This purely ceremonial function, however, is but an interlude in his otherwise more mundane and infinitely more arduous working life, which is spent almost exclusively – he is also an officer of the Most Noble Order of the Garter – within the House of Lords end of the Palace of Westminster.

He is responsible for its security; for the upkeep of the inside and outside fabric of all its buildings; for the allocation of its rooms; for the doorkeepers, attendants, police and all other staff not connected with the actual proceedings of Parliament, their supervision and welfare; and to a large extent for the welfare of the peers themselves. The office rotates between the three services. The previous Black Rod having been an Army general, this time it was the Air Force's turn.

It follows, therefore, that the Black Rod of the day is a man of some influence in the House of Lords and, to a lesser extent, in the whole of the Palace of Westminster. Successive holders of that office have been immensely liked, and very much an integral part of the day-to-day life of the House, but the same could not yet be said of the present incumbent. Sir Alastair MacRodrick had got off to a rather shaky start.

And, by the end of the meal, I had gained no greater insight as to the true nature of his character than I had before.

'Do you play piquet?' Rodrick's voice pulled me sharply back to reality. I had been subjected to one of those lulls one sometimes gets at dinner parties during which Alastair had been trying to extract some sort of conversation out of Rannie on his other side and Rodrick himself had been absorbed with Catriona. 'In my opinion it's the finest card game – certainly for two – that there is.'

'Er . . . I'm afraid not. I did as a boy, but I can't remember very much about it.'

'Oh, you'll soon pick it up again. I'll teach you after dinner. Harumph! If you'd like me to, that is?'

'Very much,' I said.

The door was opened at that point and I heard the sound of bagpipes, distant at first but growing progressively louder as the piper came down the corridor towards us.

Rodrick leant towards me.

'We don't do this every night. This evening's in honour of the first visit to the castle of the son of my old friend Derry Mallicent.'

In through the door came Dougal wearing a bonnet now, kilt swinging, cheeks inflated, marching slowly round and round the table as he played. He marched, as indeed I had earlier noticed him walking, with a sort of rolling lope which somehow I found incredibly smart. He played four or five different airs, some standing, some marching; with the last one, the loping pace became very slow indeed.

'That's a *piobaireachd* he's playing now,' Rodrick murmured to me. ' "Larna the Green", it's called, composed when my forebear and his men were exiles in Jamaica, at a time when there didn't seem to be much hope of any of them ever seeing Scotland again.'

The pipe music came to an end and Rodrick pulled himself to his feet and drew an additional chair up to the table, putting it between his own and mine.

'Nach gabh thu dram, a Dhughaill 'ic Ruaraidh?'

'Gabhaidh gu dearbh, 'ic Ruaraidh Mhoir.' *

The head stalker raised his full glass to Rodrick, then to each of the rest of us in turn, and swallowed it at one go. Then he got up, inflated his pipe again and, still with that rolling lope of his, marched off round the table and out through the door to the strains of the same air that he had come in to. The sound faded gradually, getting softer and softer until it finally died away altogether after what seemed a long time and a great distance.

* * *

'On our way from the dining-room, the whippet an ever-faithful shadow at his heels, Rodrick paused in the hall at a full-length portrait of a young man in full highland dress. Lace jabot and lace at his wrists, his plaid, kilt and stockings were all of what I was now beginning to recognise as the MacRodrick tartan, predominantly green in background but surmounted with the odd blue square enclosed by bars of black, the whole interlaced both horizontally and vertically with thin single white lines alternating with double lines of red. His tasselled goat-hair sporran was silver mounted and his right hand rested on the basket-hilt of his broadsword. In his left was his bonnet, decked with a little sprig of what seemed to be a tangle of narrow leaves, grass-like and grey-green, with three brown and white feathers rising from it. In the background loomed the vague shape of what I assumed to be Castle Rodrick.

* 'Will you not take a dram, Dougal MacRodrick?'
  'I will indeed, Mac Ruaraidh Mor.'

'My great-grandfather, Ranald,' he said, 'painted by Sir John Watson Gordon at the time of his installation as Chief of the Clan MacRodrick. To the best of my knowledge, we're the last clan that has carried on the ceremony, father to son, through the centuries. That's sea buckthorn,' he pointed to the sprig on the bonnet, 'our clan badge – the three eagle feathers are the prerogative of a clan chief – and that's the rear of the castle, where all large clan gatherings take place. Harumph! Come on, I'll get out the cards.'

He led us down a passage and through a door into a small room in which every available inch of wall-space was lined with old leather-bound books, save for where a dimly lit half-length portrait of yet another MacRodrick hung over the fireplace; a log-fire glowed and flickered in the grate. He sat me down in one corner of the room at a walnut card table, inset with green baize. Then he took a modern leather-bound box out of the single drawer, extracted the two packs of cards that it contained and laid them face down on the table.

'The game of piquet, said The MacRodrick, is played with a pack of only thirty-two cards, eight in each suit – ace, king, queen, knave and ten down to seven – the other twenty having been discarded from a conventional pack beforehand. And the game is in two phases, scoring on the cards in your hand – as in poker – and winning on tricks taken on the table – as in bridge or whist. Each player is dealt a hand of twelve cards face down on the table and the remaining eight, known as the *stock*, are spares to be divided between them. Clear so far?'

'I think so.'

'Right. Scoring on the cards in your hand can be done in one of three ways: by having more cards in your longest and strongest suit than your opponent has in his – this is known as your *point*; by having a higher sequence of three or more consecutive cards in the same suit; or by having better fours or threes of cards of the same face value, but only aces down to tens. Only one of the two players can score in each of these three categories. The game on the table is simplified by the fact that there are no trumps, so the higher card in the suit led always wins the trick. OK?'

'Yes, it's coming back to me now.

'Good. A *partie*, that's the equivalent of a rubber, consists of six deals, three for you and three for me, that's about as much as I can manage these days. And we jot down the scores for each deal,' he patted a note-pad beside him on the table, 'as we go along. Piquet's a game you really ought to play for money but, as you will see, the scores can get quite high at times.' He looked up at me anxiously. 'A penny a point suit you?'

'Fine,' I said.

'I think the best thing would be for us to start playing and you can pick up the rest as we go along. Cut for first deal.'

I drew the knave of hearts, he the king of spades.

'Ah, my deal, that makes you what's called the "elder" hand. The dealer's always the "younger". You'll see the difference between them in a moment.'

He shuffled the cards and I put out my hand to cut the pack to him, but he stopped me with a gesture.

'Lesson number one, when you play piquet you never cut the cards after shuffling. It was the great game in France during the eighteenth century and the French court never cheated. They took a particular pride in that.'

He dealt out the cards in threes to me and to himself alternately.

The back of each card bore a design of a stylised piece of greenery with the three eagle feathers protruding from it, the whole surrounded by a rectangular band of MacRodrick tartan.

'Sea buckthorn?' I asked.

Rodrick nodded.

'My brother gave me these cards. He always seems to beat me, nowadays,' he said.

When he had completed the deal of twelve cards each, he separated the eight remaining ones into five cards and three, laying the five face down beside my hand and the three beside his own.

'These are the *stock*. Now you, having the elder hand, have the option of changing up to five of your cards, discarding them face down on the table and taking up a similar number from your *stock*. If, however, you decide to change less than five, you can look at those from your *stock* that you don't need and then put them face down on top of my three. I, the younger hand, would then have the option of changing more than my original three. Right, we'll have a look at our cards, then.'

I picked up my hand and sorted it into suits.

♠ 9, 7
♥ A, 9, 8
♦ J, 10, 9, 8
♣ J, 10, 7

'All right,' said Rodrick, 'remember what you're looking for when deciding what to discard. You have to consider your *point* first, that's your longest and strongest suit; if yours beats mine, you score one point per card. Sequences can be more valuable – from three to eight consecutive cards in the same suit: they are called a *tierce*, a *quart*,' he pronounced it 'cart', 'a *quint*,' 'cint' with a hard c, '*sixième*, *septième* and *huitième* respectively, *tierces* and *quarts* scoring three and four, and *quints* and above an additional ten, making fifteen, sixteen, etc., instead of five and six. Finally, you have threes or fours of aces, kings, queens, knaves and tens, threes scoring three points each and fours, fourteen; it is usual, therefore, to refer to these, not as "four knaves" for example, but "fourteen knaves".'

'Yes, I remember that,' I said.

'But don't forget the game on the table as well, when you're discarding. All right, how many cards from your *stock* are you going to take?'

I looked at my hand again. Diamonds would have to be my *point*, I needed all four of those. With the ace of hearts I could do without the nine and the eight. The seven of clubs would have to go and the nine and seven of spades.

'All five, please,' I said.

I took out the discards, put them face down on the table and picked up my *stock*. It consisted of the ace of diamonds, nine of clubs, seven of diamonds, ace of spades and king of hearts. I added them to my hand.

♠ A
♥ A, K
♦ A, J, 10, 9, 8, 7
♣ J, 10, 9

Rodrick put his own discards down the table, took up his *stock* of three and arranged them into his hand.

'I'm having the lot, too,' he said. 'Now we come to what is known as "the call", a declaration of the cards in our hands that could score for us, you as elder hand starting and giving your *point* first. Supposing you have five hearts, you call "a *point* of five"; if mine is in diamonds and consists of four cards, I just say "good" and you score five; whereas, if I have six or more in mine, I say "not good" and that amount is what I'll get when I add up my score after you've finished. If, on the other hand, I too have five cards I say "making?" and we both add up the values of our respective cards, allowing eleven for an ace, ten for court cards and tens and face value for nine, eight and seven, and the highest score wins. If both add up to the same amount, the *point* is "divided" and neither of us scores.'

I glanced at my hand.

'I've got a *point* of six,' I said.

'*Good.* That's six points. Count as you go and give me the suit.'

'Six, then, in hearts.'

'Now the sequences and again I use the "good" or "not good" procedure.'

'Yes, I've got a . . . what's a sequence of five? A *quint.*'

'*Good.* Now if the highest card were an ace, you'd say a *quint* major, but if a king you'd say "a *quint* to a king". And again the suit.'

'To a knave in diamonds,' I said. 'Six and fifteen, that's twenty-one. And a *tierce* to a knave in clubs?'

'Yes, that's *good* too. Once your highest sequence is *good* you can count any lesser one too even though, as in this case, I've got three higher *tierces* myself.'

'Twenty-four, then. And three aces?'

'*Not good.* All right then, play your first card and say "twenty-five". You score one for leading a card, win or lose.'

I played my ace of diamonds.

'Twenty-five.'

'I've got fourteen queens and three kings,' said Rodrick and he threw his queen of diamonds down to join my ace. 'Seventeen.'

He beamed at me.

'Not too difficult, was it.'

'Not so far,' I said.

I played my seven of diamonds. 'Twenty-six.'

Rodrick took it with his king. 'Eighteen.'

Then he played his ace of clubs. 'Nineteen.' I threw in my nine of clubs. 'Twenty-six.'

His king of clubs, 'Nineteen.' My ten, 'Twenty-six.'

His queen, 'Twenty.' My knave, 'Twenty-six.'

His eight of clubs, 'Twenty-one.'

I looked at what was left in my hand for a moment. I played my eight of diamonds. 'Twenty-six.'

Then Rodrick played his queen of hearts. 'Twenty-two.' I took it with my king. 'Twenty-seven,' I said.

'Harumph!' he said. 'It was too much to hope you'd have discarded that one. The rest are yours, I think?'

'I'm afraid they are,' I said. I laid down my ace of hearts, ace of spades, knave, ten and nine of diamonds. 'Twenty-eight, twenty-nine, thirty, thirty one, thirty-two,' and Rodrick threw in his knave and ten of hearts, and king, queen and knave of spades.'

'Twenty-two for me,' he said. 'Now you also get one point for taking the last trick, that's thirty-three. You've won more than half the tricks, seven to my five, that's called "winning the cards", there's ten more points for that, forty-three. Congratulations.' And he wrote down the scores forty-three to twenty-two on the note-pad by his side.

'There *are* other refinements, of course. If we'd got half the tricks each, the "cards" would have been divided and nobody would have got the extra ten points, but if one of us wins all twelve of 'em – that's a *capot* – he scores an additional thirty, making forty in all. And if one player should get thirty points both in call and play before the other has scored any, it's called a *pique* and he counts sixty instead of thirty. Whereas, if he scores thirty points in call alone, that's a *repique* and he counts ninety.'

Stirrings in the memory of my distant past began to arise.

'Isn't there something called a *rubicon*?' I said.

'Yes, but we'll not be doing with that for the moment. You've more than enough to remember at one time already.'

He picked up the other pack of cards and handed it to me.

'Splendid,' he said. 'Your deal now, my elder hand.'

While I was shuffling the pack, I took a quick glance round at the others. Catriona, a newspaper open on her lap, was talking to Black Rod on the sofa by the fire. Malcolm and Roddy were playing backgammon in the far corner of the room, Rannie standing drooped over them. From the look on the latter's face, it was clear that he was less than pleased that it was not he who had been invited to play.

Then I dealt out the cards in threes as Rodrick had taught me and divided the *stock* into his five and my three.

'Remember as you discard that you're the younger hand,' he said. 'Aim at keeping a winning card in as many suits as possible or, however much you score in the call, you might lose that and more in the play.'

I found it rather endearing that Rodrick was obviously enjoying the whole thing enormously and, as so often happens, his enthusiasm was infectious. I found myself agreeing that, as a card game for two, it would be hard to beat.

There was one glorious moment when my fourteen tens outpointed his threes of aces, kings *and* queens.

'Harumph!' I made sure you'd have discarded at least one of those,' he said.

Rannie had now replaced Roddy at the backgammon table opposite Malcolm but things were obviously not going as well for him as he had no doubt expected and he appeared no less miserable than before. It was now Roddy's turn to be the onlooker and the smugness all too evident on *his* face indicated a malicious pleasure at his brother's fate. Glancing back to my host, I found that he too was watching them.

I caught his eye and he gave a despairing shrug to his shoulders.

'Just look at them,' he said.

The last game of the *partie* finished and The MacRodrick busied himself with adding up the scores.

'That's it,' he said, underlining the totals. 'A hundred and five for you and a hundred and twenty-two for me, I'm afraid. So I win . . . '

He sat back and watched with manifest delight as I took the change out of my pocket and counted out to him the sum of seventeen pence.

'Thank you very much.' He glanced at his watch. 'Harumph! Long past my bedtime. Good night, all. Come on, Amanda.' He got up and, followed by the whippet, left the room.

*   *   *

I began to put the cards away in their case with a certain amount of regret – as a new-found enthusiast I would happily have gone on playing – when Malcolm walked over and joined me.

'Care for another game?'

'Very much,' I said.

Black Rod had gone up to bed shortly after his cousin and Catriona, still on the sofa, was reading her copy of the brightly coloured *Oban Times*. Roddy and Rannie were now locked in acrimonious battle with each other over the backgammon table across the room.

'A pound a point suit you?'

It was a bit of a step-up from Rodrick's penny but the last thing I wanted to do at this stage was to show myself in a poor light in Malcolm's eyes.

'All right.'

'Club rules, of course?'

I wasn't too happy about that one either, not having the slightest idea as to what it implied. But . . .

'Of course,' I said.

We cut the cards, giving me the deal and Malcolm the first elder hand, and my confidence grew as the play proceeded. The size of the stakes certainly added a great deal of excitement to the game. Malcolm won the first hand of the *partie* by a small margin and I the second by a rather larger one.

He didn't seem to be playing anywhere near as well as his brother and by the end of the fifth hand, my score was standing at eighty-eight to his seventy-eight.

He got up from the table.

'Have to pop out for a moment. Won't keep you long, old boy.'

He was indeed back almost immediately, and when he was sitting down again, I passed the pack of cards to him; he shuffled it almost absent-mindedly and sat with it motionless in his hand for a moment. The light from the fire was flickering on gilt and old leather in the surrounding bookshelves. An intermittent click of dice continued from across the room.

'Gettin' a bit dull, don't you think,' he said. 'How about uppin' the stakes a little?'

'What do you suggest?'

'What would you say to a fiver a point?'

'Well, I don't know about that,' I said.

'Come on, old boy, where's your sportin' spirit? It's the last deal in the *partie*. You're already ten points ahead of me and you *have* got the elder hand.'

To hell with it, I thought.

'All right,' I said.

Suddenly the whole atmosphere of the room changed dramatically. Roddy and Rannie left their game of backgammon in mid-play and came over and stood beside our table. Catriona put her paper down beside her on the sofa and watched from where she sat.

Malcolm dealt out the cards slowly and deliberately. I waited until he had finished and, determined not to show any sort of emotion, picked mine up and sorted out my hand.

♠ A, J, 10, 9, 7
♥ A, J, 8 7
♦ A, 8, 7
♣ —

Not bad at all, I thought and not much doubt about the discard either. Spades would be my *point*. With the two aces of hearts and diamonds, I could afford to throw the knave, eight and seven of the former and the eight and seven of the latter. I hadn't got a single club but, for an elder hand that didn't really matter.

'I'm taking all five,' I said.

'Same with my three.' Malcolm fingered his jaw. 'More if I could get 'em,' he said.

I threw out my rejects, picked up the *stock* and looked at them. I drew the nine of clubs, queen of diamonds, eight of spades, seven of clubs and king of diamonds.

♠ A, J, 10, 9, 8, 7
♥ A
♦ A, K, Q
♣ 9, 7

It didn't look too bad at first sight. I'd have to play those spades carefully, though. I began to work out some sort of a plan while I was waiting for Malcolm to finish sorting his own hand.

'*Point* of six,' I said.

'Makin'?'

I did a rapid mental calculation.

'Fifty-five,' I said.

'*Not good*. Mine makes fifty-nine.'

'Then I've got a *quint* to a knave.'

'*Not good*.'

'And, finally, three aces.'

'I was afraid of that.' Malcolm grinned ruefully. '*Good*,' he said.

I led my ace of diamonds. I had decided to make the three points in diamonds before playing any spades and to keep my ace of hearts in reserve to deal with the high cards in that suit which my opponent would undoubtedly still have.

'Four.'

Malcolm threw down the nine of hearts.

'Let me see, now. A *point* of six and a *quint* major, both in clubs. Twenty-one,' he said.

Next, I played the king of diamonds, 'Five,' followed by the queen, 'Six,' to which he replied with the ten of hearts and the eight of clubs, 'Twenty-one.'

Then I led my knave of spades, 'Seven.'

'Ah, that's better,' he said, and took it with his queen. 'Twenty-two.'

As I had expected, he then led his ace of clubs, 'Twenty-three,' followed by his king, 'Twenty-four.'

I replied with my only clubs, the seven and the nine,

Malcolm then played the remainder of his clubs in order, the queen, 'Twenty-five,' knave, 'Twenty-six,' and ten, 'Twenty-seven.' I was having to think carefully now and I replied with the seven, eight and nine of spades, my score remaining at seven.

Roddy and Rannie were leaning over the table rather in the manner of a brace of vultures, one sardonic, one sulky, but both exuding the discomforting impression that they were lusting for the kill. I hadn't got the slightest idea why. I was under the impression that I'd been playing a poor hand remarkably well in the circumstances but, even so, my sense of misgiving grew.

Malcolm led his king of hearts.

'Twenty-eight.'

I took it with my ace.

'Eight,' I said.

I led the ace of spades.

'Nine.'

Malcolm played the king.

'Twenty-eight.'

Finally, the ten of spades.

'Ten.'

Malcolm put down his last card, the queen of hearts.

'Twenty-eight. Cards divided, so your one for the last trick makes that twenty-eight to eleven. Thank you very much, I enjoyed that,' he said.

I got up from my chair and went and looked over his shoulder as he added the final points to the running score. He was now leading by a hundred and six to ninety-nine. Seven points in it, thirty-five pounds – could have been worse I supposed.

I took out my wallet.

'What rotten luck! Only one short of the hundred. You've been *rubiconed*, old boy,' he said.

Oh God, I thought, what's coming next?

He was still busy with his pencil.

Then, 'I make it fifteen hundred and twenty-five you owe me.'

'WHAT!'

Malcolm peered down at the score card. 'I *think* I've got it right, old boy. Your score added to mine, plus a hundred, multiplied by five; you did agree to club rules, didn't you? Yes, one thousand, five hundred and twenty-five pounds.'

I didn't even bother to check. I felt pretty certain that, at this particular point in the game, both his mathematics and his interpretation of the rules of scoring would turn out to be scrupulously correct.

'Never mind,' he said. 'Give you your revenge one evenin' at White's. You are a member, of course?'

There was nothing in his tone to imply it, but the threat was there. No

London club takes kindly to one of its members failing to pay his gambling debts.

'Will you take a cheque?' I said, as one who had carelessly omitted to provide himself with such a sum in actual notes.

'Of course. Tell you what, old boy, make it out for the round fifteen hundred and we'll call it quits.'

I wrote out the cheque very legibly for the full one thousand, five hundred and twenty-five pounds.'

He took it, glanced at it and made to give it back to me.

'I said fifteen hundred, old boy.'

I shook my head.

'I pay my debts,' I said.

I was delighted to see that, just for a moment, I had him at a disadvantage which was worth every penny of the extra twenty-five quid.

He stuffed it in his pocket with rather bad grace and left the room without a further word.

Roddy looked across at me.

'Give you a game,' he said.

'No thanks, I think I've had about enough for the moment.'

He grinned.

'Perhaps you're right. You'd better learn how to deal first. I'd only take you to the cleaners like my father did.'

My brother gave me these cards. Always seems to beat me, nowadays. Had Malcolm also provided himself with a matching set that he'd got stached away somewhere? *You'd better learn how to deal first. I'd only take you to the cleaners like my father did.* Did Roddy *want* me to know that his father had somehow fixed the cards and what a mug he thought me for allowing it to happen?

'I was told by your uncle,' I said, 'that the French court didn't cheat.'

'Yes, and look where it got them,' Roddy said.

*   *   *

As soon as the two boys had left the room, Catriona got up from her sofa, came over and looked up at me anxiously.

'It seems an awful lot of money. Can you afford it?'

Although I was seething inwardly at the behaviour of Malcolm and his all too blatantly legitimate progeny and appalled by the scale of it, I somehow didn't want Catriona to be aware of it. I was getting to like her more and more each time I saw her.

59

'No, but it's uncomfortable rather than terminal,' I said.

We put out the lights and went out and up the staircase together. At the top Catriona, who's room was farther down the corridor than mine, paused outside my door.

I kissed her briefly and then, putting a hand on each of her shoulders, with a little more feeling.

She disengaged herself gently.

'See you,' she said.

My bedroom struck icily cold as I walked across to the window in the darkness. The far lights of Lochbuie House formed gleaming pinpoints. Lord Lovat's cave must be somewhere at the base of that black mass over to the right and the waning moon was reflected brokenly in the turbulence of the intervening Sound of Larna.

Through the glass, I could hear the muffled roar of the waves crashing against the shore below.

I groped my way back to the bedside, felt for the table-lamp and turned it on. Then I undressed, put my clothes away in the enormous mahogany cupboard in which the results of my earlier unpacking seemed pitifully inadequate for both drawer and hanging-space. Then back to the all enveloping softness of the enormous four-poster double bed.

I put the light out again and lay there fuming, more at my own stupidity in allowing Malcolm to take such an enormous sum off me than at him. Just at what point could I have stood up to him and called a halt to what must have been a well-planned operation in time?

Even as I turned it over and over in my mind, I was aware of the futility of doing so.

Deliberately I turned my thoughts back to Catriona instead.

'See you,' she had said.

In my imagination, but so vivid that it was almost impossible to be certain as to whether or not it was all really happening . . .

I heard the sound of footsteps approaching along the corridor outside. There was a gentle tap on the door. The handle turned and the door opened almost imperceptibly.

'Derek . . . ' *a tentative whisper,* ' . . . are you awake? It's me, Catriona. Can I come in?'

The door opened more widely and then shut again.

A slim shape was just discernable as the footsteps approached the bed.

A slight shiver.

'It's cold out here.'

I folded the edge of the bedclothes back invitingly.

There was a pause.

Then the sound of a garment slipping to the floor.

The figure, more defined now, leaned over me. I could feel the warmth of her soft breath as she lowered her face to mine. Then . . .

Suddenly, I felt bitterly ashamed of myself and the daydream disintegrated. What was I doing, with Julia only three weeks dead, lusting after a girl that I hardly knew, had only met so recently? I turned over and, determined now to make my mind as much of a blank as possible, drifted into sleep.

CHAPTER FOUR

It had served its purpose, though. I was woken the next morning by the heat of the sunlight magnified through the glass of the window on to my pillow, after a night of uninterrupted and, as far as I knew, dreamless sleep. I got up, dressed and went down to the dining-room.

Breakfast any time after nine, I had been told, but it was well after half-past and it looked as though I was the first there.

I found that I was amazingly hungry. There was a choice consisting of halves of cold grouse, bacon, eggs and kidneys, or kippers that could only have come from Loch Fyne. I am ashamed to say that I had all three.

After a final cup of coffee, I decided that I would explore the outside of the castle. I went through the door that led into the inner courtyard, down the steps and out into the clear dry chill of the October sunshine. The archway in through which we had been driven the night before was to my right and there was another smaller arch to the left and I walked across to it and out through that.

I was now in a flat gravelled arena some sixty yards square, bounded on three sides by a waist-high stone wall and I walked slowly round it in an anti-clockwise direction. It was broken only by a flight of steps on the western side leading to a path at the bottom which disappeared out of sight, no doubt to join the drive up to the castle at some point. Lower down was the tumbling river just visible trough the vivid red and yellow autumn tints of the surrounding trees and across that the hill rose steeply to the skyline – was that a golden eagle hovering over it? – which I judged must be some mile and a half away.

To the south the slope was more gentle, down to the shores of a loch to which the river broadened out several hundred yards away and which ran as far as I could see. To the east across several miles of choppy sea lay the islands of Seil and Easedale, the hills of mainland Argyll rising clearly behind them; I leaned over the wall to look downward and immediately wished that I hadn't: from its base the cliff fell sheer to the rocks on the shore far below. The whole of the remaining side was made up of the south face of the castle, the vague shape of which I remembered from the portrait in the passage the night before, a raised terrace running along three quarters of its breadth from the right.

I could see now why the castle was sited where it was – in the old days of clan warfare it must have been pretty well impregnable from every direction.

'Mornin', old boy. Enjoyin' the scenery?'

I turned to see that Malcolm, in tweed coat and yellow corduroy trousers, had come up beside me. I could swear that the pink carnation he wore was fresh that morning. Perhaps he brought up his own refrigerated supply.

'I was,' I said.

I realised that it must have sounded rather ruder than I had intended, but after what he had done to me last night, he could hardly expect to be the companion of my choice.

Malcolm, however, didn't seem to have noticed.

'This is where each new chief is installed after the death of his predecessor. All members of the clan who can attend are gathered in this area below, the more senior seated over there to the right. The actual ceremony takes place on the terrace up there, by the Otter Stone which has been sacred for all time to the Clan MacRodrick. Look, you can just make it out, that lump of granite that stands up slightly in the centre.'

He paused and I suddenly realised that every trace of affectation had vanished from his voice. He had drawn himself up to his full height and there was a dreamy look, almost of wonder, on his square-jawed face. Then he went on.

'The first signal for the ceremony is a horn blown by a single trumpeter standing by the base of the flag-pole up yonder and at that the whole gathering rises. Then the procession appears through the small archway there, three pipers leading, playing "The MacRodricks' Salute to Larna", the clan march; after them come first the standard-bearer, then the clan bard, followed by the most distinguished elder of the clan and finally the new chief himself, in full dress with three eagle feathers in his bonnet. They pass up the steps to the terrace and gather round the Otter Stone.'

Against my will, I was becoming totally fascinated and I could almost visualise the sequence of events as Malcolm described them.

'As the new chief stands with his head bowed, the clan elder girds a sword-belt holding the ceremonial claymore round his waist and places a white wand in his left hand. Then he takes his right hand and raises it to the crowd below, declaiming loudly, "Clan MacRodrick, I here present unto you Malcolm MacRodrick of MacRodrick . . . ",' he broke off and turned to me, 'er . . . for the sake of example,' he said and he had the grace to look slightly shamefaced about it, ' " . . . MacRodrick of MacRodrick, the undoubted Chief of this Clan, inheritor thereof by the Laws of God and Man, who is willing to accept the Chiefship".' At that point, the whole gathering roar out together, God bless our Chief and us for his cause.'

He paused again and looked up at the terrace.

'There's a lot more ceremonial of course, but that's the important part of it.'

At that moment, I noticed The MacRodrick, cromach in hand and the whippet Amanda at his heel, coming through the small archway under the castle and walking towards us, accompanied by Catriona. But Malcolm's eyes were still fixed on the terrace with its central Otter Stone as though entranced. Clearly he was living out in advance the scene that would undoubtedly be enacted there at some time within the next few months.

'All my tenants will be there,' he said. *If they know what's good for them*, his tone implied.

'MALCOLM!'

Malcolm MacRodrick spun round guiltily and I was forcibly reminded of that devastating scene in Shakespeare's *Henry the Fourth Part Two*, where the young Prince Hal is caught out by his dying father in the act of trying on the crown.

'A word with you.'

The two brothers walked off a pace or two.

'*Chuala mi gu'n do bhuidhinn thu mòran airgid bho Derek Thyrde an raoir. Dé 'na bh'ann?*' Rodrick said.

'*C'arson nach buinninn? Bha fhios aig an amadan de bha e dèanamh.*'

'*Cha robh fhios aige air na riaghailtean ceart. Cha do dh'ionnsaich mi cho fad sin e.*'

'*Thoill e na chaill e, ma tà.*'

'*De na chaill e?*'

They were obviously speaking Gaelic and pretty acrimonious Gaelic at that. Rodrick's voice had assumed a sternness of which I would not have believed that mild-mannered man capable. I turned to Catriona and was about to speak when she put a finger to her lips.

'*Cóig ceud deug nòta, ma dh'fheumas fios a bhi agad.*' Malcolm fingered his chin. '*Uill a dh'innseadh na fìrinn, cóig ceud deug 's cóig air fhichead.*'

'*Cha dèan duine sam bith rud mar sin air aoigh 'san tigh agamsa. Feumaidh tu thoirt air ais dha gun dàil.*'

'*Cha b'urrainn dhomh sin a' dhèanamh, eadhon ged bu mhath leam. Bhiodh e a smaointinn gu'n robh mi toirt a' chair às.*' Malcolm sounded conciliatory now.

'*Bhitheadh fios aige gu'n tug thu an car às. Dìreach mar thu a' toirt a' chair asam fad bhliadhnachan.*' Rodrick paused. Then, '*Uill ma tà, nì mi furasda dhuit e. Thoir dhomsa an t-airgiod mus fàg thu an caisteal agus gheibh mi doigh air a thoirt air ais dha.*'

Malcolm MacRodrick stalked off without another word and his brother came back to Catriona and me.

'Sorry about that. Family business,' he said. 'Now, Derek, would you like to see the bull I've got for you?'

'Very much,' I said.

'Good, we'll go down to the steading. You'll come too, Catriona?'

She looked down at her shoes. 'I don't think I'm quite dressed for farmyards. I've got a letter or two to write, if you don't mind,' she said.

*   *   *

'There he is, now,' said The MacRodrick.

We were standing in a slushy yard which would indeed have played havoc with Catriona's shoes. The grey granite farm buildings had grey corrugated iron roofs, some tinted with the rust of age to a rich autumnal red. Nameless pieces of obsolete farm machinery lay rotting contentedly around them. A collie was sniffing at the wheels of a blue Land-Rover. There were four of us, Rodrick, Andrew Cameron his farm manager, another man who was holding the bull by a halter and myself.

Seamus Ruadh the tenth of Kilpatrick was a truly magnificent beast, with wide-spread horns, perfectly matched, on a head held proudly high, straight back, broad hindquarters and a shaggy but immaculately groomed coat of a fiery red colour that glowed in the sunshine. He had clearly had as much care spent on him to prepare him for my approval as had his half brother Ossian the third for the Oban sale two days earlier. All the disappointment that I had since been feeling about having been outbid for the latter instantly fled.

'Will he suit you, do you think?' said Rodrick anxiously.

'I couldn't ask for anything better,' I said.

'Good. I said I'd let you have him for five thousand, three hundred, didn't I?'

'Yes.'

Even at that price I reckoned I was getting a bargain.

'I made a mistake.'

I did my best to prevent the instant feeling of dismay from showing on my face. What with last night, I'd be hard put to it to afford very much more.

'Harumph!' Rodrick continued. 'Seamus here is priced at three thousand, eight hundred and fifty guineas. Is that not right, Andrew?'

The farm manager's face was expressionless.

'It is that, Mac Ruaraidh Mor.'

'Yes, but . . .'

'Not another word, Derek. You'll have a sound enough foundation there on which to base your new fold of Highlanders. You can't imagine how much pleasure it'll give me, just thinking of that,' he said.

* * *

Catriona took me on one side as we went into the dining-room.

'There's a boat coming at four o'clock to take Malcolm and his two boys and Alastair back to the mainland and I thought I'd go with them. How about a walk after lunch until then?'

'I'd like that,' I said.

At The MacRodrick's suggestion, we decided to climb the hill directly across the river from the castle.

'You'll get a grand view from the top,' he said. 'The river itself and the loch it runs out of are a continuation of the Caledonian Fault line. That's the one that runs south-west all the way from the Moray Firth, through the three lochs that split the mainland, Lochs Ness, Lochy and Linnhe, then through Loch Spelvie and Loch Buie on Mull and on through Larna to the Sound of Colonsay.'

'Shall we take Amanda?' I said.

Rodrick looked doubtful.

'You can try. You'd better have her on a lead, though. To begin with at any rate.'

He rang a bell and in a couple of minutes a great big beaming blowsy woman who could have been anything from her late twenties to early forties appeared.

'This is Dougalina . . . ' he pronounced it to rhyme with 'finer', ' . . . my housekeeper. Dougalina, you've not met Lord Thyrde.'

We shook hands.

'Could you lay your hand on Amanda's collar and lead, do you think?'

'I could that, Mac Ruaraidh Mor.'

She walked over to a small table that was within a yard of where Rodrick was standing, opened a drawer, took out the required articles and put them triumphantly into his hand.

'That's you.'

'Harumph! I'll be losing myself next,' The MacRodrick said.

He fitted the collar round the whippet's neck, to her all too evident disgust at what she clearly regarded as an insult, and handed the end of the lead to me.

I gave it a tentative tug but Amanda immediately lay down and glued herself to the ground, where she remained unmovable.

Then she looked reproachfully back up at her master.

'Go with him then,' he said.

At that Amanda did get up and follow me, but adopting a crouching attitude as she walked with her blue fawn tail tucked miserably between her legs. It was only when Catriona and I had crossed the courtyard and gone out through the arch that led to the clan-gathering ground that she started trotting more or less contentedly at my heel.

'I've never heard the name "Dougalina" before,' I said.

'She's Dougal MacRodrick's daughter.'

'Yes, I gathered that.'

'For a daughter to be called after her father, she just has an "ina" tacked on to the end of his Christian name.' Catriona grinned. 'It's a habit we Scottish girls have,' she said.

We went down the steps, turned right at the bottom along a mown grass path to the drive, crossed the river by the bridge over which we had been driven by Dougal the night before and skirted the village of Kilpatrick by a track that led up the hill and through the trees on the other side.

I already knew from what she had told me in the sleeper train the week before that Catriona was involved in the politics of Larna but no more than that. I found it difficult to believe that she could be on the opposition side, but this would now be the last opportunity I would have to find out exactly where she did stand. I didn't want to say anything about my own involvement until I could be certain so I thought it wiser to approach the subject in a roundabout way.

'You knew our host out on the island, I suppose?'

'Everybody knows him out on the island,' she said.

'Incidentally, I'd give a lot to know what he and Malcolm were saying to each other this morning. They were speaking Gaelic, presumably.'

'They were.' Catriona looked up at me. 'I've been going to Gaelic classes out there for some months, but neither of them were to know that.'

'Really? What was it all about, then?'

'Let's see, now. He started by telling Malcolm that he understood he'd taken a lot of money off you at cards last night.' She grinned. 'That was my doing, I'm afraid, I may just have let something out about it. Well, Malcolm admitted it and told him how much, but tried to justify himself. Then the laird . . . everybody refers to him as the laird up here, when they're not calling him Mac Ruaraidh Mor . . . said he wouldn't have a guest of his treated like that and told Malcolm he'd got to pay it back.'

'Phew! And how did Malcolm take that?'

'Not very well, actually, said if he did that you'd think he'd cheated you. Then the laird inferred that that was exactly what he had done and furthermore that he'd probably also been cheating him too over a number of years. But he told him he'd make it easy for him and that if he gave him a cheque for the whole amount before he left the island, he'd find some way of giving it back to you.'

'He's already done it,' I said.

I told her about the bull that I'd bought from him that morning suddenly undergoing a dramatic reduction in value.

'Pedigree cattle, like racehorses, are sold in guineas – a guinea equals one pound and five pence in modern money. I worked it out on a bit of paper before lunch and the amount by which he reduced the price in guineas came out in pounds to exactly the same as Malcolm took off me at piquet last night – to the nearest fiver, that is. What do you think of Malcolm otherwise?'

'Not a lot,' said Catriona. 'Do you know anything about the political situation out in Larna?'

'A little,' I said. 'It's the Larna National Party against the People's Progressive Movement, if I remember rightly.'

She nodded.

'Well, I'm a member of the LNP while Malcolm MacRodrick's hand in glove with the PPM. I'd never met Malcolm before but what I've seen of him here bears out everything I've ever heard about him. My people don't trust him one little bit.'

We were approaching the last of the trees and the grey-brown shape of a roe deer chose that moment to jump out on to the track ahead of us. We stopped and watched as it turned and went up it for several paces. Then, just as a quickly, it turned again and disappeared off it on the other side.

I noticed that Amanda's head had turned to follow it round as it went in order to watch it but she had stayed stock still and I hadn't felt the slightest pressure from her end of the lead.

As we were now some distance from the road and any possible danger from traffic, I waited until we were well beyond the point of the roe's disappearance and then, greatly daring, I removed Amanda's lead. She stayed obediently at heel.

Then, a little further up, 'Run on,' I said.

The whippet cantered happily off, pausing every now and then to sniff about her, but every time she reached a turn in the track or a fold in the hill, she paused and watched me patiently until I had risen high enough always to have her in my sight.

Catriona and I walked on up in companionable silence.

This manoeuvre on my part was mainly to give me time to think before reverting to the subject of Larna. Dare I confide in her in the same way that I had done to such good effect with Geoffrey Robertson on the train from Glasgow to Oban? She, if anyone, would be a perfect ally but, if I made the wrong decision, a far more dangerous adversary. And, with Catriona, it had to be now or the chance might not come again.

Some hundred yards further on, to my absolute horror, a blue hare got up almost at Amanda's feet and bounded away across the heather. After an initial start of surprise, the whippet gazed after it and then looked back at me as though for permission. 'Stay!' I said, and miraculously she obeyed.

Amanda!

Catriona?

There was a cairn at the highest point of the hill and the whippet stood beside it, waiting goodly for us. By the time we came up to her, I had made up my mind.

The view was really staggering.

Below us was the castle, like a toy fort highlighted in the sunshine, its diminutive square flag fluttering against the spume-speckled blue of the sea beneath, and in the distance beyond it was the mainland, very much as I had been able to see it that morning over the wall that bounded the clan-gathering ground. To our immediate south, the hill rose from the lochside, gently at first and then more steeply until it reached a plateau very much higher than the point on which we were standing and, although I had no field glasses with me, I reckoned I could make out deer moving on its skyline as it dipped to the west. To the north lay the Sound of Larna with the high hills of Laggan beyond that.

'Look, Catriona, I've got to talk to you. You more than anybody will appreciate that nothing I tell you must go any further,' I said.

We sat down on the cairn. Catriona watched me in complete silence as I talked, the breeze in her silken black hair, her fine-boned honey-brown face tilted up towards me. The whippet had positioned itself on my other side so that my right hand could rest on its head.

I told her about everything. The briefing I had been given, the task to get close to The MacRodrick and to try and find out what he intended to do about his property on the Caribbean Island. The chance meeting with Geoffrey Robertson and his alternative suggestion that I should seek to persuade Rodrick to alter the succession to the clan chiefship itself. His turning out to have been a schoolfriend of my father's which had led to the offer of this other bull and the consequent invitation that had given me access to the island.

When I had finished, Catriona grinned.

'Snap! I've been acting under almost identical instructions. But mine were from ZH – his name's Zechariah Hall but everybody calls him that – the first minister of Larna and leader of my party,' she said.

'You've spoken to the laird, then?'

'Yes, I had breakfast with him in his sitting-room upstairs this morning. Before we came out and joined you and his brother on the clan-gathering ground. For all the good it did me,' Catriona said.

'What did he say?'

'Much the same as he did to your people. Like you, I didn't know that it was possible to alter the succession, but he told me that he couldn't leave the Caribbean possessions away from the clan chiefship. And he told me that the LNP mustn't worry, because everything would turn out all right in the end.'

'So what are you going to do now?'

'Go straight back to Larna to report progress . . . or rather the lack of it. That's why I'm taking up the chance of leaving by this boat that's coming this afternoon. How about you?'

'I'm hoping to get a chance to talk to the laird this evening, after you've all gone. How do you rate the chances of your party, the LNP, at the elections after independence?'

Catriona frowned and was silent for a moment or two.

'Not too bad at the moment. The opinion polls have been worrying, of course, but the PPM have been promising the earth to everybody. We all know that they're just out to "buy" votes and they've actually been doing quite a lot already. They've got hold of a lot of money from somewhere and they are doing up selected shacks in all parts of the island as an earnest of delights to come.'

'What was the latest opinion-poll figure, do you remember? The chap from the Foreign and Commonwealth Office who briefed me did tell me.'

'Forty-seven per cent to thirty-nine.'

'But . . . how do you know the PPM and their paper, what's it called, the *Voice of the People*, haven't been fudging the figures?'

'Wouldn't do 'em much good if they had. The latest informed intelligence is that publishing the results of polls doesn't have much net effect on the actual vote when it comes; some people react one way, some the other – *bandwagon* versus *underdog* – and they tend to cancel each other out. And, in any case, the United States has been taking an interest in Larna lately and the CIA's been funding its own private polls which they pass on to us . . . and they coincide all too closely with those of the PPM, damn it.'

'Who leads the People's Progressive Movement?'

She wrinkled up her nostrils in distaste.

'A nasty little man called Septimus Baker, he'd stoop to anything. We call him "Septicus" and I think he knows it, that's probably why he likes to be known as "Sep". But ZH has been holding his own up to a point by sheer personality.'

'He's a good chap, Zechariah Hall, is he?'

'Not far short of a saint. The islanders out there respect and trust ZH implicitly but they adore The MacRodrick and the combination is almost irresistible. If the elections were held now, I reckon we'd still get in for a certainty.'

'And later? Supposing Malcolm were to succeed Rodrick in the meantime?'

'Hard to say. The chief of the clan really does carry an enormous amount of weight out there and always has.'

'What do you make of their cousin Alastair? He seems to be the only possible alternative to Malcolm as Rodrick's successor.'

'I liked him. But nobody on the island knows anything about him and, from what I've seen here, he seems to get on equally well with both brothers so perhaps he's just not interested. How about you?'

'I've seen a bit of him at the House of Lords of course, he being Black Rod. But nobody seems to know anything about him there either. I got on Alastair/ Derek terms with him last night, but other than that I'm none the wiser.'

Something that had been worrying me ever since the situation in Larna had first been brought to my attention came into my mind.

'Isn't there a governor-general or something? WIAD, the Head of the West Indian and Atlantic Department of the FCO who briefed me, never mentioned him. Where does he fit in?'

She smiled.

'Governor, actually. We'll have a governor-general after independence if our lot get in, whereas if Septicus does and declares a republic, it'll be a high commissioner. No, the governor's always taken second place to The MacRodrick of the day. I'm told that being Governor of Larna has always been regarded as the most dead-end job in the entire Foreign and Commonwealth Service and the present one's no exception. He's just a cipher, really, and it's not surprising your chap didn't mention him.'

'So the whole thing really might depend on our host still being alive when the elections take place?'

Catriona nodded gravely.

'It might,' she said.

She looked at her watch and stood up.

'I'd better be getting back down now, or I'll miss the boat. Tell you what, let's keep in touch and compare notes. With me out on the island and you at Westminster, we may just be able to achieve something together.'

She gave me her address and telephone number in Larna and I gave mine, both in London and the country, to her.

My disappointment at not spending another night under the same roof with Catriona was slightly tempered by the possibility that, being alone with Rodrick at the castle, I might just be able to learn something of interest and advantage that night.

*　　*　　*

We played piquet again after dinner.

'Club Rules, this time, I think,' he said, as he got out the cards.

At the end of each *partie* of six deals, he explained, the winner normally subtracts his opponent's score from his own and adds a hundred to the difference. But if the loser's total comes to less than a hundred, he *adds* the two scores together and then the extra hundred points on top of that, and that is called 'winning a *rubicon*'.

'So you see that, even without a *rubicon*, the scores can be quite high. That is why I thought we would leave that particular rule out first time round, but with the advantage of hindsight perhaps that was a mistake.'

The laird was watching me keenly and I couldn't be quite sure whether or not I detected that twinkle in his eye.

'And we'll still stick to a penny a point, if you don't mind,' he added.

Even so, I found myself being *rubiconed* again and paying him out the sum of three pounds, seventy-eight pence!

I had been hoping to talk to him about the object of my visit during dinner, but the ubiquitous Dougal had been with us the whole time and somehow I hadn't liked to. I was wondering how to bring up the subject now, before he went off to bed. Luckily, he saved me the trouble.

'Do you know my other Larna?' he said.

'I've never been there. Nor anywhere else in the Caribbean for that matter.'

'You've missed something.' Rodrick sat there, shuffling and reshuffling the cards mechanically as he spoke. 'I'm going out there next week. It'll be the last time, I'm afraid, but I'd like to see my boy's grave again before I die.'

He gave a brief shake to his head.

'Ridiculous really. To look at me now, the way I feel even, you'd think I'd got a year or two yet left in me. But the doctors give me four or five months at the most, possibly far shorter than that. Linitis Plastica, they call it, "Leather Bottle Stomach". It's a sort of strangling cancer and that's what they tell me it makes the stomach look like,' he said.

'I am sorry.'

'Don't be. Dougal's coming out to the island with me. I never stop thinking how lucky I am to have him.'

'He certainly seems to be a marvellous person,' I said. 'Head stalker, butler, piper . . . '

'Nurse, too. He's a relation of mine, actually. All members of a clan are meant to be related to the chief . . . and a lot of them are, going back over the centuries. But Dougal really is. My great uncle, my grandfather Rodrick's youngest brother, was his great-grandfather. That makes Dougal my second cousin once removed. My son Ranald's third cousin.'

He stared at the fire for quite some moments.

Then, 'Harumph! You didn't know Ranald, did you? He'd be quite a bit older than you. Before your time at Eton?'

'I think so. I'm sure I never met him,' I said.

There was another long pause.

'Tell me about Larna,' I said gently.

'Marvellous place, I adore it. Didn't suit my wife though, never would go out there after the first few times, soon after we were married. We've always been happy enough together here, though . . . until she died back in June, only a matter of weeks after Ranald. She only ever had the one child and I think losing him was the main cause of her death.'

The MacRodrick reached forward to put a hand on my shoulder and this time the twinkle in his eye was unmistakable.

'We make a right pair, don't we, you and I. A couple of old widowers together. Perhaps that's why we get on so well,' he said.

I was struck by an instant conviction that about that he was almost certainly right.

'But, what about Larna and its Independence Bill?' I said. 'I get the impression that the government here are quite worried about it.'

Rodrick smiled.

'That's the impression they gave me too. Well, if any of 'em get to know you've been talking to me, you can set their minds at rest on that score. Everything will be all right, you have my assurance on that.'

Like my overlords I had the severest doubts about that but there was something about the tone of absolute certainty with which he said it that precluded any other approach from me on that subject. If I pressed him any further now and raised the subject of who was to succeed him, I knew instinctively not only that it would be unproductive but also that he'd realise that I was more than I purported to be, a guest invited on the spur of the moment after a chance meeting. And after all the kindness that he had been showing me, I'd been feeling more and more awful about doing what was tantamount to spying on my host.

The one message that I must take back was the vital importance of getting the Larna bill through Parliament as quickly as possible.

'But if you are interested . . . ?'

'Very much so,' I said.

'I've got ZH, that's Zechariah Hall the first minister of Larna, coming over here in a month or so. John J. MacRodrick, the president of the American Clan Society, will be staying at the castle as well, in fact the object of his visit is to bring the two together. What about coming up here again then?'

'I'd love to.'

'Good. I'll be in touch with you then, just as soon as we've got a date settled. I don't suppose you'll be going back to your job at the House for a while yet?'

'Well, the Opening of Parliament's next week,' I said. 'It's purely formal, of course, but my job as Deputy Chief Whip carries with it the appointment of Captain of the Yeomen of the Guard, who's always part of the procession. I think I really ought to be there at least for that.'

CHAPTER FIVE

The procession was moving in slow time up the Royal Gallery, through banks of seated spectators. In front of them, lining the route on either side, were spaced members of The Queen's Body Guard of the Yeomen of the Guard, of whom I was the captain. Known as 'The Oldest Guard', it was made up of retired warrant officers and sergeants wearing Tudor hats, doublets, breeches and stockings, and armed with partisans, the infantry weapon of the period, all virtually unchanged since the time of the first Elizabeth.

My own uniform consisted of a double-breasted tailed scarlet tunic, with a stand collar and gold epaulettes, aiguillettes, embroidery and sash, known as a coatee, skin-tight overalls of dark-blue cloth, with a wide gold oakleaf stripe over the side-seams and long-spurred wellington boots; my sword was slung on the left and I carried a black silk cocked hat with its plume of swan feathers in one white-gloved hand and my stick of office, ebony mounted and tasselled in gold, in the other. To my right marched Tom Lavenham, who, as Captain of Her Majesty's Body Guard of the Honourable Corps of Gentlemen-at-Arms, 'The Nearest Guard', composed of retired field officers, was more or less similarly dressed, his being the cavalry, mine the infantry, version of army full dress circa 1836. But he, poor chap, had to carry a bulky cavalry sword with its steel scabbard in his left hand, leaving his right to cope with his heavy brass helmet, surmounted by its high plume of longer white swan's feathers, as well as his gold stick.

The Royal Gallery, one hundred and ten feet long, forty-five feet wide and forty-five high, decorated and gilded from floor to ceiling throughout its entire length, is in reality only a passage. It's sole purpose in life is to enable the Sovereign, crowned, robed and accompanied by her great officers of state in full dress, to walk in procession from the Robing Room at one end, through the Princes' Chamber at the other and thence into the chamber of the House of Lords, there to meet the Lords Spiritual and Temporal and the Commons, in Parliament assembled, at the State Opening of Parliament. These four rooms, the most magnificent in the entire Palace of Westminster, were conceived by Barry the architect and Pugin his designer with this one annual occasion in mind.

There was an air of almost tangible drama and solemnity as the procession moved slowly forward. The point of the stick in my right hand tapped the thick blue carpet noiselessly, in time with each pace of my left foot. When we had shambled through the un-dress rehearsals the night before under the patient guidance of the Earl Marshal, it had been hard to believe that anything remotely approaching the impressive could come out of it, but with the metamorphosis from workaday clothes into the butterfly colours of pageantry, so had our very movements transformed themselves into an entity of military precision.

To my immediate front was the lord-in-waiting on duty, wearing his scarlet and ermine parliamentary robe and keeping pace with, on Tom's side, the navy-blue-and-gold figure of the Vice-Admiral of the United Kingdom. Some way ahead, I was dimly conscious of The Queen herself on the arm of the Duke of Edinburgh, the bejewelled Imperial Crown shimmering on her head, with her train held by four scarlet-frocked pages of honour, preceded by an admiral of the fleet and a cabinet minister bearing the Sword of Honour and the Cap of Maintenance respectively. Beyond them again were the scarlet-uniformed Lord Great Chamberlain and the Earl Marshal of England in faded ducal robe, carrying wand and baton of office respectively, they alone of the whole procession walking backwards so as to be able to face their Sovereign all along the way.

We turned into the Princes' Chamber, the route here being lined by the Gentlemen, Tom's boys – dressed like him except that they wore their white-plumed brass helmets and held tall seventeenth-century ceremonial battle-axes, and it was at this point that the procession split, entering the chamber of the House of Lords by each of the two doors.

We spaced ourselves in our allotted places to the right of the throne while The Queen and the Duke mounted the steps and turned to face the assembled peers in scarlet and ermine, peeresses in long evening dress, long white gloves and glistening tiaras, judges of the High Court in their scarlet robes and members of the Corps Diplomatique, accredited to the Court of St James, each in national or ceremonial dress, all of whom had risen at her entry.

The pages of honour arranged the long velvet train of her robe so that it lay displayed down the steps to her right.

She bowed to the House as a whole.

'My Lords, pray be seated.'

Tom and I stood there with the other members of the procession on our side of the throne as everybody else resumed their seats. Alastair MacRodrick,

The Gentleman Usher, in full court dress of black velvet and lace and holding, sloped on his shoulder from one black-gloved hand, the ebony rod from which he takes his name, came to the bar of the House at the far end. He bowed to The Queen, turned about and left the chamber to summon 'the faithful Commons' to the bar.

We could hear the cries of 'Hat's off, strangers' fading progressively down the corridor as he passed along his way.

A low murmur of conversations arose around the chamber. I couldn't help glancing across to the bench on the far side where the viscountesses sat and the place among them which I knew was to have been occupied by Julia. I could visualise her there now, in the new pale blue dress that she had bought specially for the occasion, with the Mallicent rocks, reluctantly surrendered to her by my mother, around her slim neck and surmounting her adorable light blonde hair.

After a long pause the cries of 'Hat's off, strangers' could be heard approaching again. This time they were accompanied by the shrill chatter of a hundred voices. I could never help wondering whether the Commons were genuinely unaware of just how much noise they were making or whether perhaps they did it on purpose.

The doors were flung open and Black Rod reappeared, ushering in the Serjeant at Arms bearing the Mace of the House of Commons, Madam Speaker in gold-bedecked gown, the Clerk of the House, the Speaker's Chaplain and her Secretary. Together, these five bowed three times to the throne as they approached the bar. Then the rest of the Commons arranged themselves behind and around them.

Charles Fortescue the Prime Minister and Albert Wainwright, Leader of the Opposition, were in the forefront. Behind them stood the Foreign and Commonwealth Secretary – I had an appointment to be debriefed by him early that afternoon. Among the others I could just pick out Geoffrey Robertson and, a little further off, Malcolm MacRodrick – by his carnation and his tie.

As soon as they were all in, the Lord Chancellor in his ceremonial wig and robes and carrying his Purse left his place to my front right and mounted the steps to the throne. There he knelt to Her Majesty, took out the official copy of the 'Gracious Speech' and presented it to her. Then he rose to his feet and took the three more precarious paces backwards down again.

'My Lords and Members of the House of Commons . . . '

There was complete silence in every part of the chamber and galleries, as in a clear, level, voice The Queen began to read.

In common with the other front-bench members of all parties, I had already heard the contents the night before, behind closed doors and under conditions of the strictest secrecy. Both Houses would hear it again that afternoon, repeated by the Speaker and the Lord Chancellor, before they began to debate the motion that 'An humble address be presented to Her Majesty thanking Her for Her Most Gracious Speech'. The passage that read 'A bill will be introduced to provide for the independence of Larna' came about a third of the way through.

*   *   *

The room belonging to Her Majesty's Principal Secretary of State for Foreign and Commonwealth Affairs is the most imposing of any occupied by a member of the cabinet, not excluding the Prime Minister himself – and rightly so. Imparting an aura of spaciousness combined with elegance and taste, it is the place to which the holder of that office summons an ambassador of a foreign power to complain to him about any unacceptable conduct on the part of his principals, and a certain amount of grandeur lends weight to such an occasion. Percival Strickland's own appearance and stature were such that they needed all the help in this respect that they could get.

He was a fussy, pompous little man with a fussy, pompous little moustache, unimpressive at the dispatch box and in cabinet alike, and the only reason that anyone could give for him having been able to acquire and hold down such a position was that his meticulous attention to and knowledge of the slightest detail made him an unusually good negotiator abroad.

'Well now, Lord Thyrde, perhaps you would give me your report on the success, or otherwise, of your . . . er . . . mission.'

He was seated behind a large eighteenth-century walnut desk, the flat red-leather top of which was clear except for a silver pen-and-ink stand, five telephones and a blotter. A yard to his right and a respectful pace back, sat Jack Singleton, one of his parliamentary under-secretaries of state and the FCO minister responsible for Asia, North America and the Caribbean, whom I had met briefly on a number of previous occasions. I was facing them from a chair on the other side of the desk.

I gave them a brief run-down of my visit to the Scottish Larna, leaving out any reference to Geoffrey Robertson and, apart from the bare fact of her presence on the island, to Catriona Campbell.

When I had finished, Percival Strickland was silent for a moment.

'So . . . having been afforded an ideal opportunity to do what you had been instructed to do, namely to ask Mr MacRodrick why he was not prepared to ensure that his Larnacan possessions would bypass his younger brother in one way or another, you neglected to do so.'

He picked up one of the pens from the silver stand and tapped it peevishly on the red leather in front of him.

'*Why?*'

'I told you,' I said. 'I got the impression that it would be unwise to do so.'

'*You got the impression that it would be unwise to do so.*' He repeated the words slowly and with emphasis. 'Be so good as to tell me just what exactly gave you that impression.'

'Well, it's difficult to explain really,' I said, 'but in my job as a whip you get to know instinctively whether something's going to work or whether it would be totally counter-productive. This was one of the latter occasions. I just knew,' I added lamely.

'*In your job as a whip, you get to know instinctively? You just knew?* Let me tell you, Lord Thyrde, as a relatively junior member of this government, your "job", as you're pleased to call it, is to carry out the instructions given to you by superiors and not to start varying them in order to suit some passing whim of your own.'

The Parliamentary Under-Secretary leant forward in his chair.

'Hold on, Secretary of State. Derek did at least get himself invited to stay with The MacRodrick *and* managed to remain on good terms with him at the end of it. That's more than you can say for any of the rest of us.'

Mentally chalking up to Jack an award for extreme gallantry, I awaited the inevitable explosion. Sure enough, his overlord started swelling visibly like an affronted game-bird. Then, almost immediately, he subsided again.

'Be that as it may . . .' . He looked back at me. 'You say that, in your opinion, it is of vital that we should take the Independence Bill through Parliament as quickly as possible.'

'Very much so, Secretary of State,' I said.

'That shouldn't present much difficulty. In fact, it might have been possible to get the bill through before this last session ended, but Larna only started asking for independence in March and, what with their legislature having to pass a referendum bill, the holding of the referendum itself, the constitutional conference here in London, the drafting of the bill and the subsequent Order in Counsel, together with obtaining the necessary approval of our own cabinet committees at all these stages, the earliest possible moment for the first reading of the bill in the House of Commons would have been the .

twelfth of July. With the Summer recess intervening and the date for the new Opening of Parliament already fixed for today, the whole thing would have been just too tight.'

He had reeled all this off without referring to a single note and my opinion of him underwent a certain amount of up-grading.

'So what's the timing likely to be now?' I said.

'Let me see. Stop me if I get any of this wrong, Jack. The first reading in the Commons is tomorrow?'

'No, it's on Monday,' Jack said.

'Monday then, that's the first of November.'

From the slightly smug expression on the Foreign and Commonwealth Secretary's face, I reckoned that he been aware of that fact all along. 'Well, allowing seventeen days for the bill to go through the House of Commons, with another fourteen for the Lords, brings us to the second of December with Royal Assent possibly on the same day. The order bringing about the general election in Larna would be submitted to the Privy Council the day after, the third; they could meet to approve it on the tenth; three weeks for it to come into force, the thirty-first; but you couldn't expect a largely Scottish-orientated island to begin such an important general election campaign on New Year's Eve. That would start on Monday, the third of January, with the election itself taking place on the twenty-fourth.'

I had been jotting down the dates as he gave them to me.

'Election campaign in Larna, January third to January twenty-fourth,' I said.

'That's right. If all goes well, that is. What I have given you is the most optimistic estimate.'

I didn't like the sound of that. January would be late enough as it was. After that every day might count.

'What could go wrong, then?'

Percival Strickland paused for a moment.

'Getting the bill itself through Parliament will be the only real problem, because everything else would follow automatically. But thirty-one days to cover the two Houses is the bare minimum and even that couldn't be achieved without the full cooperation of the opposition. Added to that the main programme of government legislation for this session is a full one and some of it more than usually controversial.'

'Such as the Ancillary Services Bill?' I said.

It was a measure designed to privatise a large and varied assortment of minor government organisations, none of them important enough to warrant a bill of their own, and it was one which I knew was expected to arouse a great deal of anger and resentment among the opposition parties.

The Secretary of State nodded.

'I don't suppose the Larna bill will take a very high priority compared with that.'

He started tapping on the table with his pen again.

'Will The MacRodrick be fit enough to go to Larna for the elections?'

'I very much doubt it, not as late as January. He's out there at the moment actually, but he says it's the last time. No, the really important thing is that Malcolm MacRodrick, who's bound to be there, shouldn't himself have become chief of the clan by that time, with all the immense authority that that would give him.'

Percival Strickland coughed.

'I am fully aware of that,' he said drily.

'There's one other thing,' I said, 'apparently Zechariah Hall is holding his own at the moment, but the People's Progressive Movement are making all sorts of promises. It's only a matter of time before Septicus . . . er, Septimus Baker . . . ' I amended hurriedly, but Percival Strickland was on to it like a flash.

'We do not use nicknames in this department, particularly not derogatory ones, for members of Commonwealth countries,' he said. I caught Jack's eye and he winked at me. 'And it may surprise you to know that both the Parliamentary Under-Secretary of State and I do have a certain amount of knowledge about what is going on in Larna.'

'Yes, I'm sorry. That was stupid of me,' I said.

Jack Singleton saw me out into the passage.

'Thank's for coming to my rescue, back there,' I said to him. 'I thought for a moment it was going to be pretty sticky.'

Jack grinned.

'Percy's not such a bad old boy when you get to know him.'

'I suppose not. He really does appreciate the urgency of all this?'

'I shan't be letting him forget it. Anything else I can do for you?'

'There is one thing,' I said. 'You know that first list of events that Percival Strickland reeled off, the Larnacans originally deciding to ask for independence, the referendum they had out there, the constitutional conference here in London, etc. You couldn't possibly let me have all that down on paper, with the exact dates of each?'

'I'm sure I could.'

'And would you add to it the approximate time when The MacRodrick's terminal illness was first diagnosed, together with the date of his son Ranald's death?'

Jack whistled.

'You think there might be a connection?'

'Don't you?'

'What's your next step then?'

'Black Rod, he's still the key figure in all this. If by some happy chance Malcolm is to be bypassed for the chiefship, he seems to be the only possible alternative. I've asked him to dinner at Pratt's tonight,' I said.

*   *   *

Pratt's Club, largely due to the compact size of its premises and consequently of its membership, is probably the most exclusive of all the men's clubs in London. It was founded a century and a half ago by the seventh Duke of Beaufort who, feeling the need for a place where he and his friends could find food, drink and relaxation into the early hours of the morning, took to frequenting the basement kitchen belonging to his retired steward, Pratt, who let out rooms in a narrow three-storey house off St James's Street. And it is this kitchen together with the dining room that leads out of it, with a change of duke but certainly not of atmosphere, that still forms the nucleus of Pratt's today.

I led Black Rod through the hall, past the billiard table laid out as always ready for play but somehow never used for that purpose, and down a flight of stairs to the basement. Georgina took our orders for dinner from the largely breakfast-food menu and we went over and established ourselves at a secluded table in the corner, where one of the Georges soon brought drinks over to us. Traditionally, club servants at Pratt's whatever their real names might be are invariably addressed as 'George', a rule to which Georgina, the lady who is the present incumbent of the stewardship, forms only a minor exception.

Alastair MacRodrick took a sip of his whisky and soda.

'This is very good of you, Derek. Now, how can I help you? What was it you wished to discuss with me,' he said.

I glanced around the familiar room. Chairs and tables of dark-stained wood imbued with the patina of age, prints and cartoons on the walls interspersed with antlers and cases of stuffed birds and fish, cheerful china plates arrayed on an old oak dresser, all this forming a perfect time-capsule of the mid- to late-nineteenth century. There were some twelve or fourteen other people spaced around it, some in groups of twos or threes talking and drinking, others by themselves, turning the pages of magazines or newspapers.

'Well . . . ' I said.

I had given a considerable amount of thought to how I could best sound out Black Rod on the subject of Larna and had still not come up with a satisfactory solution. I certainly couldn't take him into my confidence in the same way I had Geoffrey Robertson and Catriona Campbell, or still worse say or do anything that would lead to his suspecting the true nature of my involvement. If he was on the side of Rodrick and the LNP he would be more than justified in resenting the fact that I had inveigled my way into the castle under false pretences. Even if he was genuinely uncommitted on the subject which – after a lifetime spent in the services followed by his recent appointment to the Royal Household, both of which involved the strictest political neutrality – was not unlikely, the same would apply. Whereas, if he should turn out to be a closet supporter of Malcolm and the PPM, the dangers involved in such a course were self-evident.

My best chance lay in making it sound convincing that my interest in what was going on in the Caribbean island had been aroused at some point between the time when the laird and I saw off the boat that carried him, Malcolm and Catriona back to the mainland and now.

'I had a fascinating time talking to our host after you all left, the other day,' I said.

'I'm sure you did.'

I looked across at him questioningly.

'You made quite a hit with Rodrick,' he said.

'Well, it turns out that he and my father were at school together.'

'No, it's more than that.'

Black Rod spoke softly and evenly, without a trace of inflection in his voice. In appearance there was little about him to remember. Yet even in the dark-blue pin-striped suit that he was now wearing, that undefinable quality of his presence – a remote suggestion of menace was the nearest that I could get to it – was still discernible.

'I've seldom known him take to anyone quite so quickly. You know he's dying, I suppose?'

'Yes, he told me. And also that he was going off to the Caribbean Larna for the last time. I understand there's a bit of trouble out there at the moment.'

'Trouble?'

'Yes. My people were in a bit of a flap about it this morning. Over who's going to win the election after independence.'

'Oh, I see.'

I waited for him to go on but it soon became apparent that he wasn't going to.

'Have you been to Larna much yourself?'

Alastair shook his head.

'I was born there, as it happens. But there was never a lot of opportunity all the time I was in the Air Force. I took my elder boy, David, out for a visit though, during this last recess – his brother, Jamie, was away on some school expedition of his own.'

He held the remains of his whisky and soda up to what little light there was and studied it intently.

'Have another,' I said.

'Eh? No, really. Thank you very much.'

Alastair put the glass down on the table in front of him.

I tried again.

'Do you know Zechariah Hall?'

'Well, yes. I've met him.'

Another pause.

'And the other chap, Septimus Baker?'

'No.'

There was a periodic trickle of members returning from the dining-room and a similar outward movement of others leaving to take their place.

'They tell me that The MacRodrick is adored by the islanders and carries a great deal of influence among them,' I said.

'That's true, certainly.'

'And he's done a lot for them.'

'Well, yes.'

There was a certain amount of hesitation in his voice, so again I waited . . . and this time he did go on.

'I'm telling you this in strict confidence, Derek, because you like him and I know he likes you, but although he has the welfare of Larna and its people always in the forefront of his mind, he may not always be acting in their best interests.'

'How do you mean?'

'He's against change in any form – likes to keep things as they are. Tourism, for instance. Larna ought to have an international airport of its own by this time, instead of just a shuttle from Jamaica.'

'And The MacRodrick's been blocking it?'

'Well, he hasn't exactly encouraged it. And there's Larna's natural resources too, it has vast deposits of bauxite – nobody knows quite how much. A few years ago, certain extraction rights were given to a company formed for that purpose but they were hedged about with so many restrictions that it just didn't prove viable.'

'I see,' I said.

'Don't misunderstand me, I have nothing but admiration for my cousin, but he's set in his ways. Spent a lot of his life out there. Too much, some may say.'

'Too much?'

It had not been quite clear which of the two preceding sentences the words had referred to.

'In some people's view,' Alastair said.

I decided to press on.

'None the less, he'll be a hard man to follow. Incidentally, who does succeed him? Someone was telling me that when the chiefship of a clan changes, the next in line is not always chosen automatically.'

'I believe that to be the case.'

'What about Malcolm then? Is it likely to go to him? Or is there a chance that . . . '

George, confound him, chose that of all moments to come back and tell us that our dinner was ready in the dining-room next door and we both stood up.

'I'm afraid that that is something on which it wouldn't be right for me to speculate,' he said.

The politeness of his tone was irreproachable, but I still sensed that the words 'or you either' were implied even though left unsaid.

The one communal table in the dining-room, large and rectangular, was crowded, which effectively put an end to any further questioning. I noticed Tom Lavenham, my boss as Chief Whip, sitting diagonally across the table from me and I suspected that his presence there was not entirely fortuitous. I had gone straight from the FCO to see him in his room in the House of Lords that afternoon, the first opportunity that I had had since my return from Scotland to fill him in on everything that had been happening, and I had mentioned my assignation with Black Rod here tonight.

Alastair's whole manner underwent an instant transformation. From the potted shrimps that were awaiting us in our places, through the mixed grill to the welsh rarebit, he was attentive, informative and uniformly charming. But as soon as we had finished the latter, he turned down my offer of a glass of port outside, pleaded unfinished work to catch up on back at his flat on the top floor of the House, thanked me and left.

I returned alone and disconsolate to the corner table, where I was joined after a moment or two by Tom, bearing two brimming glasses of vintage port. He sat down and stretched out his long legs under the table in front of him.

'I saw you talking to your new friend, Derek. Did you get anything out of him?' he said.

'Yes and no.' I told him about Black Rod's reservations over Rodrick. 'Apart from that, he clammed up completely. Perhaps I didn't handle it very well.'

'Ah! Well, I've been doing a bit of ferreting myself.'

Tom paused briefly for a sip of port.

'When the last Black Rod was coming up to retirement, we were sent the usual list of suitable candidates by the Establishment Committee at the Ministry of Defence so that we could recommend one of them to The Queen for appointment to succeed him. There wasn't a lot to choose between them, as I remember, and we picked this chap largely because he was a first cousin of The MacRodrick's. He had a good enough record, though – here I've had it written down for you.'

He passed me a sheet of typed A4 paper and I ran my eye down it.

1933   Born, Larna, WI.

1945–50   Educated Loretto.

1951   Aircrew cadet RAF, selected for pilot training.

1952   Awarded pilot's wings, commissioned on eight-year engagement, initially as pilot officer. Posted for operational training to Meteor Photo Recce OCU.

1953–7   Completes tour in RAF Germany with Hunter Fighter Recce Squadron, converts to Canberra PR aircraft.

1958–60   Flies numerous upper-air research missions in Pacific area, specialises in very high-altitude operations, recommended for permanent commission and detached on exchange posting with USAF to Langley AFB, Va.

1961–3   Appointed to permanent commission, detached to HQ Near East Air Force on intelligence and recce duties relating to Iraqi threats in Persian Gulf area, attached in '63 to MOD Operations Staff following promotion to squadron leader.

1964   One year RAF Staff College, Bracknell (married at this time, 2 s).

1965–7   Posted to Operations Staff, RAF Germany, responsible for photo and fighter recce operations.

1968–70   Six months Joint Services Staff College, promoted wing commander, appointed to command squadron equipped for long-range electronic operations worldwide (awarded Air Force Cross, 1970).

1971–3   Served at MOD with Central Staff, Policy and Planning, with particular responsibilities for Belize and general Caribbean area.

1974–6   Promoted group captain, converts to Harrier aircraft, appointed to command RAF Germany Harrier base. Competes at Bisley, 1975, wins the Queen's Trophy (awarded CBE, 1976.)

1977–80   One year at Royal College of Defence Studies, posted to head special MOD Policy Planning Team as air commodore, followed by appointment as Assistant Chief of Staff Policy SHAPE with the rank of air vice-marshal.

1981–90   Senior appointments in UK and at various NATO headquarters. Assistant Chief of Defence Staff, MOD. Commands Allied Tactical Air Force Central Europe (KCB, 1984). Assumes overall responsibility for RAF personnel and training.

1990–2   Promoted to air chief marshal as Commander in Chief, NATO Air Forces, Europe (awarded CCB, 1990).

I folded it up and put it away in my pocket.

'Well, that explains one thing,' I said. 'All those hush-hush jobs. Why nobody seems to know very much personally about a man with a record as distinguished as that.'

'Yes and after you left me this afternoon it suddenly occurred to me that there might have been some particular reason for him being put on the list for the job of Black Rod in the first place. There was. I got in touch with a pal of mine in the MOD and the answer came just before I left for here this evening.'

'And . . . ?'

Tom Lavenham's eyes glinted.

'They thought they ought to put him in because he was The MacRodrick's first cousin,' he said.

*   *   *

87

I went down to Thyrde on the following day.

As I turned the corner off the main road and started up the drive with its long lime avenue that led to the sprawling stone house, I felt the uplifting of my heart that never failed to materialise when I returned after an absence of anything more than a couple of days. This time, however, it was tempered with a certain amount of anxiety. How was I going to react to seeing Julian again – he had after all been the innocent cause of his mother's death and which would take precedence in my feelings for him, that or the fact that in him Julia had left something of herself behind?

I went straight up to the day nursery, unchanged since it had been my own. The pictures on the walls, some childhood fantasy some religious, all in pastel colours and liberally bedecked with foxes, rabbits, squirrels, hedgehogs, owls and ducklings, just as I remembered them. Over by the playpen stood my old rocking-horse, with his sweeping white tail and red leather saddle bright against the faded piebald of his body, waiting patiently for not-too-distant use.

The group round the cot had turned and frozen into a tableau as I pushed the door open.

On the outside, clearly redundant, stood Sally Nichols, Julian's pretty brown-haired nanny. She smiled at me and shrugged her shoulders in mock helplessness.

Next was the usurper – my mother – over from her own house in the next-door-but-one village and fussing over a succession of diminutive white outer garments.

'Derek, *darling*. How lovely! Come and look at him.'

Nearer still, sitting upright in adoring and unrelaxing vigilance by the cotside, was Bridget, her smooth-coated tricolour show collie bitch. 'Widge' for short, she had always regarded me with the sort of mindless affection she displayed to her own puppies. Now however, as I approached the cot, she twisted her upper lip and gave a light warning growl.

I looked down into the cot at the tiny occupant, eyes shut for the moment, face chubby and waxlike, thumb firmly in mouth.

'It's time for his afternoon walk,' said my mother. 'Come on, you can push his pram for him if you like.'

She lifted Julian out and when she and Sally had inserted him into what seemed to me to be an inordinate amount of woollen clothing, we all trooped down the back stairs to where a well-blanketed pram was waiting. With a great deal of cosseting, she arranged him into it to her satisfaction. Then she reached down her Barbour coat from a nearby peg.

'I say, do you mind most awfully . . . just this one time, if I take him by myself,' I said.

My mother nodded. 'Of course,' she said and started hanging up her coat again. Sally Nichols smiled understandingly at me. I gave an apologetic stroke to the collie Widge's head.

Outside the sun was shining and I pushed the pram at a steady rate down the back drive. Suddenly I noticed a number of red splodges in the distance, blending perfectly into the colours of grass already dappled with fallen autumn leaves under the trees ahead of us. The Highlanders! I had been told on the telephone that they had arrived safely but until now it had totally gone out of my head.

'Come on, old boy,' I said to Julian. 'Let's go and talk to the moo-cows.'

His piercing blue eyes glared back at me with all the accumulated wisdom of his five-and-a half weeks.

Suddenly I realised that I needn't have worried. Yes, the fact of his birth by a thousand to one chance *had* been the root cause, however indirect, of his mother's death. Yes, there were already signs that he had a great deal of his mother in him and, in that respect alone, he would be someone to value always. But, above all, even at this age, Julian was very much his own person – to be loved and cherished for himself alone.

I wheeled the pram down to the part of the drive that was nearest to the Highlanders.

Seamus Ruadh the tenth of Kilpatrick was lying there chewing contentedly, but his head with the magnificent spread of horns was alert, his eyes watchful. He was surrounded by his seven well-matched wives, some lying down, some standing and grazing. Together they set off the parkland to perfection and I had an immediate feeling of gratitude for the set of circumstances that had brought about the fulfilment of the long-standing ambition of mine to own a fold of pedigree Highlanders, which I might otherwise never have taken the trouble to achieve.

Highland bulls are renowned for their even-temperedness but, even so, just at this moment I had my new charge to think of. With a certain amount of regret therefore I wheeled the pram back towards the house, while the moo-bull, still chewing, followed us only with his eyes as we went. My mother was standing outside the door waving urgently as we approached.

'Derek,' she called when we were within earshot, 'telephone! Catriona somebody. I couldn't quite catch the second name.'

*   *   *

89

'How have you been getting on, since I saw you last?' said Catriona.

I told her.

'How about you?'

'Well, not at all badly, actually. The laird's been more of a success than ever over here these past few days. He's left now but he's been touring round the whole island with ZH and gaining an enormous amount of popularity for the LNP.'

She paused for a moment.

'But do you know what bloody Septicus has done now? The *Voice of the People* should have published their latest poll results this morning. But instead of the 'how are you going to vote' figure they gave the percentage replies to a number of questions that they had put to the people they interviewed. *Which of the following do you consider will be the most important issue at the forthcoming general election – one, the economy, two, unemployment or three, the relief of poverty? Which of the following will best achieve that – one, developing tourism, two, developing mineral resources or three, providing grants to bring local amenities up to standard? Under which of the two parties, one, the Larna National Party or two, the People's Progressive Movement?* While the votes were almost equally divided between each of the three parts of the first two questions, when it came to the third almost seventy-five per cent answered, "two, the PPM," didn't they?'

'But . . . I thought you told me a couple of weeks ago that the latest informed intelligence was that publishing the results of polls doesn't have any effect on the actual vote when it comes?' I said.

I heard Catriona's chuckle.

'Obviously the latest informed intelligence didn't bother to tell Septicus. Be that as it may, we had the results of *their* latest poll from the CIA., this morning. Us fifty-five per cent to their thirty-three, with twelve per cent "don't knows" – swung back almost eight points to the June figures where we started!' she said.

'That sounds hopeful.'

'So far.' She sounded doubtful. 'When did you say the election was likely to be?'

'About the twenty-eithth of January with any luck. But the campaign proper would start on the seventh. Will the effect of the laird's visit last until then?'

'I hope so. The trouble is that ZH might let things slip again – he's so unworldly and just won't put himself forward, while Septicus adores the limelight. But he's going to Scotland to pay a return visit in a week or two, that's bound to be good for publicity here and may just keep the general euphoria going for a bit.'

'I know,' I said. 'I've got an invitation to go back to the castle when that happens.'

'Lucky old you. I adored the Scottish Larna. Not that it wasn't lovely to get back here again.'

'What's your Larna like, then?'

'A sort of dream. You only appreciate just how much when you've been away from it. From the misty blue-green heights of the Hills of the Eagle down to the sparkling azure of Laggan Bay, with its washed white-gold sands that ring Kilpatrick Town, and the rattle and bustle of the town itself, happy, friendly, flamboyant – I love it all.'

'It sounds like paradise.'

'Yes, but it's got a snake in it, remember. You must come out here once all this is over. Promise, Derek?'

'I'll do that,' I said.

*   *   *

'Everything all right?' said my mother, as I joined her in the drawing room. Then, without waiting for an answer, 'You are going to be able to stay for a bit this time, a week or two, I hope?'

I shook my head.

'I'm afraid not,' I said. 'I've got an awful lot going on in London just at the moment – from this coming Monday onwards. I really can't afford to be away.

CHAPTER SIX

' . . . and I have every confidence,' said the Minister of State for Transport, 'that this will be more than enough to satisfy my right honourable friend,'

It would have to be.

From my seat in the Peers' Gallery of the House of Commons I could see that the hands of the clock above the Speaker's Chair were standing at exactly half-past three This had been the reply to the last supplementary question, from an elder statement of his own party on the bench below the gangway, to the last question on the order paper that there had been time to reach, and a more than usually dull question-time was irrevocably over. The main business of the afternoon, the fourth day out of six of the debate on the motion that An humble address be presented to Her Majesty thanking Her for Her Most Gracious Speech, had yet to begin.

In the meantime two government bills were to be read a first time.

'Ancillary Services Bill.' Madam Speaker glanced towards the government front-bench.

The Secretary of State for Trade and Industry half rose in his place and nodded.

'Independence of Larna Bill.'

Jack Singleton, for the Foreign and Commonwealth Office, did the same.

And that apparently was it.

I went down the stairs and out into the Commons lobby.

'Ah, Derek.'

I turned to see my old friend Geoffrey Robertson approaching.

'I knew your party had gone mad on privatisation, but don't you think even this government are going a wee bit far with the Ancillary Services Bill? I assume it's that you're here to see get its first reading?'

'That and one other,' I said.

Geoffrey grinned.

'Tell me about how you got on since I saw you last.'

He took me by the arm and led me to one of the green-leather benches over in the corner.

'I got absolutely nowhere about the succession to the clan chiefship. The laird simply refused to discuss it. He just reiterated what he's been saying to my overlords all along, assuring me that everything would turn out all right in the end.'

'And that was all?'

'Well, I'm invited back at some unspecified time in the near future to meet Zechariah Hall who's coming over.'

'Ah, ZH,' said Geoffrey.

'He's quite a chap from all I hear.'

'He certainly is. Particularly compared with Septicus and his PPM crowd.' I smiled.

'I got my head bitten off by old Percy Strickland for calling him that last week,' I said. 'Have the LNP got many more people of ZH's calibre?'

Geoffrey shook his head.

'That's the pity of it. The other leading members are all right as far as they go, but there's no one to touch ZH. I'm told that one of the younger ones is somebody to watch, though. A girl with a Scots-sounding name – not that that is anything very unusual in Larna.'

'Not Catriona Campbell?' I said.

'Campbell, yes, that's the one. I knew I had some reason for disliking the name. You've heard about her too, then?'

'I've met her. She was at the castle when I was staying there.'

'And what did you think of her?'

'Absolutely first class,' I said. 'She and I . . . '

I became aware of footsteps approaching from behind me just at that moment and Geoffrey put a warning hand on my knee.

'Good afternoon to you, Mr Former Attorney-General.'

I turned to see the square-jawed face of Malcolm MacRodrick beside me.

'Ah, who have we here?' He took a step backwards as I stood up. 'The Deputy Chief Whip of the House of Lords, no less! We are keepin' distinguished company, Geoffrey.' He turned back to me. 'How are you, old boy?'

'All right. Thank you.'

I was finding it difficult to simulate a great deal of pleasure at his unexpected presence and I could think of no possible reason as to why I should try.

'Well, I'm sure the two of you have matters of great importance to discuss, so I won't be takin' up any more of your time.'

Geoffrey watched him in silence as he walked off down the corridor.

Then, 'I was not aware that you were acquainted with our Malcolm MacRodrick.'

'I wasn't. He was staying at the castle too. I met him there,' I said.

I told him about the piquet incident and its aftermath.

'My, you have been busy. I don't trust him, him and his pink carnation and his fancy way of speaking . . . I beg your pardon, *speakin'*! And his Old Etonian tie. I've never seen you wear one, Derek.'

'Hardly anyone does nowadays. It's a pity really because the colours are so good. The black with pale blue diagonal stripes goes with practically anything.'

'Well, as I say, I don't trust him. I'm told he's already borrowed up to the hilt on his expectations of becoming clan chief and he's bound to have a massive stake in the People's Progressive Movement getting control in Larna. He knew what we were talking about all right and I wouldn't be at all surprised if he's up to something.'

'Yes,' I said. 'And I've got a pretty good idea what it is.'

'Oh. And what might that be.'

'Well, the key to the whole thing seems to be timing. It would be very much in Malcolm's interest to seek to delay the bill and consequently the start of the general election campaign in Larna for as long as he possibly can. For two reasons. In the first place, there'd be a better chance of his having succeeded Rodrick by that time and he himself would have acquired the almost mystical influence that successive clan chiefs have always had over the islanders and be in a position to exercise it on behalf of the PPM.'

'Aye, that figures. And the second reason?'

'Not quite so important perhaps, but The MacRodrick's just returned from what he says will be his last visit to Larna and Catriona tells me that he spent most of the time touring the island with ZH, thereby giving an enormous boost to the Larna National Party. There'd be more time for that to wear off. And apparently the People's Progressive Movement have been spending a lot of money they've managed to get hold of from somewhere on projects likely to buy popularity and, similarly, there'd be more time for that to take effect.'

'What's the programme as it stands now then?'

Like Percy Strickland, by this time I knew it off by heart.

'Seventeen days in the House of Commons, today's the first of November, so that brings us to the eighteenth. Fourteen days in the Lords, that's the second of December. Those estimates are pretty optimistic but if the government *can* keep to that timetable, I understand the rest would follow automatically. Royal Assent also on the second, submission of the Order in Council to the Privy Council on the third, the Privy Council would meet to make the order on the tenth and it would come into force three weeks later with the general election in Larna on January the twenty-eighth.'

Geoffrey thumped his knee with his right hand.

'That's it then. You said that the second of December was only an optimistic estimate. Both Houses must rise for the Christmas recess by the twenty-third at the latest. That means that Malcolm's only got to delay the bill in the Commons for just over three weeks, an easy enough matter for a man of his parliamentary experience, and it won't have completed its parliamentary stages until after the recess. We've been promised the full three weeks for that, this time, so he'll have set back the whole programme for six weeks, nearly a month and a half.'

'Oh my God,' I said. 'That would mean the election campaign in Larna starting in mid-February with the election itself well into March. Incidentally, talking of timing, what do you make of this?'

I passed him over a sheet of A4 paper with the Foreign and Commonwealth Office letter-heading on it. 'It's the sequence of events in the early stages that led to this bill coming before us today. I asked Jack Singleton for it when I saw him last week and it came this morning.'

Geoffrey glanced down at it.

1st March	LNP and PPM ask for independence
16th March	HMG asks for referendum in Larna
24th March	RODRICK'S ILLNESS DIAGNOSED
31st March	Larna legislature passes Referendum Bill
22nd April	Referendum held
12th–26th May	Constitutional conference in London
6th June	RANALD'S DEATH IN MOTOR ACCIDENT IN LARNA
11th June	Authority sought to instruct parliamentary counsel
23rd June	Drafting of bill and Order in Council
5th July	Approval of Legislation Committee sought
12th July	(First reading could have been held in the House of Commons, but just not enough time for it to go through all its stages in both Houses before the end of the session)
1st November	First reading in the House of Commons

Geoffrey Robertson looked up from the paper. 'The People's Progressive Movement would have had no means of knowing that The MacRodrick was suffering from a terminal illness at the time they started pressing for independence.'

'That's true,' I said. 'They must have been confident at that stage that the popularity that they were earning . . . or buying, rather . . . would have been enough to carry them through. But with Rodrick known to be on the way out, they might have jumped at the chance of getting rid of Ranald too. As clan chief, he would have carried almost as much influence with the islanders as his father. Do you think that Malcolm would go as far as murder, or at least condoning it, if the circumstances were right?'

Geoffrey shook his head.

'Until a short time ago I'd have said "no". But now . . . well, I just don't know,' he said.

* * *

Back in my room in the House of Lords, I sat at my desk and gave some thought to the conclusions that Geoffrey Robertson and I had come to.

If we were right about Malcolm seeking to delay the Larna bill going through Parliament for as long as possible, the three weeks which would give him the added advantage of the length of the Christmas recess would certainly be his first target. Three weeks didn't sound very much but compared with the seventeen days that had been provisionally allotted for its passage through the House of Commons, it would certainly take a bit of doing. On the other hand, for someone of Malcolm's experience it would not be impossible.

All public bills have to go through a number of different stages in both Houses on their way to becoming law.

The first reading, as with the Ancillary Services Bill and the Independence of Larna Bill this afternoon, is purely formal, bringing the bill to the notice of the House and causing it to be printed. The second reading is to debate the principle of the bill as a whole and, in the House of Commons at least, it may be rejected outright in the division lobby at this stage. The committee stage, which with an independence bill would be taken on the floor of the House, is to enable the individual provisions of the bill to be examined in detail and amended where it is thought to be necessary. The report stage is to re-examine the bill in the light of any changes that may have been made to it in committee and to consider whether any further amendments may have become necessary. The third reading is to decide whether the bill as amended at committee and report is still acceptable to the House and it is not unknown for one that has been unopposed at its second reading to be rejected at its third. Failing that however, the bill would be passed forthwith.

The second reading of the Larna bill was down for Monday, the fifteenth of June, a fortnight today (with committee on the following day and report and third reading the day after, making up the seventeen days). As all the political parties at Westminster, together with the two in Larna, were on record as being in favour of independence, the principle of the bill was not in dispute and there didn't seem to me to be any opportunity for delay at second reading. The committee stage however was a different matter, because that is the point at which a campaign to delay the progress of a bill has the best chance of success.

The traditional method is to put down a large number of amendments and to arrange for them to be spoken on by as many members and at as great length as possible. Delay has always been regarded as a legitimate weapon for use by an opposition but it is equally incumbent on them to allow the government to get their business through. Procedural devices have therefore been evolved over the years, such as 'selection of amendments' by the Speaker, who can thereby eliminate any whose sole purpose is to delay rather than to improve, and the 'guillotine', a maximum timetable imposed by a vote of the House on the remaining stages of a particular bill. But Malcolm's parliamentary skill would surely enable him to devise amendments that Madam Speaker would find it difficult to reject and the House as a whole might well consider that the use of the guillotine would not be appropriate in connection with an independence bill.

Furthermore, it only needed one amendment to be carried in committee to ensure that there would be a full-dress report stage on which further opportunities for delay would present themselves, rather than it being taken formally as just a part of the remaining stages on the following day. Altogether, it would be of the utmost importance to watch every move that Malcolm MacRodrick might make and seek to counter it immediately. He would be likely to give some indication in his speech on second reading of the lines he intended to take during the remainder of the Commons stages and, until then, there didn't seem to be very much more that I could do but wait.

The procedures in the House of Lords vary in a number of minor ways from those in the Commons, but it would be soon enough to worry about them when the time came.

* * *

97

'Hello, Derek?'

Catriona's next telephone call had come three days later, on the Thursday afternoon.

'I don't know whether its got anything to do with the independence business or not. You know we've got vast deposits of bauxite here in Larna, which have never been developed?'

'Yes,' I said, 'oddly enough Black Rod was talking about it the other night. Incidentally, what is bauxite? I didn't have the face to let on to him that I didn't know.'

'It's one of the principal sources of aluminium – bauxite has formed a large part of the Jamaican economy for a long time. Some years ago, something called the Larna Mining Company acquired the development rights, but somehow it never got off the ground. Well, it's now being said that the company's been taken over by somebody, but nobody seems to know who.'

I made some notes on my blotting pad.

'Thanks. I'll ask around.'

'I thought I ought to mention it. It just seems an odd time to be doing it with everything in the melting-pot like this,' she said.

*   *   *

And it was at nine o'clock on the following Wednesday evening that I had an urgent message to go and see Geoffrey Robertson in his room in the House of Commons.

'Sorry to ask you to come all this way to see me, Derek, but what I've got to tell you couldn't be said on the telephone. Nothing but bad news, I am afraid. Would you like me to dress it up a bit for you, or shall I give it to you straight?'

I had followed with difficulty the tortuous way given in his directions, along corridors and up staircases, and we were sitting on either side of his desk in the muted light shed by its green-shaded lamp.

'Straight, please,' I said.

'Here it is, then. Malcolm MacRodrick has been invited to join our front-bench as an additional spokesman on foreign and Commonwealth affairs with the direct purpose of his taking the Larna bill through this House for us. The shadow cabinet, which met tonight, agreed to make an official request to the government for the second reading, which was as you know to have been taken this coming Monday, to be postponed for a fortnight, so that Malcolm can fly to the Caribbean, see the situation out there for himself and get himself properly briefed on the subject. Our Chief Whip rang up yours the moment shadow was over to pass on the request and Henry Chanter rang back half an hour later to say that the government were prepared to agree to it.'

'*What!*' I said. 'They can't have done.'

He nodded.

'It's only too true, I'm afraid, my source for all this was impeccable. The second reading is now to be held on the twenty-ninth of November; it will be in the usual Thursday business statement to the House tomorrow. Malcolm MacRodrick's won himself two out of the three weeks he needs before he even starts.'

'But . . . what on earth do your people see in him?'

'I've often wondered that myself. Him being a MacRodrick, for one thing, there's a bit of the snob in all of us, you know.'

He paused for a moment.

'Then, there's his links with Larna, the supreme example of a model British colony.'

'But surely,' I said, 'the very reason they've decided to support the Larna People's Democratic Movement is because they're against feudalism and all that sort of thing in the first place.'

Geoffrey Robertson put the palms of his hands together as they rested on the leather of his desktop.

'I know it sounds inconsistent, Derek, but to have the chief of a clan, particularly one of the status of the MacRodricks, in the Parliamentary Labour Party would be a tremendous feather in our caps. It would do more to consolidate the position we already hold in Scotland than anything else would.'

He looked across at me almost appealingly.

'Don't think too hardly of my colleagues, Derek. They *want* to believe in him.'

I stood up.

'Yes, I can understand that,' I said. 'Well, thank you, Geoffrey, it really was good of you to let me know so quickly. I'd better get straight back now though to see what, if anything at all, can be saved out of the wreck.'

*   *   *

I found Tom Lavenham standing by the carved wooden cabinet in which he kept a selection of bottles and glasses. It had been designed by Pugin as a repository for the Mace of the House of Lords but when, not many decades ago, considerations of security had caused it to be redundant for that purpose, it had found its way into the room of the Chief Whip of the day. Tom had turned as I came in, an empty glass in one hand and an open bottle of whisky in the other.

'Have a drink, Derek.'

'Yes, please. A large one,' I said.

I had kept him informed, on whips' terms, about my previous conversations with Geoffrey Robertson and I gave him a verbatim account of this latest one.

'So,' he said, when I had finished, 'just let me make sure that I've got it right. Thanks to the blithering stupidity of our friends down the corridor, the opposition only have to delay the bill for one extra week, which with Malcolm MacRodrick in charge they could do on their heads in committee, and the general election in Larna, which should have been held on the 28th January will now be on the 11th of March at the earliest. By which time, Rodrick MacRodrick will almost certainly be dead, Malcolm will have become chief of the clan, the People's Progressive Movement will win hands down . . . and goodbye Larna?'

'That's about it,' I said. 'But it's probably far too late to do anything about it now.'

Without a word, Tom sat down at his desk, picked up the receiver of his telephone and punched in a four-figure number at its base.

During the brief pause that followed, he glanced up at me.

'We'll see about that,' he said.

Then he spoke into the mouthpiece.

'Get me the Chief Whip, please.' The 'Chief Whip', unless otherwise specified, applies to the Government Chief Whip in the House of Commons. 'No, now . . . Well, get him out of his meeting then,' he said.

There was a slightly longer pause.

'Hello, Henry.' Henry Chanter had been Commons Chief Whip since the last general election, some eighteen months before. 'What's this I hear about the Larna bill? . . . I've got Derek Thyrde with me . . . Never mind how he knows, is it true – that's the main thing? . . . Well, do you realise what this will mean? . . . Let me spell it out for you, then.'

I had met Henry Chanter on a number of occasions, mostly in the presence of Tom. I could hardly say that he and I were yet on terms that could be described as friendship. Nonetheless, while Tom Lavenham explained the situation at far greater length and with a certain amount more acerbity than the brief summary that he and I had agreed before he made his telephone call, I couldn't help being sorry for the hapless recipient at the other end of the line.

'If you're prepared to see over three hundred years of quite unprecedentedly successful colonial rule thrown away for the sake of five minutes peace with the opposition, I'm not . . . What do you mean it's all settled? It's not been before cabinet yet, has it? . . . Well, I happen to know that the Lord President will be raising it at the meeting tomorrow.'

The Lord President of the Council, a former Chief Whip of the House of Commons, was also Leader of the House of Lords, Tom's boss and mine. If Tom Lavenham said that Tony, Lord Dysart, would be raising something on the following day in cabinet, raise it he would. Nothing could be surer than that.

'Who's just come in? . . . Oh, the Prime Minister. Would you like me to have a word with him? . . . Just as you wish,' Tom said.

Tom Lavenham picked up a pen and started tapping it slowly and but rhythmically on the desk in front of him.

'Hello . . . Well, thank you, Henry. And thank the Prime Minister too . . . Oh, he's gone, has he?'

He put down the receiver, stood up and went over to the cabinet for the whisky bottle.'

'Let me fill your glass up for you, Derek.'

Thomas, Earl of Lavenham was far too dignified a figure ever to assume what could be described as an expression of smugness, but he came as close to it now as I had ever yet seen him.

'You don't do fifteen years in this job without gaining a certain amount of influence,' he said.

*　　*　　*

It was on my way back from passing on the good news to Geoffrey Robertson that I met Jack Singleton in one of the corridors.

'Derek! I really don't know how I'm going to break this to you.'

'Don't worry,' I said. 'I think my news may be slightly more up-to-date than your's. The second reading of the Larna bill will go ahead as planned, this coming Monday.'

I told Jack about Tom Lavenham's telephone conversation with his Chief Whip and its outcome.

I had just finished when Malcolm MacRodrick walked past us. There was none of the 'Derek, old boy,' or affected chumminess, about it this time. He swept by without a word, hardly glancing at us as he did so, but the expression on his face was confirmation enough of the success of Tom's intervention, were any to be needed.

'I somehow don't think that chap likes you,' Jack said.

*   *   *

All this was on the Wednesday. On Thursday morning, the summons from Rodrick MacRodrick arrived. I was to be at the castle on Friday evening – the very next night.

CHAPTER SEVEN

It was Dougalina, broad and beaming, who met me off the boat and I saw why the moment she showed me into the drawing-room. The head stalker himself, already in kilt and doublet, was standing protectively behind Rodrick's chair. There was a noticeable change in the laird's appearance after – how long was it? – barely three weeks.

Even in that short time, he looked distinctly frailer and more bent, his clothes hung on him even more loosely and the skin on his face had taken on a transparent quality. But his eyes still sparkled and the manner of his welcome was every bit as warm as before. Dougal stepped forward and put a hand under his elbow to help him, but The MacRodrick shook him off impatiently and, gripping his cromach with both hands, levered himself up to his feet.

Amanda, the whippet, inched forward and insinuated a damp experimental nose into my hand.

'Good of you to come at such short notice, Derek, with the second reading of the bill on Monday too. Don't worry, I'll not let you miss the sleeper train on Sunday night. This is Lord Thyrde, gentlemen. May I introduce the honourable Zechariah Hall, first minister of Larna, and John J. MacRodrick from the United States . . . '

'Junior,' put in the American in a voice like a megaphone.

'Er, John J. MacRodrick *Junior*,' added the laird accommodatingly, 'and Alastair of course you know.'

I had not been expecting Black Rod to have come up this time as I knew how difficult it was for the holder of his office to get away from London while the House was sitting. The president of the American Clan Society, bluff and burley, exuded goodwill and cheerfulness. With Zechariah Hall, however, from the very first moment I knew instinctively and beyond any doubt whatsoever that I was talking to a quite exceptional man.

The first minister of Larna was wearing an ordinary English dark suit, with a white shirt and nondescript tie. He was a tallish figure, thin but not excessively so; his face was a shade or two darker than Catriona's and his short curly hair had faded into an iron grey. He possessed the kindest pair of eyes that I had ever seen.

'I've been looking forward to meeting you, sir,' I said. I had been wondering exactly what I was going to say to this almost legendary figure, but in the event it all came quite naturally. 'I've heard a lot about you.'

He gave a brief deprecatory gesture with his right hand that I was later to realise was one of his customary mannerisms.

'Please . . . ZH,' he said. 'Everybody calls me that. I would esteem it a kindness, Lord Thyrde, if you would do so too.'

His voice had a soft gentle quality about it but none the less it carried an unmistakable air of authority.

'Derek,' I said.

He nodded gravely.

'Very well . . . Derek. I too have heard much about you, from our mutual friend Catriona Campbell.' He smiled. 'She has done nothing but sing your praises ever since she returned to our island. I understand that you are helping us and I welcome this opportunity of being able to express my thanks to you personally.'

'How are things going?' I said.

'Well, I thank you. And with you? The Independence Bill – will we have long to wait for it?'

'We're doing our best,' I said. 'With any luck we'll have it through in time for the general election to be held at the end of January.'

I hoped that I wasn't being over optimistic. Since our recent victory over Malcolm and his delaying tactics, I had been having a nasty feeling that things were going almost too well to last.

'So long!' ZH shook his head sadly. 'None the less, I understand that the correct procedures must be followed. Equally,' he glanced over to where the laird had resumed his seat and was now deep in conversation with Black Rod and John J. MacRodrick, 'I know that you are aware of the sad reasons that we have for urgency.'

'I am indeed,' I said.

'As you probably know, I have never myself been convinced of the need for independence. We have always been proud of our close connection with the mother country and everything that we might conceivably want for Larna could have been achieved equally well as a Crown colony. But,' he gestured with his right hand again, 'all that is now in the past. We have much to do and if, God willing, our people in Larna give us their backing, the sooner we can make a start on it the better. Mr John J. MacRodrick tells me that he and his Clan Society intend to give us all the help they can.'

*   *   *

I had an opportunity to talk to John J. MacRodrick Junior at dinner.

This time, it was Dougalina who brought in the dishes. Her father left his position behind the laird's chair at the head of the table for as long as it took to help her, but resumed it again as soon as they had been handed round. ZH was on Rodrick's right with Alastair beyond him, the American was on his left and I was on his other side.

'Do you know Larna, Derek?'

John J., he had asked me to call him that, spoke not only with great distinctness but also, as I had already experienced, in a voice several decibels louder than any other that I had ever heard.

'I've never been there,' I said.

'Me neither,' John J. bellowed. 'But I certainly intend to.'

He had a shiny bald head with a collar-length fringe of sandy-coloured hair hanging from ear to ear below it.

'You may have heard of our Clan Society of which I have the honour to be president. Well, since I retired back home in Miami, I'm happy to say I've had more time to give to it. And, if the right people get in,' he gave me a wink so broad that his right eye was all but shut and nodded his head in the direction of the first minister, 'we have great plans for Larna.'

'Yes, so Mr Hall was telling me.'

'Ah, ZH,' he said. He lowered his voice to a tone that he no doubt considered to be that of a confidential murmur but one which could still have been heard without much difficulty from the far end of the room, 'There's a man!'

John J. reverted to full voice again.

'Well, I don't want to boast but I must tell you that between us we control a considerable amount of funds in our little society. We're considering a number of projects out there and it seems that a new airport is one of the chief priorities. Then there's . . . '

By the time that dinner was over, I had been treated to such a comprehensive run-down of the business opportunities on the island that, had I been able to take it all in, I would have acquired full mastery of the Larnacan economy, past, present and in the halcyon days of independence that lay ahead.

*   *   *

'Tell me, Derek, how's Seamus Ruadh the tenth of Kilpatrick getting on with those new ladies of his?'

'Splendidly, when I last saw them. They look marvellous in the park at Thyrde. I can't thank you enough,' I said.

We were in the library, finishing our coffee, and had formed ourselves into two informal groups. Black Rod was on one side of the fireplace with ZH and John J. MacRodrick, the latter contributing more to the conversation in volume than the other two together were doing in content. The laird and I, with Dougal in attendance, were on the other.

'Harumph! Only too glad to have been able to help. The old boy should be just what you need,' Rodrick said.

At that moment, the door was thrust open and an unusually flustered and aghast looking Dougalina appeared in the doorway. She stood there for a moment, her vast bosom heaving, twisting a dishcloth round and round in her hand.

Then, 'The . . . the gentlemen, Mac Ruaraidh Mor,' she said.

Malcolm MacRodrick, the inevitable tie and buttonhole to the fore, thrust his way past her and strode into the room followed by a short bouncy little black man with spectacles and large floppy red-and-white-spotted bow tie.

The laird collapsed back into his chair as though someone had hit him and it was left to Malcolm to make the introductions.

'My cousin, Alastair MacRodrick; our kinsman from the United States, John J. MacRodrick; and . . . who have we here . . . Lord Thyrde. I say, Derek old boy, you do keep gettin' around, don't you? No need to introduce my brother or Zechariah Hall, of course. Dr Septimus Baker, gentlemen, whom I know you'll all be overjoyed to meet.'

He glanced towards his brother.

'I see you've already dined, Rodrick old boy. Don't worry about us. Sep and I managed to get ourselves somethin' to eat on the way.'

The laird's innate good manners came at once to his rescue. This time he did let Dougal help him up to his feet so that he could go forward to welcome his uninvited guest. ZH was before him though, holding out both arms, gripping Septicus's right hand with his own and laying his left on the other's shoulder, rather I suspected, to that individual's momentary discomfort. John J. MacRodrick's honest face was looking appalled, Black Rod's as inscrutable as usual. When it came to my turn, I shook the little man's limp hand dutifully and retreated into the background . . . it had become a situation, I decided, with which I was totally unqualified to cope.

I was joined there some five minutes later by the laird himself.

'Tomorrow isn't going to be quite as easy as I'd expected, Derek. Would you like to go out for a day's stalking? It'll only be hinds now, I'm afraid, but they could do with the culling.'

'I'd love to,' I said.

'Harumph! That's settled then. I'll arrange for Dougal to take you.'

'But . . . won't you be needing him yourself?'

'Not a bit of it. He'll pick you up in the gunroom at nine-thirty in the morning.'

It seemed to me that there *was* one minor consolation. At least Malcolm didn't seem to have brought Roddy and Rannie with him this time. It only needed them to make the party complete.

*　　*　　*

The gunroom had that welcoming atmosphere about it, common to all of its kind. It smelt in equal proportions of old leather and gun-oil. Framed Spy cartoons in various tones of grey and faded pink filled every available inch of the walls.

One of them particularly caught my eye and I walked over to look at it. It was of an elderly gentlemen, with a benign expression and side-whiskers, wearing an archaic looking tweed coat, breeches and leggings, and holding a rifle. It was captioned *The Laird*.

'Good day to you, Lord Thyrde.'

I turned to see that the imposing presence of the head stalker had somehow manifested itself and was now dominating the room.

'I see you're admiring one of my favourite pictures.'

'Good morning, Dougal,' I said.

'That's Ranald MacRodrick, he's my own great-great-grandfather, believe it or not. He smiled. 'If all the tales they tell about him are true, there's many another living on the island today as could say the same, but in my case it's legitimate. My great-grandfather was his youngest son.'

I looked at the picture again and then back to Dougal.

'I can see the likeness,' I said.

'Well, it's a grand morn for the hill and we mustn't be wasting it standing here blethering.'

He walked over to a steel cabinet and unlocked it with a key from his pocket. Then he took out one of the rifles from inside it, worked the bolt-action and handed it to me. It had a workmanlike feel to it and the metal and woodwork toned in with each other, both imbued with the patina of age.

'I think this one might suit you best. It's a Rigby 275. Try it and see how you think you might get on with it.'

It had been a year or two since I had handled a rifle and I weighed it up in my two hands and turned towards the window. It fitted snugly into my shoulder and, with my finger over the trigger-guard, I glanced through the telescopic sight to a point just above the distant horizon. As I did so, the slight aura of apprehension that had been with me since I got up that morning, instantly disappeared.

'I've another here which you may like better. This one's a Holland and Holland 240. I'd sooner you used the Rigby, though.'

I tried the second rifle in the same way. Somehow it didn't give me quite the same feeling of confidence as the other one had. I put it down on the oilcloth-covered top of the table that filled most of the middle of the room and took up the Rigby again.

'No, I'll stick to this one, thank you,' I said.

There was a noise at the door and the American came in.

'Morning, Derek,' he bawled. 'Off out for a go at the deer, are you.'

He picked up the discarded Holland and Holland, turned it over and studied it before putting it up to his own shoulder.

Then he looked round and beamed at me.

'Takes me back to my old hunting days. Quite a crack shot I was then, I can assure you. Wish I were coming with you,' he said.

*   *   *

It was a fine frosty morning, as we walked across the bridge. The leaves were off the trees now and the birches were of a reddy-brown colour, rimed with sparkling white. Dougal paced himself with the old wooden-handled cromach held in one hand, a telescope slung over his other shoulder together with the rifle in its canvas slip. I had wanted to carry it myself but he had been adamant, doubtful perhaps as to whether I had quite enough experience to be trusted in that way.

We skirted the top of the village of Kilpatrick and came to the steading where I had first met Seamus, my highland bull. The stonewalled grass parks around it were brim full of black-faced sheep. Dougal noticed me looking at them.

'Aye, they've been gathered for the dipping before being put out with the tups,' he said. 'It'll be no bad thing for us today. Sheep out on the hill can give the alarm to the deer quicker than anything.'

After another ten minutes or so's steady climb, we paused.

'Now, we'll just try a shot or two at the iron stag to give you the feel of the rifle,' he said.

He pointed over to where, against the point where the hill started to rise more sharply, there stood a cut-out in red rusty metal the outline of which did indeed represent a sideways-on caricature of a stag. We lay down on a grassy knoll and Dougal took the rifle out of its slip and put a white cardboard box of ammunition from his pocket open on the ground beside him. Then he loaded the magazine of the Rigby with three brass-cased cartridges, pushed home the bolt leaving one of them up the breech and handed it over to me.

'That's exactly a hundred yards from here. Now, aim at a point just above and behind the beast's shoulder. That should get him clean through the heart.'

The feeling of apprehension returned in full measure – more than anything, I realised, I wanted to earn the head stalker's respect. I brought the butt of the rifle up into my shoulder, glanced through the telescopic sight and lined up the point where its thin black lines crossed with the appropriate part of the metal beast in relation to where I judged its shoulder to be. Then I held my breath and gently squeezed the trigger; the impact of the recoil was far more gentle than I had expected through the tweed of my coat.

Dougal focused his telescope.

'Not so bad,' he said. 'Perhaps a wee bit too far back. An inch, inch and a half, maybe.'

I worked the bolt action to eject the spent case and feed the second cartridge into the breech and repeated the procedure with the necessary adjustment in aim.

'That's good enough,' said Dougal. 'Come over and take a look.'

I applied the safety-catch to the rifle, scrambled to my feet and we walked over the hundred yards of intervening heather to where he pointed out the two silvery-coloured indentations made by the soft-nosed bullets, the second exactly two inches to the left of the first.

'You'll have done this before, I'm thinking.'

I tried not to preen myself too obviously over what was clearly a rare compliment from such a man.

'Yes,' I said, 'I did have several days at the stags a year or two back.'

'Well, you'll find a hind much the same. And as with the stags, we'll be looking for a beast in poor condition, or one with a calf in poor condition. Something that's not likely to improve the herd.'

Dougal loaded the magazine of the Rigby with three more cartridges, leaving the breach empty and making four in all, replaced it in its canvas slip and we walked along the wide path that wound its way upwards. On either side of us, the technicolor green of moss-covered stones and tree-stumps formed a vivid contrast to the mid-brown tapestry of twisted stalks of dead bracken from which they protruded. I realised that we were going the same way that I had come with Catriona on my first visit, when I reached the point where the whippet, Amanda, had been so unexpectedly obedient over the blue hare.

I told Dougal about it.

'Aye, there's not many whippets will behave half as well as that Amanda,' he said. 'She's fond enough of the laird and he of her. You should have seen the two of them together when we got home from the other Larna.'

'How did you get on out there?' I asked.

'Well enough. The laird and I have been out there together many a time in the past. This time was a sad trip for me, though.'

'I'm sure it was.'

'Still, I expect to go back yet, from time to time, for I've good friends out there, acquired over the years.'

'Mr Hall? You'd have met him there, I suppose?'

'Aye, him more than most. That's a good man, if ever I saw one.'

'And what about the laird? Did he enjoy it?'

'Well enough, don't you fret. He was determined from the first to make the most of it.' Dougal wiped the sleeve of his old tweed coat across his forehead. 'And make the most of it he did.'

I had a feeling that the head stalker must have played no small part in this himself. Care and companionship he would have provided in full measure. But I was pretty sure that advice and level-headedness, whenever they were called for, would have been there as well.

'He's very much liked over there, I hear.'

'He is that. Though, "loved" would be the more appropriate word for it, every bit as much as he is here and that's saying a deal. Now then, here we are at Spy Hill,' Dougal said.

We had reached the cairn that had been the objective of Catriona's and my walk and we found a boy in his early 'teens, introduced to me by Dougal as 'Young Angie', waiting for us, holding a dun-coloured pony by its bridle. The rest of its harness consisted of a deer-saddle, chunky-looking with a pommel at either end, on which to carry a beast home.

I was getting my breath back as I looked down at that splendid view again. The reddy-brown blocks of larch trees stood out against the evergreen of Scots firs and spruces in the valley we had come from and the castle was visible beyond it. The distant ribbon of loch wound away from us until it lost itself somewhere to the south.

Dougal settled himself among the prickly dark-brown stubs of a bank of heather bushes and took out his telescope again. He held it steady against the lower part of his cromach and started methodically sweeping the high ground that lay to the south. Every now and then he paused and nodded, murmuring 'Aye' to himself under his breath.

Then he raised himself slightly and passed the telescope to me.

'You see that rock against the skyline yonder with the green bit to this side of it, that's pretty well a mile from here. Well, five-o'clock of that you'll see the head of a corrie. There's a party of hinds grazing there.'

I borrowed his cromach and steadied the telescope against it as he had done and, after a certain amount of adjustment managed to get it into focus.

'Yes, I can see them,' I said.

'Well just about the middle of them there's a sway-backed one, a wee bit greyer than the rest.'

'I think I've got her. The one with the dip in her back? She's got her head up and she's looking this way?'

'Aye, that's the one, we'll go for her first. Then two beyond her, at two o'clock of where she's standing, there's a poor-looking one with a calf no better than she.' I nodded. 'If there's time and if she gives us the chance, we'll take her next.'

We stood up and Dougal slung rifle and telescope over his shoulder again.

'The wind's from the south-west, which'll suit our purpose just fine.'

He leant on his cromach and pointed as he described the route we should take, down to the bottom of the slope in front of us, up by a steeper part on the far side, along a number of gulleys until we could be within shot of the corrie where the hinds were.

'We should be able to get within a hundred and fifty yards of the beast herself, no more.' He turned to the pony-boy. 'Go to the head of the loch, Young Angie, you know the place?'

Young Angie ran the fingers of one hand through his hair and grinned.

'Aye, Dougal,' he said, cheerfully.

'Wait for us there till you see the smoke and come for the beast then.'

'Aye, Dougal,' he said again. 'Good luck to you, Lord Thyrde, sir,' and he and the dun-coloured pony made off down the hill in the direction from which we had come.

The first part of our own journey was downhill too and relatively easy. Apart from my nailed boots sliding about as I scrabbled over rocks, that is, and sinking to their tops into spongy little bogs of spagnum moss from time to time. The wind in the form of a gusty breeze was pleasant on my face.

'How about the elections in Larna?' I said to Dougal. 'Did you get any impression when you were out there, as to how they might go?'

'Hard to tell. They're not like us, the Larnacans.' He turned to me and smiled. 'We're known as "Larnochs" here, same as folk from Mull are "Mullochs", and maybe the word "Larnacan" is what they call a corruption and comes from that.'

We walked on in silence for quite a number of paces.

'Don't misunderstand me, Lord Thyrde. They're our own folk and they're not simple, the Larnacans, but they can be swayed by considerations. For generations they've learnt to respect the MacRodricks and do as they do. But now that Septimus Baker, he's no Larnacan, comes and tells them different, and a new notion's always a temptation to the young. And, if the chief of the clan should ever be for change himself . . . ' he paused, 'ah well, they're good at heart notwithstanding, and maybe it'll all come out right in the end.'

We were reaching the burn at the bottom now.

'Take care you don't get your feet wet,' said Dougal, 'you've a good way to go yet.'

I did as he told me even though there wasn't a lot of point in it. The water from the innumerable little bogs had come through the laceholes of my boots and my feet were wet through already. Actually I was glad of it because, with the degree of exercise that was involved in hill walking, the refreshing coolness was a welcome relief.

Beyond the burn the hill climbed steeply and the next twenty minutes or so was a period of pure slog.

Dougal led, and although he himself was covering the ground with effortless ease, he glanced backwards from time to time to see how I was doing and kept his own pace matched to mine. I certainly had no breath for further talking even if there had been the opportunity for it and for the first time I was glad not be carrying the rifle. The steepness of the climb and the unaccustomed angle between foot and leg brought into play muscles in my ankles, calves and thighs that I never even knew I possessed and each one of them made itself felt to an extent that it ached almost to screaming point.

A thirst began to develop itself and proliferated with every step.

I achieved a certain amount of relief by spending quite some minutes in devising in my imagination a succession of more and more exotic liquid taste sensations that might best satisfy it, in the unlikely event of course of all the ingredients being available in such a place at my command. This came to an abrupt end, however, with the realisation that a simple pint of draught fined bitter beer at room temperature from a pewter tankard outran all the rest.

False summits succeeded one other in abundance, each appearing to be the actual top of the climb but only giving way, as one approached it, to yet another ahead.

Just as I was becoming reconciled to the fact that I was now in a sort of hell and the punishment for past sins had condemned me to going on like this for ever, Dougal stopped some twenty yards ahead of me, turned round and beckoned me forward.

'Look there, now.'

I went up and stood beside him and immediately wished that I hadn't. We were standing on the brink of what seemed to be a precipice, the ground falling away almost sheer immediately to the front of us. Some sixty feet below us, wings magnificently out to their full spread, a golden eagle lazed round in circles. Far below him again the rippled silver surface of the loch sparkled in the sunlight. My eye had just time to take in the dun-coloured pony, a diminutive figure at its head, plodding steadfastly along the near side of the shore and engaged at this particular moment in passing a rowing boat beached on the shingle, before I retreated rapidly backwards to a point a good eight paces down from the edge.

But the head stalker was still leaning over and pointing down to his right.

'That's his nest, you can just make it out on the wee ledge down yonder.'

'I'll have to take your word for it,' I said apologetically from the safety of my new position. 'I'm not very good at heights, I'm afraid.'

'Ah, you soon get used to it.' Dougal appeared to be rather disappointed as he came back and joined me. 'I thought you'd like fine to see it. Young Mr Ranald would always come this way, when he was out on the hill.' Then as an afterthought he added, 'Mr Malcolm, too,' but with a distinct diminution of enthusiasm in his voice.

'Malcolm stalks too, does he?' I said, glad of something to cover up my sense of shame for the weakness that I was revealing.

'Aye, he's as good a rifle shot as his brother. A wee bit better, maybe. The laird doesn't stalk any more, more's the pity, but he was a fine shot himself.'

The head stalker shook his head sadly.

'This is called Ben na h Iolaire, "the hill of the eagle". That's its peak, up yonder, the highest point of the island, but we'll not be going that way else the beasts would see us. You've done well, Lord Thyrde, would you be needing a wee rest?'

As so often happens, I found that exhaustion had instantly been replaced by exhilaration.

'No, I'm fine,' I said.

'Ah well, we're past the worst now. But we'd best be quiet from here on. And keep yourself down when I give you the sign.'

So far it had merely been a question of gaining the necessary height but it was from here on that the stalking proper began.

It was with rising excitement, therefore, that I followed Dougal, copying his movements in every way. Sometimes he crouched downwards, sometimes he went on hands and knees, but mostly he walked in that rolling lope of his that had so impressed me when he had marched round the table piping at the end of my first dinner on the island. It occurred to me that it had probably originated from a life spent stalking on the hill here and, indeed, after a certain amount of time I found myself acquiring it too.

'Aarrk!'

The hoarse cry came from directly above us. I glanced up and there, at height of some forty foot and standing out clear against the blue of the sky as it circled, was the sinister black shape of a raven. Dougal beckoned me up to his side and pointed.

'That bird'll be waiting for the gralloch,' said quietly. 'They always sense somehow when you're going to kill a beast.'

'Will he disturb the hinds?' I asked anxiously.

He shook his head.

'No but we're getting close enough. We must go cannily from now on or maybe something else might.'

I watched every step that I took now, searching each piece of ground as though it might contain something that would give the alarm, and, sure enough, not many minutes later there was a sharp whistling sound and at the same time I felt Dougal's hand on my sleeve.

'Don't move a muscle,' he whispered.

I froze but, without moving my head, I followed the line of his gaze. At the top of a small rise to the front left, an old black-faced ewe stood eyeing us balefully. As I watched her, she raised her near-fore foot and brought it down to the ground again with an audible stamp.

'Now, let yourself sink *very, very* slowly down to the heather.'

Inch by inch, and moving as one person, we subsided until we were flat on the ground.

After what seemed like an age, the old ewe moved her head slightly and transferred her attention away from us. Still we lay there as, in the slowest of slow motion, she lowered her head to the ground and, with infinite fastidiousness, began to graze. Tentatively at first and then step by step, but still with maddening deliberation, she passed over the brow of the hill and, eventually, out of sight.

Dougal rose slowly to his feet.

'Aye,' he said, 'there's always one left out from the gathering. We'll eat our piece now to give her time to settle. That rock'll be a good place to rest.'

I did my best not to let my impatience show, but sitting down in the shelter of the place that Dougal had chosen, I had no sooner taken out the grease-proof-paper package with which I had been provided by Dougalina that morning, than I realised how hungry I was. There were two enormous wedges of sandwich, the crunchy fresh-baked bread buttered thickly and their filling of underdone cold roast beef, red and juicy, set off to perfection by the bite of the mustard with which it had been coated in equally generous supply.

Accompanied by long draughts of slightly bitter water from a nearby rill, I reckoned that it was among the finest meals I had had for years.

Dougal looked at his watch.

'I reckon it'll be all right now, but we'd best take care from here on.'

He led the way as we crawled up the hill, I to his left and just behind him, and he glancing over to shoulder every so often to make sure that I wasn't getting left too far behind. Some thirty feet short of the top of the ridge ahead of us, he stopped and waited for me to come up alongside him. I now had that marvellous feeling of abandon when one realises that one's clothes can only get wet through once and there's no need to worry about it for the rest of the day.

Dougal took the rifle out of its slip, gently worked the bolt action to slide the top cartridge into the breach, applied the safety catch and passed it to me.

Then he pointed to the brow of the hill, put his face close to mine and whispered in my ear.

'You see that rock, Lord Thyrde, we'll go up to either side of that and you should get a good clear shot from there.'

We inched our way forward together until we reached the top, our faces flat to the heather. With the rock to the right of me and Dougal on the other side, together we raised our heads until we could see into the corrie where the beasts were.

There was no sign of the ewe but the grey hind was still there, she stood out from among the others by her distinctive colour. At this distance the dip in her back was even more pronounced and, in addition, I could see that she had a pot belly and very furry ears. It was no wonder that Dougal had singled her out for culling.

'D'you see the one,' he whispered. I nodded. 'There's a wee stag way over there to the left of them, but he'll not be bothering us. Now bring your rifle forward very gently.'

I eased it along to a position in front of me and, an inch at a time, brought it slowly up into my shoulder. The grey hind was facing the same way as had the iron stag and, apart from the fact that she had her head down grazing, was in much the same attitude. I located the position just behind and above her shoulder and covered it with the crossing-point of the thin black lines in the telescopic sight.

Although the death of the quarry is the sole object of all field sports, and in many cases the justification for them, the actual kill is often an anti-climax. And this is never truer than in deer-stalking. It is the getting there that matters, that is the point.

'Now, make yourself comfortable,' said Dougal. 'There's all the time in the world for a good clean shot.'

I suddenly realised that the loose coins in one my pockets had formed themselves into a solid wedge and were biting into my thigh in a manner that was anything but comfortable.

'Hold on, then,' I said, and I lowered the rifle to the ground, and leaving it there, levered myself slowly backwards and down out of sight.

At that actual moment, I became aware of three sounds that followed each other in such quick succession that they were almost simultaneous: a whine above me; a *phu-ittt* as a small section of the rock, at the exact point beside which my head had just been, disintegrated; and a muffled bang from far away to my right.

'Get up, man, quick now!'

Dougal was on his feet already and I felt him seizing me bodily and throwing me and himself over the top of the rock that was between us, down to the heather stubs on the far side, and as I somersaulted over, I had a lightning impression of all the hinds, the grey one foremost among them, the lone stag, even the old black-faced ewe that had somehow materialised from somewhere, galloping off in their several directions, and at the moment I landed, there was a second sharp whine over my head and an identical, and again not quite simultaneous bang, from the same direction as the first.

I looked across at the head stalker where he lay in a semi-prone position, supporting himself on one elbow.

'Thank you very much,' I said. 'It was pure chance that the first shot missed me, but if you hadn't been as quick as you were, the second would have got me. And, with soft-nosed bullets, I'd have been splattered all over that rock for a certainty.'

'Aye, it was a good enough shot. I've a fair notion as to where it'll have come from, and it'll be fully three hundred yards, I'm thinking. There's someone out there doesn't like you,' he said.

'What'll we do now?'

'We'd best find out who it is.' His eyes glinted. 'It'll be a new experience for me to be the beast rather than the stalker, but we'll carry on in that role for the moment. If I show myself from time to time, you keep yourself down, it'll not be me he's after.'

He crawled back up the slope and reached for the Rigby 275 from the top where I had left it. When he was safely back in dead ground again, he stood up and checked the safety catch. Then, as we moved off, he held it in his two hands at the ready without putting it back in its canvas slip. From that moment on, it became incredibly exciting. The one ingredient that makes for the greatest pleasure in sport is an element of danger – a tinge of fear, as with a formidable looking post-and-rails or a stiff cut-and-laid hedge with ditch-towards out hunting, coupled with the exhilaration of overcoming it – and that was something that on previous occasions I had found lacking in deer-stalking. But it was certainly there now.

The whole thing suddenly called to my mind one of John Buchan's Richard Hannay novels set in the highlands. *Mr Standfast* was it? No, *The Three Hostages*, that was the one, the denouement of which consisted of a situation not very dissimilar to the one which we were in at the moment.

Dougal led me through a maze of gullies and other sheltered ground. Every now and then he beckoned to me to get down as he went marginally higher himself, crouching so as only to let our unknown adversary get the merest glimpse of him, and that none too obviously. As he himself had said it wasn't him that the man wanted but it would have been a fair assumption on his part that where the head stalker was, there would I be also and, in that belief, he was being coaxed forward in the hope of getting another shot at me.

And it was working.

Zig-zag back and forth though we did, our general direction was inexorably to the east.

'Do you know where he is?' I said at one point.

'No, but I know where he isn't and that's almost as good,' Dougal said.

Then, at some indefinable point, I became aware that we had switched roles again and that we ourselves were now the hunters rather than the hunted. The very last thing that our man would dare to let happen was for himself to be identified. The head stalker, with his own unrivalled knowledge of the ground in this deer forest and having started by luring him on in the precise direction that he wanted in pursuit of us, had now contrived for us to be behind him again and, like a sheepdog with a recalcitrant tup, was literally driving him the rest of the way.

Suddenly Dougal stopped, knelt down and focused his telescope. Then he shook his head, turned to me and pointed up the slope of the hill some distance ahead.

'Did you see that flash of movement? I couldn't get my glass on it but, from the shape and shade of it, it was no beast.'

'Is it him, do you think?'

'Aye, it's our man, no doubt at all. He'll have gone over the top; that's the one place he can get down to the loch. He'll be making for home, I'm thinking.' He stood up. 'Don't you fret, Lord Thyrde. There's but two ways back to the castle – round the head of the loch or back down to the bridge by the village. We'll go to the peak of Ben na h Iolaire and whichever he takes we'll get him either way.'

The view from the summit of the hill of the eagle was the most sensational we had had yet. The drop from here was even deeper and almost as steep as it had been from where we had seen the eagle himself, but somehow it didn't seem to matter now. With the wind fresh in my face and the clothes drying upon me, I stood and took it all in.

Far away to the south I could see the Sound of Colonsay and beyond it, laid out like a map, green amidst the startling blue of the sea in the late afternoon sunshine, was the distinctive shape of the island of Colonsay itself with Oronsay beyond that again. Nearer was the head of the loch and I could just make out Young Angie and the dun-coloured pony waiting patiently for the smoke signal that they would now never receive. Come to think of it, I was incredibly lucky that the deer-saddle hadn't been needed to cart my own corpse home.

Dougal was down on one knee sweeping the ground in front of us with his telescope.

'If he goes by the loch head, Young Angie will see him. He's a canny lad, Young Angie. So it's the bridge he'll be making for, I'm thinking.'

Then, after a minute or two, 'I cannot understand it. The man's just disappeared,' he said.

Without a great deal of hope I did my best to cover the same ground as Dougal was doing, in shadow as it now was, with the naked eye.

Something was niggling in the back of my mind but I couldn't quite place it. There was no sign of the eagle, but that wasn't it, and his nest which I had not seen would be covered by the overhand directly below where we now were. The boat . . .

I tapped Dougal on the shoulder and pointed.

'You see that little rowing boat up on the shingle across the loch there?'

'Aye. It's always kept there. What of it?'

'I noticed it this morning, while we were looking at the eagle. I saw it without really taking it in. But it was beached on this side of the loch then,' I said.

There was a long pause during which Dougal's face was inscrutable.

Then, 'Aye,' he said quietly, 'there's a wee ridge beyond it and he had only to get over that to be in dead ground all the way back to the castle.'

The head stalker stood up, snapped the telescope shut and returned it to its case. Then he unloaded the Rigby 275, put that back in its canvas slip and slung both over his shoulder. Finally, he turned in the direction of the head of the loch and waved both hands backwards and forwards above his head in what was clearly a standard gesture of cancellation.

I saw Young Angie raising one arm in acknowledgement and then pony and boy together setting off philosophically on their long plod home.

So ended the best day's stalking that I had yet had and was ever likely to have in the whole of the rest of my life. True, we would be going back to the castle hind-less and with an equal lack of success over our second quarry – but it is indeed the getting there that really matters. Even so, I pondered on the latter's possible identity as we ourselves started for home

As Dougal had said, he was a first-class shot with a rifle, but which of them was it?

Malcolm MacRodrick whom Dougal had declared only that day to be a better rifle shot than his brother? Alastair MacRodrick, that enigmatic character, who some twenty years before had won the annual Queen's

Trophy for rifle shooting at Bisley? John J. MacRodrick, the American, who had boasted that morning about his early prowess at 'hunting', could it be that all that ebullient bonhomie of his was nothing more than an act, a façade behind which he sought to disguise a rather more sinister character?

Septicus himself, perhaps? Probably not, I thought. Even if he were capable of such a shot, I doubted whether he would have been prepared to risk his political future by doing that kind of dirty work himself. Someone else on the island? Somehow I was convinced that that was unlikely too.

Whoever it was, it had been sheer bad luck on his part that he had failed in his undoubted object of ridding himself of the nuisance that I had recently turned out to be.

I never did have a very good sense of direction but I was slightly surprised at the way Dougal seemed to be going. As far as I could see, he was taking anything but the direct route back to the castle. But after about twenty minutes the reason became clear.

The head stalker stopped suddenly and pointed down to the ground where lay two empty brass cartridge-cases. Then he took out his handkerchief, picked them up and held them out for my inspection. Each had the motif 'H & H 240' engraved on its end.

'Aye,' he said, 'it's the laird's Holland and Holland 240 he'll have been using. I know well there's only the one on the island.'

The light was failing as we came down the last part of the slope before the steading and the glimmer from the castle windows across the river was welcoming ahead. I was imbued with that strangely pleasant feeling of exhaustion that one often experiences after a day's hard exercise spent out in the fresh air of the countryside. Suddenly Dougal stopped again, stooped down and pointed to an insignificant little bush already bare of its leaves by the side of the track.

'Do you know what that might be, Lord Thyrde?'

He picked a bit off the end of one of the thin branches and handed it to me. Holding it up to what light there was, I could make out greyish twigs with narrow reddy-brown buds like beetles crawling up them. Its intermittent thorns were fully half an inch long.

I had a sudden flash of inspiration.

'Sea buckthorn?' I said. 'The badge of the MacRodricks?'

'Aye, it is that. Maybe it's a good omen. One that'll bring us all luck,' Dougal said.

Back in the gunroom, he made straight for the gun cabinet, unlocked it, took out the Holland and Holland 240, worked the bolt action and sniffed at the breech.

'Aye, that's the one,' he said. 'There's no doubt at all.'

'Can you smell the gunpowder?' I asked.

He smiled and shook his head.

'Not once it's been cleaned. I've as good a nose as any but it's not as good as that. It's fresh oil I'm smelling.'

'So there's not much chance of our finding out who's been using it?'

He shook his head.

'Look, Dougal, I don't think I'll say anything about what happened this afternoon, then. It wouldn't do any good and it would only worry the laird unnecessarily.'

'Very good, m'lord.'

It was the first time that he had called me that.

* * *

They were all there, when I got up to the drawing-room, Malcolm, Black Rod, John J., Septicus and ZH, sitting about separately in the various armchairs and sofas. Only The MacRodrick himself was missing. They each of them turned their heads and looked up at me as I came in.

'Well?' boomed the American, excitedly. 'How did you get on?'

'So, so,' I said.

Malcolm raised his eyebrows.

'Did you get one, old boy?'

'No, I'm afraid not,' I said. 'But then again, *one* didn't get me.'

CHAPTER EIGHT

It was only when I had had a bath and was dressing for dinner that reaction began to set in.

I took longer than usual fumbling with my black tie and I was the last to come into the drawing-room. The others were already paired off, Rodrick, with Dougal behind him and Amanda at his feet, talking to Alastair on one sofa, and ZH to Septicus on another. The American and Malcolm MacRodrick were deep in conversation together in front of the fire.

At a signal from Rodrick I went over to the drinks tray and helped myself to a much needed glass of Kilpatrick twelve-year-old malt.

'Hard luck, Derek!'

I turned to find that John J., flamboyant in matching doublet and kilt of a somewhat gaudy version of the MacRodrick tartan, had come up and joined me. Malcolm, I had noticed, was again wearing his own tartan dinner jacket and trousers, infinitely more discrete in comparison, while Septicus had adopted a high-collared paramilitary coat in field grey, which was reminiscent of Communist Chinese dignitaries. ZH, Rodrick and Alastair all had on conventional dinner jackets like myself.

'Tell me about your day.'

'There's not much to tell, I'm afraid.'

I gave him an edited version of the first part of my day's stalking, ending with the accurate statement that, at the end of a long and highly enjoyable stalk something had startled all the hinds away before I could get a shot.

'How about you?'

John J. MacRodrick made a grimace. Then he adopted his confidential tone.

'I tell you frankly, Derek, I don't take much to Mr Malcolm MacRodrick. Not out of the same mould as his brother if you ask me.'

Malcolm must have heard every word of it because I saw him glare at John J. and then ostentatiously turn his back on him. As for myself, I didn't care how much anyone offended our host's brother by this time. The American seemed oblivious, however, and went on in the same marginally muted tone.

'Have you spoken with Dr Septimus yet?'

'Not properly,' I said.

'Well, you haven't missed much there either, I can tell you . . . ' and he suddenly broke off with a loud 'Hch . . . hhm'. He put a massive hand on my shoulder and simultaneously distorted his face with an exaggerated movement of his lower jaw to my left. I glanced round in that direction to see Septicus coming towards me with his hand already outstretched.

'We'll talk again after dinner, Derek,' John J. said and stumped away quickly, leaving me with the horrifying prospect of coping with the good doctor by myself.

'May I say what a pleasure it is to meet with you, Lord Thyrde. Any friend of the Chief of the Clan MacRodrick must be a friend to all good Larnacans.'

He was a ratty little man and spoke in a high-pitched voice with a suggestion of obsequiousness to it. His mouth was set in a broad smile which somehow failed to find any corresponding twinkle in a pair of distinctly chilly eyes. I noticed that beneath the spectacles a scar ran from the outside of his right eyebrow almost down to the corner of his mouth.

'Thank you very much, Dr Baker.' I shook his small bony hand for him while I was groping for something more to say. 'I've been learning quite a lot about Larna recently.'

'How gracious of you to say that, Lord Thyrde. Nothing to our detriment, I hope?' He gave an equally high-pitched little triple giggle. 'Oh, but we're being too formal, call me "Septimus".'

'Thank you,' I said again.

Still slightly dazed with delayed reaction to the events of the afternoon, I was suddenly struck by a horror that I might blurt out the name 'Septicus' without thinking and I was damned if I was going to ask him of all people to call me 'Derek', which was what he no doubt expected.

Septicus seemed almost to have been reading my mind.

'Some people,' he said, 'seem to experience certain difficulties with the pronunciation of my forename.' The smile remained fixed but the eyes were even colder if that were possible. 'So perhaps you might find it easier to call me "Sep". "Dr Sep", if you prefer it.'

'Dr Sep,' I repeated lamely, and I made an instant resolution never even to think of him as anything but that from now onwards – or at least until our mutual visit here had finished. 'Er . . . I hope you had a good flight over.'

'So kind of you to express concern for my comfort, Lord Thyrde. Passable, I thank you. In any case, one that . . . ' again that triple giggle ' . . . I am fully confident will be justified by results,' he said.

Even if I had started out undecided as to which of the two parties in Larna to support, a comparison of the personalities of their respective leaders alone would have left me in no doubt at all.

To my immense relief, Dougalina appeared in the doorway at that moment to announce dinner and we all filed in.

*   *   *

And I didn't feel a lot better as dinner progressed.

The laird sat at the head of the table, Dougal a watchful figure standing behind him, with ZH and Dr Sep on his right and left respectively. Alastair was on Dr Sep's left and I beyond him. The American on ZH's right and Malcolm on his right again.

Luckily, I was very much out of the conversation and was able just to sit, keeping myself to myself and dealing mechanically with course after course brought round by Dougalina, with their accompanying sequence of wines. Only three things did manage to imprint themselves upon my consciousness: the glint of candlelight on the framed portraits of ancestors around the walls; Rodrick hardly touching his food; and Dr Sep drinking nothing but water all the time.

Eventually, there was one of those lulls in the conversations around the table and, during it, Malcolm MacRodrick put down his glass, rested both tartan clad elbows on the table and faced me across it.

'I say, Derek, old boy, how's that young son and heir of yours gettin' on. Name's Julian, isn't it?'

'Yes,' I said. 'Very well, thank you.'

He picked up his glass again and held it up to the light of the candle nearest to him.

'Surprised you're prepared to go away and leave him for so long at a time.'

'What do you mean?' I said.

'Seems obvious, old boy. Very vulnerable they are at that age. Lot of nasty people about, these days.'

There was an awful silence.

I was briefly aware of a ring of tense faces watching the two of us, among them a sympathetic and encouraging glance from ZH diagonally across the table and a look of appalled horror from the American beside him. I heard a muted but unmistakable high-pitched giggle which came from Rodrick's other side. As for myself, in a violently accelerated state of shock I was totally incapable of reply.

'Malcolm!'

The laird was glaring at his brother who turned and looked back at him, his eyebrows slightly raised.

'Yes, Rodrick?'

'I would have you know that Derek Thyrde's son, Julian, is under my personal protection. And the same goes for Derek himself, whether or not he is under my roof at the time. DO YOU UNDERSTAND?'

'Hey, steady on, old boy. Young Derek, here, can take a joke. I was only pullin' his leg, don't you know.'

Just as he had in the cattle market, just as he did when talking to his head stalker, The MacRodrick lowered his voice and his words took on a gentle Scottish intonation which he could slip into and out of at will.

'Do I make myself clear, Colum Mac Ruaraidh?'

I found myself thinking that whereas he had used Gaelic for his previous confrontation with Malcolm, this time he had equally deliberately avoided it in order that all the witnesses round the table should be able to hear and understand.

Tall though he was, The MacRodrick seemed to have grown in stature. It was no longer the elder brother calling a younger one to order, now it had become the feudal overlord addressing a subordinate member of his clan. The two of them sat there, upright in their seats, glaring at each other across the table. For a long moment I thought that Malcolm was going to brazen it out. But then, gradually at first, his gaze began to falter and finally it dropped until it was lost into some indefinable point below him and, at the same time, his whole figure seemed to crumple and diminish into nothingness.

His words when they did come were no more than a murmur and spoken with an air of total capitulation.

'You do that, Mac Ruaraidh Mor,' he said.

Almost immediately the conversation became general again. And, as Dougalina brought in the plates and handed round the dishes for the final course, I retreated into myself again. But now I knew instinctively and with absolute confidence that the threat to my son, the very possibility of which had never occurred to me until Malcolm had uttered it, together with the danger of any repetition of this afternoon's attempt on my own life of which the laird must have been told by Dougal, were now past.

When all the other plates round the table, including my own, were empty, the laird's was still untouched in front of him. He picked up his spoon and made an experimental dig with it. Then he threw it down again and turned to the head stalker behind him.

'I cannot be doing with this, Dougal. Take it away, please,' he said.

When Dougalina and her father had finally left the room, The MacRodrick rapped on the table in front of him.

'As this evening has become something of a formal occasion, I think it calls for a formal toast.' He put both hands on the ornate arms of his carver chair and levered himself up to his feet. 'Gentlemen, I would ask you rise and to drink to the health of Our Queen.'

We stood up. Even Malcolm came to reluctant attention. Only Dr Sep remained in his seat. Perhaps some devilment had entered into the laird, because the supercilious sneer on the little man's face proved this challenge to be just more than he could take.

Rodrick lowered his glass.

'Dr Baker,' he said, 'will you please stand. We are about to drink to the health of our Sovereign.'

There was a distinct pause. Then, 'Ah yes,' he said, as he too stood up, 'a very gracious lady. How good of her to interest herself in so insignificant a little island as ours.'

'Gentlemen, The Queen,' said Rodrick.

'The Queen,' I said.

'The Queen, God bless her,' said ZH.

'God bless her,' boomed John J. MacRodrick.

But still Dr Sep had not drunk and The MacRodrick glared at him. This time there was no vestigial clan loyalty to call upon, it was a sheer trial of personalities, the one against the other. Finally, the little man did raise his glass of water and took a tiny sip from it.

Then he uttered that triple falsetto giggle of his.

'God bless her, indeed!' he said.

Just at that moment, the sound of the bagpipes, infinitely faint at first but growing with every second, reached us from down the passage. Immediately it relaxed the tension that had dominated the dining-room to a point where it was almost tangible. We were all seated in relative comfort again by the time the head stalker came in.

He marched round the table with that rolling lope of his. How much of what he played was repetition from the previous occasion I cannot say, but I did manage to pick out the plaintive notes from three hundred years ago and five thousand miles away – but for all that as fresh and evocative as the day they were written – of the pibroch 'Larna The Green'. The piper stood to attention when his programme came to an end.

'*Nach gabh thu dram, a Dhughaill 'ic Ruaraidh?*'
'*Gabhaidh du dearbh, 'ic Ruaraidh Mhoir.*'

*   *   *

The downstairs gents' at Castle Rodrick was through a door and down three steps off the passage that led from the dining-room to the library.

There were two washbasins in mottled grey and white marble against one wall and a matching-topped table covered with ivory brushes and combs, each with its engraving of eagle feathers and sea-buckthorn, along another. A pair of adjoining lavatory stalls took up the far side of the room. The laird and I having been the last to leave the dinner table, I found both these latter occupied by the time I came in.

There was a conversation passing between the two in tones that I first took for heated disagreement. My immediate reaction was to feel the discomfort of an unintentional eavesdropper and I half decided to slip away unobtrusively. Then as the sense of what they were saying became clearer I realised that, far from disagreement, what I was listening to could better be described as heated *agreement* and I thought I'd do well to stay where I was.

'We're going to destroy those honkies once and for all, aren't we?' The high excited voice of Septimus Baker.

'We can only hope so.' The deeper, more measured tones of Zechariah Hall had a touch of acerbity about them that I hadn't heard in that seemingly mild-mannered man before.

'But they still haven't woken up, have they?'

'They will have done if they've been listening to the radio.' The doors opened and the two occupants emerged simultaneously. 'If they haven't, they won't be long finding out,' said Zechariah Hall. 'Leroy's our man, that's for sure.'

Instantly the meaning of the whole exchange became clear to me and I was grateful for the fact that neither of the two could possibly be aware of the momentary panic that the first part of it had been instilling in me.

'What's the score?' I said.

'England a hundred and four for four against our four hundred and twenty,' said ZH with evident satisfaction. 'With any luck we'll be able to make them follow on. Dougalina has had the commentary on in the kitchen and Septimus here had it from her at the end of dinner.'

But for once Dr Sep seemed to be at a disadvantage.

'We mustn't let m'lord Thyrde think of us Larnacans as being so concerned over anything so trivial,' he said.

ZH shook his head.

'Derek will understand,' and a twinkle came into his eye as the little doctor scuttled off. 'You do, don't you, Derek?'

'I do indeed,' I said. 'I've never been much of a cricketer myself but a lot of my friends are.'

'Cricket means a great deal to our lives, where I come from, especially a test match against England. For the rest of the Caribbean it's a blow against their former colonial masters, whereas we native-born Larnacans see it rather as a small measure of revenge for Cullodon. It's the one truly unifying influence we have out there.' He made the now familiar gesture with his right hand. 'Talking of which, I understand that I owe you my thanks, Derek. I have been told of your adventures this afternoon, but you must not put yourself at risk on our account again.'

'I'm glad to,' I said. The more I saw of this old statesman, the more certain I became that the cause I had been asked to espouse was the just one. 'But in view of what happened between The MacRodrick and his brother at dinner tonight I think the danger's now over.'

ZH nodded gravely.

'That is my belief too and I pray that it is so. But my party, and I think I may say my country too, are very much in your debt. If ever I can be of help to you, do not hesitate to call on me,' he said.

*   *   *

Back in the library I found John J. waiting for me, standing apart from the others.

'Ah, there you are, Derek. I was wondering what had happened to you. Let's find a place where we can have a quiet talk.'

Not a lot of chance of that, I thought, as the American led me over to two chairs in the farthest corner of the room.

Just as we were getting settled into them, Alastair MacRodrick arrived bearing two cups of coffee for us.

'Thanks, Sir Ala*stair*.'

'Thank you, Black Rod,' I said.

John J. stared at me.

'What did I hear you calling our host's brother?' he said, when the latter was out of what would normally have been earshot.

'Black Rod,' I repeated.

'That's what I thought you said.'

I explained about the Gentleman Usher and the distinctive symbol of his office from which he took his name.

'Well, nothing in this country of yours surprises me any more but, back in the States, you'd never get away with calling a respected official *that*,' he said.

He leant forward and switched over to confidential mode.

'You and I can help each other, I guess. Over Larna. I reckon I've figured by this time which side you find yourself on.'

I nodded noncommittally.

'Well, I told you last night about this Clan Society of ours and the plans we have to help out there. We'd like to adopt one major project. I'll talk to ZH, of course, but I sure would appreciate your advice as to which one it should be.'

'I'd like to help, of course. But I'm not sure how much use my views would be.'

'Non . . . *sense*, you underestimate yourself. Now, there's the airport, I fancy that would be ZH's first choice. But I rather favour the idea of the mineral resources. They tell me they might have bauxite in large quantities. To develop that for the benefit of the islanders would be a contribution indeed.'

'Hold on,' I said, 'I remember hearing something about the bauxite the other day. Oh yes, there's a thing called the Larna Mining Company that had a lot of the extraction rights but somehow never got started. Well it now seems the company's suddenly been taken over but I'm not sure by whom.'

I had a sudden feeling of guilt, remembering that I'd promised Catriona to set in train enquiries about the new owners of the bauxite concessions. With other things on my mind, I'd done nothing about it. But the American seemed delighted with what little I had been able to tell him.

'There now,' he said, reverting to his full-bodied tone again, 'I said you could help and you've done so already.' Then he lowered his voice again. 'Well, if they're in earnest about the bauxite, that's one thing my friends and I won't have to worry about. It'll have to be the airport for us, after all. That'll please ZH.'

'I'd trust ZH to get his priorities right, anyway,' I said.

'Sure! ZH is a gentleman.' His habitual air of *bonhomie* deserted him as he glared across the room in the direction of Dr Sep. 'I can do business with *him*.'

'Meaning you can't with the other chap?'

'You'd better believe it. I don't mind telling you, Derek, if that Dr Septimus and his friends should win the election out there in Larna, as far as I and my Clan Society are concerned, all bets are off,' he said.

At that moment, I became aware of general movement across the room and I looked across to see the others all standing and the laird using his cromach to lever himself up to his feet and with its help coming over to join us, Amanda at his heel.

'I'm off to bed now,' he said. 'Good night to you, John J.'

'Good night, MacRory Moor.'

He turned to the rest of the room.

'Good night, Zechariah.'

'And to you, Rodrick.'

'Dr Baker. Alastair. Malcolm. You'll come up after me, Dougal?'

Then back to me. 'A word with you, Derek.'

I followed my host, as did Amanda and Dougal, but the latter only as far as the door which Rodrick shut behind me.

At the foot of the stairs he stopped and turned towards me.

'I'm sorry I haven't been able to look after you better this time, Derek,' he said.

'But you have indeed,' I said.

'Oh, that . . . ' The MacRodrick moved both hands in a deprecatory gesture. 'I'd have liked to have had another game of piquet with you but I doubt if I could manage the full six games of a *partie* now. Tell me, how's the Independence Bill going now?'

'Not too badly. If all goes well in both Houses here, the election campaign will be able to start on Friday the seventh of January with the election itself being held on Friday the twenty-eighth.'

' "If all goes well." Give me an honest opinion, Derek, just what do you think the chances are?'

'Well, it's pretty tight,' I confessed. 'It all depends on just how cooperative the opposition here are going to be.'

'The opposition! And from what I now hear, that means Malcolm. Harumph! I'd like to see the new administration in place before I die.'

He shook himself and then his composure returned.

'One bit of good news I've had, though, and I think it might please you too. Dougal brought me the mobile telephone while you were closeted with John J. just now. A message from Catriona Campbell, she's flying over tonight and she'll be with us in the morning,' he said.

*   *   *

'The little sod, I could ring his neck!' said Catriona. 'Trust Septicus to try and get in on anything ZH does. I only just heard about it in time to fly over myself and see fair play.'

We were coming out of the castle into the middle courtyard. Catriona had been closeted with the laird and various permutations of the others all morning. But the moment lunch was over she had suggested that she and I should go for another walk.

'ZH would let him get away with anything. He's so saintly I could scream sometimes. Can't see any harm in anyone . . . even him.'

'Dr Sep must have some sort of redeeming feature. No one's all bad,' I said.

'Septicus is. His soul, if he's got one, is as black as hot molten liquorice. Anyway, what's with this "Dr Sep" stuff, he's no more a doctor than I am!'

I explained to her my worries about blurting out the name 'Septicus' accidentally in his presence and the mental precautions that I had felt it necessary to take.

'I'd have used it to his face and to hell with it.' Then Catriona put a hand on my arm and grinned up at me. 'No, of course I wouldn't really. I have got some sense of responsibility and things are bad enough between our two parties already. I haven't got very long this time, where shall we go?'

'You've see the clan-gathering ground, I know, but has the laird shown you round it yet?'

'No.'

'Let me, then. It's really quite impressive. Through this archway,' I said.

Once we were through, Catriona stood for a moment breathing deeply and taking in the almost magic atmosphere of the place. The ancient amphitheatre of the MacRodricks, with its low wall hemming in three sides of it. The sound of the waves reached us clearly now, as they crashed against the rocks far below, away to our left.

Then she took my hand and led me up the steps and on to the raised terrace that was an integral part of the south wall of the castle. We walked along and inspected the lump of weathered granite in the middle. Catriona pointed down at it.

'That's the Otter Stone,' she said.

'It doesn't look very like an otter.'

'Yes it does.' Catriona was indignant. 'There's its tail, see, and its head and body curling round.'

'Rudder,' I corrected automatically.

'Eh?'

'Otters have rudders, not tails. Sorry. I was being pedantic.'

She grinned with a flash of very white teeth and stuck her little pink tongue out at me.

'Hey,' I said, 'I thought you said you hadn't ever been shown this before.'

'I haven't.'

'How do you know about the otter stone, then?'

She sat down on the paving stones immediately to the left of it. Her mouth was firmly shut but still smiling. I sat down myself, joining her on its other side.

Then Catriona relented.

'Well, I have in a way,' she said. 'You see we've got a full-size replica of the whole assembly ground built in the market square out in Kilpatrick Town, even down to the castle wall, this terrace and the Otter Stone, and I've been in and out of it since I was tiny.' She turned her head and then, starting with the castle, looked around her full circle. 'The sea's different, but otherwise I feel I've been here all my life.'

Then she drew her knees up towards her, put her elbows on her knees and her chin between her hands.

I watched her in silence as she sat there for a long time, an expression of pure bliss on her face.

' "See! how she leans her cheek upon her hand," ' I said. ' "O! that I were a glove upon that hand, that I might touch that cheek." '

Without moving any other part of herself, she reached over and took my left hand and placed it where her right had been.

'Be my guest, Romeo,' she said.

Her skin felt just as I had imagined it, firm and smooth. I pulled her face gently towards me and my mouth found hers. It was soft, warm and welcoming.

'Have dinner with me in London tomorrow night, before you go,' I said.

She shook her head.

'I can't. I'm catching an aeroplane from Glasgow – tonight.'

'Catch one from Heathrow on Tuesday instead, then.'

'Or next week, perhaps?'

Then she studied my face more carefully.

'You really meant it, Derek, didn't you?'

'Yes, I did,' I said.

She shook her head.

'I'd love to, but I can't. I mustn't let Septicus get back to Larna before me.

Not if I'm to be able to stave off any damage the little rat's planning.' Then, 'Why don't you fly back to Larna with me? Just for a day or two. It would be well worth the time seeing it all for yourself at first hand.'

For a moment the temptation was almost irresistible. And then I thought of the second reading of the bill in the Commons the next day. And the sort of tricks that Malcolm might have in mind.

'I can't either,' I said.

CHAPTER NINE

Jack Singleton, as Foreign and Commonwealth Office minister responsible for the Caribbean, moved the second reading of the Independence of Larna Bill.

He made a good enough speech.

He gave a brief history of the island from the time that it had first been taken from Spain by members of the Clan MacRodrick on behalf of the Crown in 1661. He explained how Larna had prospered throughout the years under consistently wise administration and how it had thereby proved to be an outstanding example of the benefits of colonial rule. And finally how the island had become a Crown colony in 1923 and had remained so until the present day.

I had taken care to position myself half way down the Peers' Gallery, a point from which every speaker from either side of the House would be fully visible. Malcolm MacRodrick, with his twin trademarks of tie and carnation, had sat upright and attentive in his place behind the opposition dispatch box throughout Jack's speech so far. I had noticed Roddy and Rannie in the public part of the gallery, two tiers behind me and several places along, as I came in but I don't think that either of them had yet seen me.

In recent years, Jack was saying, Larna like many another colony before her had felt that she had grown to years of discretion and was now in a position to stand on her own. To that end a referendum had been held on the island which had endorsed the principle of independence overwhelmingly; a constitutional conference had been called in London, during which all outstanding issues had been settled, except two – whether Larna should remain a monarchy or become a republic and whether or not the new state should apply to become a member of the Commonwealth – these two points being left to be decided by a general election after independence. He did not believe it proper to express a view on behalf of Her Majesty's Government on either of these points this afternoon, these were matters that the islanders themselves should be free to decide.

Jack also congratulated the honourable member for Glasgow, Parkhouse on his elevation to the front-bench opposite, a courtesy which Malcolm acknowledged with a grave and not ungracious nod of his head.

The House was about a quarter full, which was what one would have expected for a second-reading debate which was important but at the same time not one of universal interest. I could hear a distinct buzz made up of some seventeen separate desultory conversations from around the chamber. This was loud enough to be mildly distracting but had not yet reached such a pitch as would merit a rebuke from the morning-coated Deputy Speaker, who was sitting back cross-legged in the Chair, with a hand at the end of each armrest, as Jack concluded his opening speech.

'I would only end by saying this, Mr Deputy Speaker, the road to independence is a long and arduous one for those who have been campaigning so anxiously for it. I am confident, therefore, that this House will allow the process to be completed as speedily as possible. I beg to move that the Independence of Larna Bill be now read a second time.'

He sat down to a respectable sprinkling of *hear, hear!* from all sections of the House.

The Deputy Speaker sat forward in the Chair.

'The question is that this motion be agreed to?' There followed a barely noticeable but conventionally necessary pause. Then, 'Mr Geoffrey Robertson,' he said.

If Jack Singleton had deliberately refrained from expressing any preference as to the outcome of the forthcoming general election in Larna, the former Labour Attorney General clearly regarded himself as being under no such inhibition.

He outlined the quite exceptional record of Larna among all other colonies for stability and contentment over the centuries and this, he said, was never greater than under the present administration, the Larna National Party, led by that wise statesman, the honourable Zechariah Hall. What a pity it would be, therefore, to put all this at risk at the very moment of independence by embarking on a highly controversial and, in his view, unnecessary change in direction. The Larna People's Progressive Movement were on record as saying that they would opt not only to become a republic but also to leave the Commonwealth, both of which he personally deplored.

If this meant him taking sides in advance of the forthcoming general election in Larna, so be it.

For the first time the harmony of the chamber seemed to be broken. This time the murmurs of *hear, hear!* came only from among the Tory benches. These in turn prompted a distinct rustle of order papers interspersed with the odd *Oh!* and *Shame!* on the opposition side.

As Jack had done, he appealed to the House to carry the bill through all its stages without delay. He too was unable to give the real reason for urgency, of course, but he did mention the sad illness of The MacRodrick whom he was proud to count as a personal friend. He expressed the hope, and he was sure that it would be echoed by the House as a whole, that someone who had spent so large a proportion of his life among the islanders of Larna, and contributed so much to their well-being, would be spared for long enough to see the newly independent country settled safely on the road to a prosperous future.

Again *hear, hear*s, came spontaneously from all parts of the House and I could feel the atmosphere settling into peace again.

'I would only end by saying this, Mr Deputy Speaker. In some of what I have said, I know that I differ from the views of my honourable and right honourable friends. I make no apology for this. I speak for myself and myself alone, as I will always do when I believe that a particular cause is just and right.'

Malcolm MacRodrick had leaned forward in his seat as soon as Geoffrey had risen to speak, so as to be able to see him in his place on the opposition front-bench below the gangway. He watched him throughout with an expression of interested concentration. And this he maintained throughout the remaining speeches in the body of the debate.

There were five more such speeches, three from the Tory side and two from Labour. The sense of the former was clearly tilted in favour of the LNP, the latter towards the LPP. Then came the official spokesman from the Liberal Democratic bench and the winding-up speeches had begun.

Throughout this time, the House had been filling up again. Members had been coming in, singly at first, then in twos and threes and finally in a constant stream. Now every bench was full, overflowing until even the steps of the gangways were packed, and it was becoming hard to find room even among those standing at either end of the House.

Finally, Madam Speaker herself had come in, a path miraculously clearing itself for her and enabling her to beat her way through and replace her deputy on the Chair.

Part of all this could be explained by the prospect of a maiden speech from the dispatch box, but Malcolm MacRodrick, whom I had never yet heard speak in the House, would have to be something pretty special to achieve an effect anything like this. It could hardly be the attraction of the matter under discussion either, because however important the outcome to those of us closely involved, to the vast majority Larna was an obscure little island they hardly new where. What was more likely, I thought, was that what we were seeing here was an example of something that can happen in either House of Parliament, but only on the rarest of occasions, when in some mystical way members seem to be able to sense in advance the imminence of some unexpected but quite outstanding parliamentary occasion and find themselves drawn almost lemming-like back into the chamber from whatever cranny of the Palace of Westminster they happen to find themselves in at the time.

The Liberal Democrat spokesman was clearly overawed by it all.

In a rather pedestrian opening, he veered from one faction to the other before positioning himself and his party in a precarious balance between the two. After that, he could barely be heard through the rising and falling drone of chatter, which Madam Speaker made gallant but not very successful efforts to suppress. In the end, the poor man gave it up and subsided limply into his place on the bench.

The hubbub died away to give place to a silence that was almost electric.

'Mr Malcolm MacRodrick,' the Speaker said.

Every eye was focused on Malcolm as he rose to his feet. He put one hand on either side of the dispatch box before him. There was no trace of a note either on the bench from which he had risen or on the dispatch box itself.

'Madam Speaker, as this is the first time that I have had the honour to stand at this dispatch box, I feel that I should first beg the indulgence that it is customary for the House to accord to such timorous novices as myself.' There was a slight ripple of laughter at this point. 'I should also like to express my thanks to the honourable member opposite who sits for Blatchford, East . . . ', here he gave a brief inclination of his head across the table towards Jack, ' . . . for the generous welcome that he gave to me in his opening speech. Also to my right honourable and learned friend, the member for the Highlands and Islands . . . ' again he paused for a brief but friendly nod, this time to Geoffrey Robertson on his left, ' . . . for the kind things he said about my elder brother, who is not, alas, fit enough to be present in the galleries this afternoon but who I know will read every word of this debate in the *Official Report* tomorrow.'

Although Malcolm MacRodrick's twin trademarks of pink carnation and Old Etonian tie were as prominent as ever, just as had been the case in the clan-gathering ground the day after I had met him, his voice was indicative of total sincerity and without the slightest vestige of affectation.

'This is one of those rare and happy occasions, Madam Speaker, when the tussle of party politics can be laid aside and all sides of the House can speak as one. My honourable and right honourable friends have sometimes had occasion to be critical of Her Majesty's Government over such matters and, in the past, I have said harsh things about them myself. But in the present case I have nothing but praise for the way in which they have conducted the question of the independence of Larna from start to finish. I would, it is true, have been glad of rather more time between first and second readings of this bill so that I could have briefed myself rather more fully and, indeed, I submitted a request to that effect through the usual channels. None the less I fully appreciate the reasons they gave me for being unable to accede to this and I can assure them now that I hold no hard feelings over the matter.'

This was a new Malcolm, I thought, could it be that his confrontation with Rodrick at dinner two nights before had really resulted in such a seemingly fundamental change of heart? Jack was staring at him with his mouth open in amazement, Geoffrey looked frankly incredulous. But that the House as a whole was almost mesmerised by him was apparent from the constant murmurs, sometimes even muffled roars, of assent.

'I must confess, Madam Speaker, to a feeling of pride that verges on humility in being a member of the clan that has played such a significant part in the history of the island. Larna has rightly been described as the jewel in the diadem of our colonial system. And may I here put in one further word of gratitude and that is to my right honourable friend, the leader of Her Majesty's Opposition, for giving me the opportunity to take a small part in the final chapter of what must be the greatest success story that we, as a parent nation, have yet been able to achieve.'

He paused and looked down at Albert Wainwright who sat, beaming broadly, on his immediate right.

'Which brings me to what I may call the two unfinished paragraphs in that chapter. I have listened with the greatest of care to my right honourable and learned friend. He feels so passionately about the two issues still outstanding that, alone among those who have spoken, he has expressed a preference for the success after independence of one of the two political parties rather than the other – and I respect him for his sincerity over this. I, myself, am on record more than once in the recent past, while I still possessed the freedom of a back-bench member to hold an independent view on matters such as this, as expressing no less of a preference for the other and it would be vain, not to mention dishonest, of me to deny it now. As to the two issues concerned however, whether Larna should opt for remaining a monarchy or becoming a republic and whether or not she should apply to retain membership of the

Commonwealth, I find myself in agreement with the honourable member for Blatchford, East, opposite – those are matters that should be left for the people of Larna to decide.'

He paused again.

'Whatever such ultimate decisions may be – and none of us can know for certain, for it would be open to either of the political parties in Larna to have a change of heart on either of those issues – we all know with what eagerness every single Larnacan is waiting to join the adult members of our former colonial family. There is no difference between the parties here in Westminster this afternoon. I would add my voice to those of my right honourable and learned friend and the honourable gentleman on the front-bench opposite, the sooner that this bill is on the statute book the better.'

The applause went on for some minutes, and during it I saw first Geoffrey Robertson nodding his head to me in obvious satisfaction and then Jack Singleton giving me a thumbs-up sight. At last, I thought, my adopted troubles really were over. Then, just as the tumult was dying away, I became aware of a muffled choking sound that came from somewhere over my right shoulder.

I turned to see the MacRodrick boys in their seats two tiers behind me, Rannie with a handkerchief up to his mouth in a not-too-successful attempt at suppressing a giggle and Roddy with a slightly unpleasant smile on his face; the latter caught my eye and winked at me. Instantly I knew with a terrible sinking certainty that my feeling of relief had been premature. Down below, in spite of what I, and I had no doubt the whole of the House, had taken to be the peroration of his speech, Malcolm was still standing at his dispatch box.

'I say that, Madam Speaker, but I feel that I must add just one word of caution. Honourable members on this side of the House are as anxious as any to see the parliamentary formalities concluded so that this ward of ours, so newly come to maturity, may set out proudly to take her place among the nations of the world as a free and equal partner. But, after three centuries and more of paternal guardianship, of which this bill is the culmination, you might even say the whole *raison d'être*, is it too much to suggest that we should spend perhaps just a day or two more in making certain that we have got it absolutely right?'

The atmosphere had now switched to one of perplexity – I doubt if anyone other than members of his own front-bench had the slightest idea as to what could be coming next.

'The House will be aware,' Malcolm continued, 'of the very special relationship that Larna has always enjoyed with the United Kingdom and in particular with Scotland and the west coast island from which it takes its name. None of us, I feel sure, would like that relationship to be put at risk in any way. I must ask the honourable gentlemen, the minister, what will be the position of citizens of Larna with regard to access to this country after independence, both in the event of their remaining in the Commonwealth and that of their leaving it?'

Even among the government benches, there were indications that the House considered the point that Malcolm had raised to be a valid one. I saw Jack Singleton lean back and look over his shoulder to have a word with his parliamentary private secretary, seated directly behind him. The latter began scrambling over other members on his bench and making his way towards the 'box' – the wooden stall where civil servants from the department responsible for the bill that is before the House can sit, so as to be available to give instant advice to ministers should unexpected questions arise.

But Malcolm waved a reassuring hand towards Jack.

'The honourable member needn't worry,' he said, 'I don't expect him to reply today. But I felt that it was only fair to give notice that should a satisfactory answer not be forthcoming, I shall be tabling amendments to the bill at committee, or perhaps at report stage. As a member of the Clan MacRodrick, and perhaps, Madam Speaker, I should declare a personal interest in this, I feel that I cannot honourably sit by and see the islanders of Larna, who have looked to my family through the ages for advice and support, have their ancient rights and privileges eroded purely through insufficient attention being paid to them at this stage.'

He still seemed to be carrying a majority of the members with him and I suppose this was hardly surprising, for how could anyone be expected to see through deviousness of such an order? But what he was doing was standing the arguments on their heads. The very delay for which he was asking, under the pretence that it would help to preserve the existing ties between Larnacans and this country, would have precisely the opposite effect in that its sole purpose was to let the wrong party in and thereby ensure that those ties would be lost for ever.

At this point Malcolm MacRodrick did make as if to sit down . . . but then apparently he thought better of it.

'Oh yes, there is one other aspect of the bill that may be worth mentioning, Madam Speaker. Some years ago a company was formed, the Larna Mining Company, to develop certain mineral rights on the island and in particular deposits of bauxite which are believed to be present in economically viable quantities. Although this company has hardly engaged in any active development since that time, it has recently been taken over and I understand that the new owners have already committed themselves irrevocably to substantial expenditure on geological surveys and metallurgical tests. I also understand that they are now claiming that their company is in a unique position with regard to the possibility of its interests being affected by the passage of this bill. It has just come to my notice that further evidence exists which would support them in this claim.'

Now at last I did sense an instant reversal in the mood of the House. Malcolm MacRodrick had suddenly ceased to be the sympathetic figure that he had somehow gulled all sides of the House into believing he had become. The Speaker was looking at him with an expression of horror and disbelief.

She rose from the Chair.

'Order!' she barked.

Malcolm instantly sat down and looked up at her with an expression of polite enquiry.

'Am I understand that the honourable member wishes to raise implications of hybridity with regard to this bill?'

Hybridity! The one word the very suggestion of which is calculated to turn the most hardened minister into a screaming hysteric.

'I am afraid that that is the case, Madam Speaker. I should not like to see the people of Larna take this great step into independence with the taint hanging over them of not having honoured commitments made in their name.'

'This is most unusual not to say improper. Why was I not given notice of this in reasonable time before the debate began?'

'I very much regret that, Madam Speaker. But I was only apprised of the evidence concerned when it was too late for me to do so. I did however manage to have a word with the Clerk of Private Bills just before this debate began and he was able to add his support to my view that a *prima facie* case for hybridity might exist.'

This time, there was a slight pause before the Speaker rose again.

Then, 'Very well, but I do not think it would be proper for me to allow the progress of the bill to be interrupted at this stage without more substantial evidence. I shall give my ruling tomorrow. In the meantime, the debate should proceed.'

'I am more than satisfied with that, Madam Speaker. I should like to express my thanks to you for your tolerance and understanding over this matter. I would only end, then, by commending this bill to the House on behalf of my honourable and right honourable friends,' and he sat down with the air of one who has carried out a disagreeable task with unusual charm and tact.

'Mr Jack Singleton,' called the Speaker.

An ghastly-looking Jack, his face a pale greeny-grey colour, blinked at her for a moment before pulling himself to his feet. Then he made a token attempt to reply to the debate, mentioning neither access nor hybridity, and moved that the bill be read a second time. The question was put and agreed to and the House moved on to the next business of the day.

I left the Peers' Gallery as quickly as I could, taking care not to look in the direction of Roddy and Rannie and give them whatever satisfaction their two warped minds might get from such a confrontation. I wanted to get downstairs and into the Commons lobby as soon as possible so as to catch Geoffrey Robertson and seek his advice.

All bills that come before Parliament fall into one of two main categories, 'public' or 'private'. Whereas public bills, which include the vast majority of all measures introduced in the government of the day's parliamentary programme, treat everybody whose activities and interests are likely to be affected equally, private bills, which are usually sponsored by local authorities or other similar bodies, are inclined to impose different rules affecting certain specified areas, organisations or groups. The main difference in the parliamentary treatment of public and private bills, is in *committee*, public bills being referred either to a 'committee of the whole House' on the floor of the House or to a 'standing committee' upstairs, in both of which amendments are moved and discussed by members of that House of Parliament alone, and private bills to a quasi-judicial select committee whose job it is to hear petitions presented by counsel on behalf of anyone who feels that he is being singled out for unfair discrimination.

But there is a third category of bill known as 'hybrid', which would be public bills, were it not that some small part of them had the characteristics of a private bill, in that it treated certain people or bodies differently from others. In some bills a certain degree of hybridity is unavoidable and this is usually recognised and allowed for from the start, but in others the hybridity is accidental and can be discovered and pointed out either by the clerks or by individual members of one House or the other. In either case, while the rest of the bill is treated as is any other public one, that part of it that makes it hybrid must be referred to the quasi-judicial select committee, which can invariably lead to considerable – and, in particular, carefully stage-managed – delay.

I reached the Commons lobby as members were starting to stream out of the chamber, chattering excitedly at the unusual turn that the afternoon had taken, and Geoffrey, who had spotted me marginally before I had him, came straight over and joined me.

'What's all this about hybridity?' I said.

'Aye, I was hoping you'd be able to tell me that. He's out for delay, of course – playing for the three weeks or so that are necessary to delay the bill until after the Christmas recess.'

'And how long could he delay it?'

'Well, the Speaker's got to give a ruling tomorrow that there *is* a *prima facie* case to start with, without that he's finished. If she should do that, however, the bill would be referred to the examiners, whose job it would be to make the final decision. It would be at least a week before they met, to give time for the parties for and against hybridity to prepare their cases, that's one week out of the three already.'

'And then?'

'Another week at least, I'd say, for the examiners to decide whether the bill is hybrid or not. If they do, there's the select committee to be appointed, the petition to be prepared, counsel to be briefed . . . after that the sky's the limit. This Larna Mining Company really does exist, I suppose, it's not just something dreamed up by Malcolm MacRodrick for the occasion?'

'I'm afraid it does exist,' I said. 'And if the examiners find the bill not to be hybrid?'

Geoffrey Robertson thought for a bit and then shook his head.

'It'd still be pretty tight,' he said. 'The two weeks we'd have lost already are a minimum and the House still has to approve a motion for the bill to be referred to a committee of the whole House – if all this hadn't happened it would have been done automatically as soon as the motion for second reading had been carried this afternoon. It all depends on whether the report of the examiners is received before the business statement on Thursday fortnight so that the motion for committee can be announced then. Otherwise, it would have to figure in the business statement the Thursday after, with the committee stage itself being held in the following week.'

'So Malcolm would still win. Oh, my God,' I said.

'What about the fourteen days you've allowed for the bill in the Lords? Could that be cut down a bit?'

'I don't think so,' I said. 'Better assume not, for safety's sake.'

'I shouldn't worry too much, Derek, . . . yet! Madam Speaker still has to rule on there being a *prima facie* case, remember. And for the life of me, I cannot see just where in the case of this bauxite company the element of discrimination might lie.'

'What about the amendments to the bill that Malcolm's threatening on access to this country for Larnacans, then?'

'Ah, there he's certainly on less strong ground. Larnacans hold the status of CUKCs – that's Citizens of the United Kingdom and Colonies – and, as such, have been subject to immigration control since the early sixties, so the rights that he's asking the government to preserve are purely imaginary. But I would think he only brought those in to be used as further delaying tactics, a sort of fall-back position in case the hybridity ploy fails.'

'Well, thank you very much, Geoffrey. I think I'd better go off now and fill in Tom Lavenham on the situation. He's one of the best parliamentary strategists I know.'

Geoffrey Robertson clapped me on the shoulder.

'And if things should go really wrong, I'll be able to bend Albert Wainwright's ear. As a former Labour law officer of the Crown, I've still got a right to be heard on such matters. But I only want to use that as a last resort,' he said.

*   *   *

Outside Tom Lavenham's office I found Gwilym Jones, who combined the job of private secretary to the Leader of the House of Lords with that to the Chief Whip.

'Hello, Gwilym. Is the Chief Whip in?'

'No, I'm afraid not, but the Lord President is and he wants to see you urgently,' he said.

I found Tony Dysart at his desk, engaged in the perennial task of going through the papers in his two red boxes. He had short grey curly hair and an expression of intense anxiety which, as this was habitual, did nothing to alert me to any very great problems. He looked up as I came in.

'Ah, Derek, bad news, I'm afraid. Tom Lavenham's had a heart attack.'

'Oh, my God,' I said.

'It's not too bad, I understand, but he's got to be off for several months and not to be worried about anything. You'll have to take over as acting Chief Whip, of course. Do you think you'll be up to it yet, after . . . ?'

This time I knew that the anxious expression was genuine. Perhaps it always was.

'Yes, I'm sure I will,' I said.

'How's Julian?'

'Very well, thank you. I didn't see him last weekend, I had to go up to Castle Rodrick.'

'Oh yes, of course. How's the Larna bill getting on?'

'Not too well, I'm afraid. That's what I was on my way to see Tom about.'

I told him about the events of the afternoon.

'Well, being acting Chief Whip will give you added clout over all that. I haven't got half the parliamentary cunning Tom Lavenham has, but come to me if I can help in any way. As for anything else, rely on Gwilym, he'll see you through.'

'Thanks. Where is Tom?'

'Across the river in St Thomas's.'

'Would it be all right if I popped over to see him?'

'I'm sure it would. But remember, light chit-chat only,' Tony said.

*　　*　　*

'Sorry to land you with all this and at such a time, too, Derek.'

Tom Lavenham was lying in bed facing towards the window which looked out on to the river. He was considerable frailer in appearance than I'd been prepared for and his voice was faint too. But the sparkle in his eyes was still there.

'Don't worry.' I did my best to display a degree of confidence that I was in fact from feeling. 'I'm sure I'll manage. Actually I'm rather looking forward to it.'

'Trust Gwilym. He knows the ropes almost as well as I do now. How's the Larna affair getting on?'

'Could be worse,' I said – a statement that, although meant to be misleading, had the benefit of being strictly accurate – as of that moment, that is.

But it might not be tomorrow.

'Don't hesitate to get in touch if you need my advice.'

I looked out of the window and across the water to the floodlit Palace of Westminster, the well-being of the southern half of which had suddenly become my own virtually exclusive responsibility.

'I'll send over a smoke signal,' I said.

*　　*　　*

First thing next morning, I moved my things into the Chief Whip's room from my own slightly smaller one across the corridor. Tom's fastidiously neat desk-top gradually took on the appearance of a car-boot stall. Then I asked Gwilym Jones to come in and see me.

At my request he ran through my various daily duties and then the cabinet and House of Lords committees that I would be expected to attend – these being mercifully few in number – over the next week or so.

'Penny Seymour will look after you generally and do your letters for you. Then there's your weekly meeting with the Chief Whip of the Commons at six this evening. It alternates between his room and yours, tonight it's in Mr Chanter's room in the House of Commons.'

'And that's about all?'

Gwilym nodded.

Rely on Gwilym, he'll see you through. Trust Gwilym, he knows the ropes almost as well as I do now. The advice from Tony Dysart and Henry Chanter had been almost identical.

'How much do you know about the Larna situation?' I said.

'Well, I know about the goings on in the Commons yesterday, of course. And the Chief Whip . . . er, Lord Lavenham . . . has told me a certain amount about your own involvement and what you've found out. But there may be gaps in that.'

I gave him a brief résumé of everything that had happened so far.

'So it all comes down to timing,' I said. 'Let's be certain of exactly what that means. We need fourteen days for the bill in this House; could we improve on that?'

'Not without the full consent of the opposition and, for the purposes of the Larna bill, that means Malcolm MacRodrick. Let's see now . . .' Gwilym took out his diary and studied it for a moment . . . 'with both Houses rising for Christmas on December the twenty-third, we'd need to take first reading in the Lords on Friday the tenth, with the Commons completing all their stages on Thursday the ninth, at the latest. Tomorrow, Wednesday, being the seventeenth of November, they've twenty-three days to do it in.'

'And, if Malcolm ensures that they don't, we won't get Royal Assent before Christmas. That in turn means the election in Larna being delayed for about a month and a half. So everything depends on the Speaker's ruling this afternoon.'

'Not necessarily, her ruling would only be on whether there's a *prima facie* case for the bill being hybrid. It would be for the examiners to decide definitely whether there is hybridity or not and I agree with Geoffrey Robertson – I can't see how this bauxite company can be in a different position from other companies on the island. If their answer is no and if they haven't been too long in making up their minds about it, we could still just about manage it.' He paused for a moment. 'Is there any possibility of finding out any more about this Larna Mining Company?'

'That's my next job, this morning,' I said.

* * *

'Hello, Simon. Derek Thyrde, here. I've got a little job for you.'

The voice in the earpiece of my telephone spluttered slightly. Simon Shaw was my stockbroker and also a personal friend of very long standing. He had helped me out over one or two not dissimilar enquiries in the past.

'Oh, my God, not again,' he said.

'No, this is nothing difficult, I promise you. Larna Mining Company; Larna as in Caribbean, Mining as in bauxite, Company as in the sort of thing that brings in your daily pittance. It was taken over not long ago. Do you know anything about it and in particular who now owns it?'

'Not offhand. It must be a private company?'

'I should think so.'

'Hold on a minute.'

There was the sound of a turning of pages at the other end. Then, 'Yes, private company, set up about ten years ago. It's quite simple. You just go to Companies House and they'll be able to find you all the information you need.'

'I say, Simon, you couldn't be an absolute angel and get someone to do it for me, could you? My Chief Whip's been taken ill and I've been landed with the entire running of the House of Lords. And it really is terribly important; it's to do with the Independence of Larna Bill that's going through Parliament at the moment.'

There was a pause that I could feel biting into my ear.

'I suppose so. It might take a day or two, though.'

'Thank you so much. That's a very good lunch I owe you,' I said.

* * *

This time, when the Speaker rose to her feet, the House was tense, silent and packed.

'Yesterday afternoon,' she said in her clear authoritative voice, 'I undertook to give a ruling to the House on certain matters that had been raised at a very

147

late stage in the second reading debate on the bill to give independence to the island of Larna.

She paused and directed towards Malcolm MacRodrick a look of distaste such that, had I been its recipient, would have had me writhing in my seat. The fact that he had been newly appointed as a front-bench spokesman in the party of which she had until recently been a prominent and immensely respected member served only as an aggravation to the offence. But Malcolm only nodded gravely and waited for what she had to say.

'I have received representations from both sides of the House and, after long and careful consideration, I now have to rule that the Independence of Larna Bill is *prima facie* hybrid.'

For a moment or two there was again total silence, but then it was broken by sporadic cheering from the Labour benches – it must have been pure reflex action, because what they were cheering for I doubt if even they knew – and this in turn provoked angry rumblings accompanied by the waving of order papers on the government side.

But the Speaker was still on her feet.

'Mr Malcolm MacRodrick,' she said.

Malcolm rose to the dispatch box and in what, even to my biased state of mind, appeared to be an unexceptionable manner thanked Madam Speaker for her patience and fair-mindedness and immediately resumed his seat. Pausing only to cast in his direction a further brief glance that would have been worthy of the Queen of Hearts rebuking her errant rose gardeners, she then called a subdued Jack Singleton who gave notice that he would be tabling for the following day a motion to refer the bill to the examiners. The House then went on to discuss the second reading of the Ancillary Services Bill, which it appeared was the first business of the day.

I sat on in my place in the Peers' Gallery in a state of almost total shock and tried to collect my thoughts. In my new capacity as acting Chief Whip, I had sat through the whole of the House of Lords question time, before coming down the corridor to catch the tail-end of that of the House of Commons at which, today being a Tuesday, the Prime Minister had been presiding. I had nothing much more to do until it was time for the first of my weekly meetings with the Chief Whip of the Commons, at which I would undoubtedly get the most up-to-date information of today's horrors from the most authoritative source available, at six tonight

It wasn't long before the proceedings in the chamber below me impinged themselves on my consciousness.

I had long known that the Ancillary Services Bill was the most controversial measure of this current session, possibly even of the whole Parliament so far. But the noise and hubbub beneath me seemed to be reaching a state of anarchy that far surpassed anything in my previous experience. In spite of Madam Speaker's valiant efforts, the Secretary of State for Trade and Industry was hardly being able to complete a single sentence of his opening speech uninterrupted and I found myself, however unwillingly, becoming totally immersed in it.

Poor man . . . he had his troubles too.

*   *   *

'Come on in, Derek. I'm s–sorry to hear about poor Tom, but welcome to you just the same. Whisky?'

In the muted lighting of his room, restful with the Commons' green of its upholstery, curtains and carpet, my new opposite number, Henry Chanter, had got up from his desk and come forward to meet me with outstretched hand. He was a thin, rather earnest-looking man, with horn-rimmed spectacles and a very slight stammer. Tom Lavenham I knew had become very fond of him after a comparatively short time.

'Yes, please. A large one,' I said.

When he had provided us both with glasses, he signalled me into one of his armchairs and himself sat down on a sofa near to it.

'I saw you in the gallery for the Speaker's ruling this afternoon.'

'Yes,' I said. 'What on earth was it all about?'

'Apparently that utter s–sod, Malcolm MacRodrick, has got hold of some document or other that supports his accusation of hybridity. It must have been enough to convince the Speaker to a certain extent, sh . . . she'd never have backed up MacRodrick if she could have avoided it. I'm sorry, we tried to get in touch with you earlier to warn you.'

'But Jack Singleton, why did he say he was going to move that the bill goes to the examiners?'

'He hadn't got much option, and the sooner it's done and cleared by the examiners, the sooner we can get on with it.'

'Wasn't there anything else he could have done?'

Henry looked a bit sheepishly at me.

'Well, yes actually. He could have put down a motion that the application of standing orders regarding hybridity be dispensed with – there is a precedent for such a thing and on far less valid grounds than would have been the case with the Larna bill. But, with the mood that the opposition were in this afternoon, we just d–didn't dare to risk it.'

'Ah yes, the Ancillary Services Bill. Why are the opposition so worked up about it? I've never seen them in the state they were this afternoon.'

'Well it's all about privatisation for one thing, privatises virtually everything that's left in the public sector. Then it's got a "Henry the Eighth Clause" in it. Gives us the power to add any little thing we might have overlooked by order after the bill becomes law.'

'Oh, I see,' I said.

I'd had some experience of Henry the Eighth Clauses. King Henry, or one of his advisers, had hit on the bright idea of making laws by proclamation, thereby avoiding the tedious process of seeking the agreement of both Houses of Parliament. The nearest modern equivalent is to take powers in a particular bill to make additions or alterations to it by Order in Council. It is a practice that is universally detested and condemned but all governments do it – and there's a refinement to it too.

Orders laid before Parliament are of two kinds, those for affirmative resolution in which, for the order to become effective, it has to be debated and approved in both Houses, or those for negative resolution in which the order simply has to lie on 'the table' for a certain number of days after which it takes effect unless someone in the intervening period has demanded a debate and voted it down. These, in theory at any rate, come into force without any debate at all. The government of the day, therefore, invariably tries to get away with a negative order in the parent legislation, thereby avoiding the possibility of what they consider to be waste of parliamentary time for the future. The opposition of the day, however, almost invariably moves and carries an amendment to the bill changing the negative resolution into an affirmative one, so honour is satisfied and everyone is happy. It's a game that everyone enjoys and keeps us gainfully employed through the long winter evenings at Westminster.

Hence the turmoil in the House that afternoon.

'Tug Wilson was stirring it more than most,' said Henry, 'barrack-room lawyer if ever there was one. Up to every parliamentary trick there is. The opposition are bound to want to get him on the standing committee upstairs.'

'Wilson?' I said. 'Cocky little man with gold-rimmed spectacles, grey hair and a ginger-moustache?'

'That's him. Why?'

'He was one of the Labour MPs who spoke on the Larna bill yesterday.'

'That figures,' said Henry Chanter, 'always been thick as thieves with Malcolm, Tug has. N–never mind, we'll get the Ancillary Services Bill through somehow. And your bill still has top priority.

I hoped so. The remaining stages in the Commons of the Independence of Larna Bill should have been completed tomorrow, Wednesday. The motion which was to replace them would set in train procedures that might or might not delay it almost indefinitely.

The countdown of twenty-three days had begun.

CHAPTER TEN

Twenty-three days . . . and at least seven of them would have gone before the examiners would even meet to consider the matter.

'Just who are these "examiners"?' I said to Gwilym. 'Everyone seems to speak about them with bated breath as though they were tantamount to the Spanish Inquisition.'

We were sitting in the Chief Whip's room, now mine, on the following morning. Wednesday, the seventeenth of November. The day when the Independence of Larna Bill should have passed through its committee and remaining stages on the floor of the House of Commons in one afternoon.

'Usually the Clerks of Private Bills in both Houses.'

'That's a lot of help,' I said. 'From what he said at second reading, Malcolm seems to have nobbled the Commons one already. How well do you know our chap?'

Successive private secretaries to the Leader and Chief Whip of the House of Lords are seconded to that office for a three-year stint from the middle-ranking members of the clerks of the House stream, often double firsts at Oxbridge and, as such, of greater intelligence and certainly far greater security-of-job tenure than the politicians they serve.

'Very well. In fact, he's a particular chum of mine.'

'Do you think you might be able to sound him out a bit and find out just what the chances of them finding the bill hybrid are . . . and, if possible, why?'

At that moment, Penny Seymour, marginally the prettiest of the three pretty girls in the Government Whips' Office – and the one who was specifically responsible for looking after me – put her head round the door.

'I know you said that you weren't to be interrupted, Lord Thyrde, but I've got a Mr John J. MacRodrick Junior on the telephone. He says it's extremely urgent. And he won't take "no" for an answer.'

Gwilym Jones gathered his papers together and stood up.

'I think we've covered as much as we can for the moment, Chief Whip. With regard to the matter we've just been talking about, I'll do what I can,' he said.

I looked at Penny.

'Then, yes please, you'd better put him through,' I said.

She nodded and left.

I picked up the receiver as soon as the telephone rang and the strident tones of John J.'s voice came on the line.

'Derek, I'm glad I've caught you. You remember our talk up at Castle Rodrick at the weekend – about my little old Clan Society and how we can best help Larna?'

'Indeed I do.' I said.

'Well, I'd like very much to meet with you in the near future so as we can discuss it further. Might you be free for lunch today or tomorrow? Dinner, if you'd prefer it.'

I thought for a moment. It had already occurred to me that, with the baddies on the island scattering money about like groundbait in the name of the People's Progressive Movement, it would be no bad thing if we could persuade John J. and his American Clan Society to do the same on behalf of the Larna National Party. So there was nothing contrived about the regret in my voice when I answered.

'Look, John J., I'm afraid I'm in one hell of a rush at the moment. My boss has just been taken ill and I've had to take over everything from him at short notice. Could you give me a day or two to get things sorted out?'

'Sure. Next week would do just fine. I'll give you a ring then,' he said.

As I put down the receiver, it did occur to me that the enforced delay had one advantage. Well though I had got on with the American, I still knew very little about him. This was something that could be put right in the meantime.

I knew exactly whom to speak to next.

Some years ago, I had had some dealings with a United States Air Force four-star general called 'Dick' Richards who had also been a friend of my father's during the '39–'45 war.* Earlier this year, I had had a letter introducing himself from Dick's son, George, himself a full colonel in the US Air Force who was doing a stint as air attaché at their embassy in Grosvenor Square. I had asked him to lunch at the House of Lords and we had got on extremely well together from the start.

I was lucky enough to get him on the telephone first time off.

'George,' I said, 'I've got a rather sensitive political situation at the moment to do with the Independence of Larna Bill. There's an American, pretty rich I

* See *Two Thyrdes* by Bertie Denham, 1983

should imagine, who's involved in some way but only, I think, on the fringe of it at the moment. Would there be any chance of your seeing if you can find out anything you can about him . . . the point is, can I trust him and, if so, how far?'

I gave George the very few details I knew about John J. MacRodrick – that he was retired, that he lived in Miami and was president of the American Clan Society. I also added his present London address and telephone number.

'Do you think that might be enough to go on,' I said doubtfully.

'Sure, nothing easier,' George said.

*   *   *

That afternoon, the House of Commons passed the motion to refer the Independence of Larna Bill to the examiners, without any further discussion. The call from the castle came that evening. The MacRodrick himself was on the line.

'Derek, what's all this I read in the newspapers yesterday and today about the Larna bill?'

I explained as best I could about public bills and the horrors of hybridity.

'But the best advice I can get at the moment is that it's probably only a ploy of the opposition's and that at the worst it might delay the bill a matter of ten days or so.'

'Harumph! Glad to hear it. Keep me posted, will you?' he said.

*   *   *

On Thursday, I was frantically busy all day. But almost all of it was concerned with my new job as Chief Whip and the running of the House of Lords. Only two isolated parts of it had anything to do with Larna.

At one point in one of our almost non-stop meetings, Gwilym took me on one side.

'I had a brief word with the Clerk to Private Bills, Chief Whip. Not very good news, I'm afraid. Apparently the other side has got hold of some document or other which makes a finding of hybridity not so unlikely.'

'Have you seen the paper? Do you know what its about?'

'No, I had to play it rather carefully. I might be able to find out more early next week.'

I took an instant decision that, in spite of my undertaking to Rodrick, I would not worry him about this until I had something more definite to go on.

Catriona Campbell rang up later in the day.

'How's it going with you, Derek?'

I gave her a brief rundown on the latest situation.

'Well, it's not so good here either. There's a new opinion poll published this morning.'

'I thought it wasn't due for ten days or so yet.'

'The *Voice of the People* say they're going to poll weekly from now on and it's obvious why. The PPM are creeping up again. Now the figures are back to fifty-one/thirty-seven, still with twelve per cent "don't knows",' she said.

*　　*　　*

On Friday I went down to the country, to Thyrde House . . . and Julian, my son.

*　　*　　*

'Goodbye, Alastair, then – and many thanks for your help.'

It was Monday morning and I had had an early meeting in Downing Street. I was walking down the West Front corridor towards my own Chief Whip's room when I heard these words coming through the open door of the one occupied by the Gentleman Usher of the Black Rod. It was the ever-fresh pink carnation and the black tie with its pale-blue diagonal stripes that impinged themselves on my consciousness first as Malcolm MacRodrick emerged looking more than usually pleased with himself and, as soon as he saw who it was, an additional glint came into his eye.

'Hello, Derek old boy, excitin' times we do live in, wouldn't you say?'

I gazed at him stupidly in a helpless silence and watched him as he walked off down the corridor and turned the corner out of sight. It was perfectly natural, of course, that first cousins should know each other pretty well and be on casual visiting terms. But it re-raised the question that had been in my mind on and off ever since this whole business had started . . . just how much could we trust Black Rod?

Back in my own room I found Gwilym Thomas waiting for me.

'I've just been talking to John Antrobus, the Clerk to Private Bills. I've found out quite a bit more. Not very good news, I'm afraid.'

I sat down in my chair.

'Tell me the worst,' I said.

'Well, it goes quite a long way back into history. It seems that in 1693 the Scottish Parliament passed an Act for Encouraging Foreign Trade and that, subsequent to that, King William the Third issued a proclamation that was based on that act.' He took a xeroxed document out of the inside breast pocket of his coat and passed it over to me. 'Look, Chief Whip, you haven't seen this and even if you have it wasn't me who showed it to you.'

'Of course not,' I said.

I unfolded it and read it through slowly.

His Majesty, understanding that certain peers and gentlemen, in-dwellers in this his ancient Kingdom, are willing to engage themselves with great sums of money in a trade with the island of Larna, to be exercised from this Kingdom, and being mindful of the encouragement given thereto by the Act for Encouraging Forraigne Trade, doth by these letters present constitute William Hamilton, earl of Ruglen, James Campbell, earl of Irvine, John Graham, Lord Lynedoch, Archibald Seton, viscount of Kingston and Ranald mac 'ic Ruaridh to be one body incorporate and a free incorporation, by the name of the Company of Scotland trading to Larna. Providing always that each of the said undertakers shall subscribe an equal proportion of the fund or capital, stock subscribed shall be devised up on the male heirs of their body and upon none other, so however that if there are no heirs male of any of the undertakers, his stock shall pass in equal proportions to the remaining undertakers or their heirs as aforesaid; and that the Company shall perpetually be assured of their free trade in any goods whatsoever to and from the island of Larna, to carry it on without any manner of restraint or prohibition, free of all customs, taxes, cesses, supplies or other duties or prohibitions imposed or to be imposed.

Then I read it through a second time.

'I see,' I said. 'Look Gwilym, I know that I'm probably being extremely dense, but how exactly does this affect the hybridity issue?'

'Quite simply. Apparently, the original company ceased trading well before the Act of Union in 1707. Equally, all the peerage lines named have since died out in the main line and accordingly Rodrick MacRodrick, as the direct male successor to the original Ranald, will have scooped the pool, such as it may be. But the rights conferred on him, as they relate to minerals and in particular to the excavation of bauxite, he will almost certainly have passed on, albeit unwittingly, in the concessions that he himself has made to the Larna Mining Company. Furthermore, the long title of the Independence of Larna Bill includes, among other provisions, the words, "to regulate trade between Larna and the United Kingdom" and "to impose duties of customs on certain goods or categories of goods imported into the United Kingdom".'

'And all this is enough to make the bill hybrid?'

'In John Antrobus's view it is,' Gwilym said. 'It's highly unlikely that there's another company in Larna that stands to lose rights as valuable as these.'

He left me to my not very happy thoughts; during the course of the next forty minutes or so, I received three telephone calls in what seemed like quick succession.

The first was from my stockbroker friend, Simon Shaw.

'Derek? I've managed to locate this Larna Mining Company of yours.'

'Oh good,' I said.

'Not so good, I'm afraid. The new ownership is in nominee names. Look just how important is it to you?'

'Absolutely vital,' I said. 'It's now become the key factor in the Independence of Larna Bill which is going through Parliament at the moment and it could be the direct cause of the baddies getting in after the first election out there. Why?'

'The nominees are a highly reputable firm of solicitors and one of the senior partners is an old schoolfriend of mine. It's just possible that I might be able to squeeze something out of him – in strictest confidence, of course.'

'I would be most awfully grateful.'

'I'll ring you back,' he said.

The second call was from Colonel George Richards, the air attaché at the American Embassy. He came straight to the point.

'John J. MacRodrick Junior,' he said. 'Nobody's ever been able to pin anything on him but, over the years, he's been strongly suspected of having had his finger in any number of undesirable pies – the Mafia, Columbia drug barons, you name it. My advice to you is don't touch him, he's poison.'

The third was from Simon Shaw again.

'I've got it.' He sounded mildly triumphant. 'The new owners of the Larna Mining Company are some six or seven in number . . . quite a consortium. I can give you the names of all of 'em, if you like, but the lead man is a John J. MacRodrick Junior,' he said.

*   *   *

I rang up The MacRodrick that afternoon.

The first thing I did was to pass on George Richards' warning about John J. MacRodrick. He was predictably appalled by it. But, after the initial shock had worn off, I somehow got the impression that he wasn't altogether surprised.

'There's something else, I'm afraid, an old seventeenth-century document's turned up that might give us a bit of trouble,' I said. 'Listen, I'll read it to you. "His Majesty, understanding that certain peers and gentlemen, . . . '

' " . . . William Hamilton, earl of Ruglen,' Rodrick interrupted, 'James Campbell, earl of Irvine, John Graham, Lord Lynedoch . . . " I know the one. What of it?'

'Well, it seems the whole case for the bill being hybrid is based on that,' I said.

'But . . . there was a second proclamation rescinding it at the time of the Act of Union. Those examiners of yours are bound turn it up if they're worth their salt. Anyway, my brother Malcolm knows all about it, he and I were discussing it only a week or two ago, why doesn't he put 'em right?'

'Er . . . , I'm afraid it was Malcolm who produced the document in the first place.'

'Harumph!'

There was a long uncomfortable pause, which eventually was broken by me.

'Could you get me chapter and verse about the second document and where it can be found? It might save quite a bit of time.'

'I'll ring you in the morning,' Rodrick said.

*   *   *

Gwilym Thomas was waiting with me in my room, the next morning, Tuesday the twenty-third of November, when the call came through.

I jotted down the details as Rodrick gave them to me: *10th December 1706. Antiquities Museum, Brook St, Glasgow.*

Then I passed the slip of paper to Gwilym who stood up immediately.

'I'll take this to John Antrobus. He's promised to pull out all the stops,' he said.

A little later on, my telephone rang again.

'I've got John J. MacRodrick Junior on the line,' said Penny Seymour's voice.

'I'm not in.'

'Right-ho.'

'Oh, and Penny . . . '

'Yes?'

'If ever that man *should* ring up again, you haven't seen me, you can't find me and you don't know where I am.'

My weekly meeting with the Chief Whip of the Commons, at my end of the palace this time, was scheduled for six o'clock that night.

*   *   *

Henry Chanter arrived half an hour late.

'I'm terribly sorry, Derek. Bloody people!' he said.

'Trouble?'

'You could say so. The Ancillary Services Bill, again, needless to say. The committee of selection met last Wednesday and, just as I feared, the opposition managed to persuade them to include Tug Wilson on the standing committee on the bill, and not only him but two others of almost equal trickiness. Then, the standing committee met today to consider our 'sittings motion', enabling it to sit mornings, afternoons and evenings – normal practice in a bill of this size and complexity – and they've started to gib at that.'

I gave him a drink and he relaxed into an armchair.

'I've just come down from there now. How long will you need for it in your House?'

'Ten weeks at least, a lot depends on how long you take. I'll check up with Gwilym. When do you want it through by?'

'Easter, if possible. But that's enough of my problems. What's the latest situation about the Larna bill?'

'Not too bad,' I said.

I told him about the MacRodrick document and Rodrick's revelations about it. I tried, unsuccessfully I fear, not to let too much smugness show in my face.

'The examiners meet tomorrow. With any luck they will find it not to be hybrid straight away.'

Henry finished his drink and stood up.

'That's one piece of good news, at any rate. But do see if you can get them to issue their report before the business statement in the Commons on Thursday afternoon. That way, we'll be able to take the committee and remaining stages early next week.'

*   *   *

On Wednesday, the twenty-fourth of November, the examiners did indeed find the Larna Independence Bill not to be hybrid.

*   *   *

On Thursday the twenty-fifth, Catriona rang, after lunch our time, after breakfast her's.

'One interesting development out here,' she said, 'the police have been ferreting about among the bits of the car that Ranald MacRodrick was killed in and they're pretty certain now that it had been tampered with. They came across the near-side-front stub axle some twenty yards away from the rest of the wreckage, didn't like the look of it and sent it off to an accidents forensic laboratory. It seems that the wrong size hub-bearings had been fitted and that would have made them overheat, seize up after fifty miles or so, and sheer off the stub axle and the wheel with it – they reckon it had been done deliberately.'

'Then it *was* murder,' I said.

'Yes, and they've got a witness of a sort. A "fix it" job like that would have taken between three and four hours. The car had been in the garage for a major service a couple of days before and the mechanic, whom the proprietor swears to be totally reliable, came in an hour earlier than usual the next morning to finish off the job and surprised a European on his way out.'

'Malcolm?'

'Could be. He's known to be something of a motor-car freak and he was certainly out here at the time. Trouble is the mechanic has now clammed up completely, seems to have been got at in the meantime – threats to his family and all that – and they don't think he'll be prepared to give evidence until after the election and then only if the PPM don't get in. Can't blame him really. And the latest opinion-poll figures came out in the *Voice of Larna* this morning. Forty-nine to forty-one, the worst yet.'

I did a rapid mental calculation.

'Which still leaves ten per cent "don't knows". Hell!' I said.

'Never mind, Larna National Day's tomorrow week. There's a ceremony held round the Otter Stone in the replica of the clan-gathering ground out here to celebrate – it's the governor's big day – and the PPM have always boycotted it. The euphoria in the days leading up to it may well influence next Thursday's poll.'

'That's something. I'll drink to its success in Kilpatrick twelve-year-old malt. I'm getting quite a taste for it.'

'You must try Kilpatrick twelve-year-old rum,' Catriona said.

*   *   *

The business statement in the Commons that afternoon confirmed that the committee and remaining stages of the bill would take place next week on Tuesday the thirtieth.

*   *   *

'Why not Monday?' I asked Henry Chanter when I confronted him in the Commons lobby afterwards.

'Steady on, Derek, you're becoming paranoic, you know. The Consolidated Fund Bill's on Monday which takes all day. And I can't move that?'

'Why not?'

'Because if I did every single government department would run out of cash. That's why. And, if it's any consolation to you, Malcolm MacRodrick was absolutely livid when I insisted on taking the Larna bill as early as that.'

*　　*　　*

'I've got the Valley of Dreams Club on the line for you,' Penny Seymour's voice said in my earpiece that evening.

'The *what*?'

Penny repeated it.

'All right. You'd better put 'em on,' I said.

'Lord Thyrde? My name's Monique Fourier, I'm a friend of Catriona Campbell's. She's given me a message for you.'

Her voice was intriguingly husky.

'But . . . I was talking to her on the telephone only this morning,' I said.

'I know. She told me. No, this is something that is written and can only be delivered personally by hand. Could you come here at ten o'clock tonight? Valley of Dreams Club, Wesker Place, off Regent Street, you can't miss it.'

'I suppose so,' I said.

There was indeed no mistaking the place. It had *Valley of Dreams Club* scrawled across its entire frontage in sloping joined-up writing of a vivid pink neon. When I knocked at the door a little wooden flap was pulled aside and a pair of eyes peered through a grill at me in a manner redolent of vintage black-and-white B movies.

'Are you a member, sir?' It was an elaborately refined voice.

'No, Miss Fourier asked me to come here.'

The door was opened to show a bulky woman in a high-cut emerald-green satin evening dress, with a choker made of three parallel strings of large imitation pearls and silver-grey hair piled into a woven dome atop her head.

'Follow me, dear, if you please. Monique's expecting you,' she said.

Round a diminutive dance-floor were crammed dimly lit tables, their chairs upholstered in dark-red velvet. Some were already occupied by men, each with a hostess in attendance, but at one sat a lone figure engaged in eyeing speculatively the group of as yet unspoken-for girls who were filling in the time by chatting together. At the far end of the room, a six-piece all-girl band was playing muted rock.

Monique, as I had expected, was black. Her skin was darker than Catriona's but she reminded me very much of her. She didn't seem quite to fit in with the other girls – they were all of them pretty but she in a far less brassy way; she was wearing a simple classic-cut light-blue dress, the severity of its lines relieved by a single silver brooch in the form of a monogram, consisting of the letters M and F entwined.

When the old girl in green satin had left us, Monique patted the bench-type wall seat beside her invitingly.

'I'm afraid you're expected to order champagne,' she said, her tone was anxious. 'Do you mind?'

'Of course not.'

I beckoned over the girl who was hovering nearby for that purpose and ordered a bottle for her and a large Kilpatrick twelve-year-old malt whisky for me.

I poured out some champagne for her and picked up my glass of whisky.

'Sorry not to join you, but I don't like it,' I said.

Monique took a sip and made a face.

'Neither do I, really, but need's must. Look, Derek, it's not safe to talk here and I can't leave before midnight, but I thought we could go back to my flat then and I could give you the stuff I've got for you there.'

'If you don't mind . . . ?'

'Would you like a picture of yourself and the lady, sir?'

A tall girl in a miniskirt, fishnet tights and holding a camera had come up to our table.

'No, thank you,' I said.

'Come on, dear, there's no obligation, you know,' and she raised the camera to focus it on Monique and myself.

'I said "no thank-you",' I said and held the palm of my hand out flat towards the camera lens, then I turned to Monique with a warning glance and urgently shook my head.

She glared at the camera girl. 'Cut that out, Mary,' she said sharply. 'You heard the customer say "no".'

The girl's face took on a sulky expression but she lowered her camera and walked off.

I put my hand over Monique's.

'Thank you. Let's dance,' I said.

There were one or two couples on the floor and, as we joined them, the music changed to a sequence of thirties' slow foxtrots. Monique was a dream dancer, reacting to my every movement almost before I had made it. In the marginally brighter light coming from the band, I could see that she was indeed very pretty but she somehow missed being attractive. Perhaps it was in my mind only and arose from her being so like Catriona without actually being her. I remember thinking that her hair had an odd smell to it which I couldn't quite place.

We arrived back at our table some time later and I was pulling it out from the bench seat to let her in when, quite by chance, I glanced into the looking-glass with which the wall behind it was lined. I caught a brief glimpse of a long thin face with an expression of malicious glee on it peeping out at us from behind a pillar across the room behind me and then being withdrawn again, but not before I had unmistakably identified it as that of Rannie MacRodrick. I was equally certain that he was unaware that I had seen him.

I sat beside Monique in silence for a minute or two.

Obviously this whole thing was a ruse engineered at the instigation of Malcolm MacRodrick . . . and I had fallen for it. But what should I do now? I hadn't yet seen a male employee about the place, but they must have some form of chucker-out who could no doubt reverse the usual process and prevent me from leaving until whatever it was that they had in mind for me had taken place.

The only thing, I decided, was to go along with it for the moment and hope to make an escape on the way to her flat.

At midnight precisely we left and the green-satin lady called a taxi for us. On Monique's instructions I gave the driver an address off Primrose Hill. He was a thickset man who looked at me with an expression of intense disapproval, verging on disgust, which I must say rather surprised me . . . I had always found London cabbies to be more than usually broadminded about nocturnal peccadilloes in the past.

It was all a matter of timing now. I had already come to the conclusion that if I tried to leave the taxi in the middle of the journey, the girl would shout for help and accuse me of having interfered with her, which could be, to say the least, embarrassing. I waiting until the driver had to pull up at a set of traffic lights.

Then I took out my wallet, ostentatiously searched through it and tapped on the partition.

'Look, I seem to have run myself rather short of money. Do you take credit cards?'

The cab-driver didn't even turn his head.

'Don't know about that, mate.'

'What about this one?' I said, and I passed through to him a piece of plain white card of approximately the right size and shape on which I had managed to scribble a rough message while I was still in the night-club.

I think I am being set up. When the girl gets out can you be prepared to drive on quick, soon as I ask?

The driver held it out to his right, so as to be able to read it in the light of a street-lamp.

Then he turned back towards me, his face expressionless.

'That'll do nicely, sir. As they say,' he said.

As soon as we drew up outside Monique's address, I got out of the taxi, walked round to the near side, opened the door for her to get out and then started to close it again.

'Hold on,' I said, 'I think I've left my umbrella inside.'

I pulled the door open again, climbed in as though to reach over towards where I had been sitting and suddenly slammed the door shut behind me. At the same moment, without waiting for me to say anything, the cabby had the taxi in gear and we shot forward. Then the door of a black Mercedes, parked under a lamp-post some thirty yards ahead of us was thrown open, and I saw a figure that I almost immediately identified as Roddy MacRodrick jump out of it and stand in the middle of the road, both hands in the air – a camera with a formidable-looking flash attachment in one of them – in a vain attempt to stop us.

He managed to leap aside again to safety just in time.

The cab-driver was obviously enjoying the whole thing enormously.

'Knocked his camera out of his hand, didn't I?' he said. He looked round at me with raised eyebrows. 'Been to that Dream Valley Club before?'

'No,' I said.

'What was they after, sir? Blackmail?'

'No, I don't think I was going to be given the option of buying myself out of it. The object of the exercise was to discredit me. And they damned near succeeded.'

The cabby chuckled.

'You don't know the half of it, mate. The gaff's chock full of bleeding woopsies – blokes dressed up as women – even the old witch in the entrance hall. That "girl", as you call her, were one of 'em,' he said.

*　　*　　*

All this time, upstairs in the House of Commons standing committee, the government had been running into even worse trouble over the Ancillary Services Bill. Apparently, our whip on the bill had insisted that they sit that night beyond ten o'clock, and this had infuriated opposition members with trains and sleepers back to their constituencies to catch. Point-of-order after point-of-order had been raised right up to midnight and no progress at all had been made the whole day.

But I wasn't to hear about that until the Monday morning, when Gwilym Thomas just happened to mention it by the way.

CHAPTER ELEVEN

Monday, the twenty-ninth of November, eleven o'clock in the morning, eleven days to go . . . and that was counting today.

I sat at my desk, still shaken by the events of Thursday night. Not only by the highly embarrassing confrontation with a transvestite in his flat that I had only just been spared but also by what would have been its inevitable aftermath. I could visualise the headlines now. TOP TORY PEER SURPRISED IN GAY LOVE NEST. The possibilities were too awful to contemplate.

The telephone rang. It was Henry Chanter on the line. He came to the point straight away.

'Look, you're not going to like this,' he said. 'There's been another slight hiccough over the Independence of Larna Bill. You know that the committee and remaining stages were to have been taken in the Commons tomorrow, Tuesday.'

'*Were* to have been?'

'Well yes, we've had to postpone it for a week until Tuesday, the seventh of December.'

'*What!*'

'Now steady on, Derek, it's only for a week.'

'Didn't somebody once say that a week was a long time in politics,' I said bitterly. 'But for heaven's sake, why?'

'In the first place, the Labour Party have been pressing for more time so that they can organise a petition out in Larna . . . over the "access to this country after independence" issue. And petitions have always been taken very seriously in the standing orders of our House. But it's a combination of a number of things, really.'

'Such as?'

'Well, you know we've been running into even more trouble over the Ancillary Services Bill?'

'Yes. Gwilym's just been telling me.'

'We've enough on our hands over that, for the moment, and we can't have two major rows going on with the opposition at the same time. Then there's another thing. Malcolm MacRodrick got quite a lot of support from our own back-benchers over "access". If we tried to press on, and it came to a division, we might well lose it.'

'I suppose so.'

'Anyway, it's too late now. Malcolm's on his way out to Larna already and if we changed our minds again, at the last moment, we really would be accused of bad faith. Never mind, Derek, it still leaves us plenty of time; we'll do it on our heads.

'No it doesn't, it leaves us exactly three days.'

I heard Henry's chuckle in my earpiece.

'Three days is *quite* a long time in politics,' he said.

*   *   *

On Tuesday, it was my turn to go down to Henry's room in the Commons for our weekly meeting.

The last thing I wanted was to talk about the Larna bill – I didn't trust myself to do so with any degree of self-control in the circumstances.

'How are things going with Ancillary Services?' I said.

'Rather well, actually. The standing committee's been making a bit of progress at last. Got through quite a number of amendments during the course of the day.'

'That's good.'

But Henry Chanter looked worried.

'I'm not so sure,' he said. 'At the same time, Tug Wilson and his boys have been calling for a number of assurances from the government in relation to the code of practice applicable to the services to be privatised and the terms and conditions for their various staffs. And they want these to be presented at the next sitting of the committee, the day after tomorrow.'

'That seems reasonable.'

'Not *un*reasonable . . . on the face of it. The trouble is that it's not giving the government much time to produce the information they're asking for. If they're in earnest, we shouldn't have a lot of difficulty in persuading them to hang on for a bit, but they may just be setting up an excuse for further disruption.'

Henry took a long drink from his glass of whisky and water.

'Anyway, that's something we'll be finding out soon enough,' he said.

*   *   *

Catriona Campbell rang up late on Thursday afternoon. The results of the latest opinion poll had been published that morning. It was not the sort of news we'd been hoping for.

'Our forty-seven per cent to the PPM's forty-six with only seven per cent "don't knows",' she said. 'The LNP are still in the lead . . . by a whisker. That's something to be grateful for, I suppose.'

I must confess that it came as an enormous shock to me.

'But . . . why?' I said.

'You know Malcolm MacRodrick flew out here on Monday?'

'Yes, I heard about it at the time,' I said.

'Well, since then, he's been seen everywhere, doing everything. He hasn't said much, nothing to quote anyway, and keeping his neutrality as a Westminster shadow minister he hasn't even talked to Septicus as far as I know. But the *Voice of the People* has been running great spreads on him, every day.'

'Saying what, then?'

'Oh, how the illness of the present chief is to be regretted, but how lucky we are to have his brother out with us instead. You know the sort of thing. How much the island can expect from him once he becomes Chief of the Clan MacRodrick, making over land for the benefit of the ordinary people, all intelligent guesswork, of course, and photographs by the hundred.'

'And that's what's caused the change in the polls?'

'I would think so. And if his presence as mere heir apparent can achieve all this, just think what he'll be able to do once he becomes chief. Thank goodness we've got the Larna National Day tomorrow, that might still turn the tables a bit.'

'Will you be going to the ceremony, yourself?'

'Wild Septicuses wouldn't keep me away,' she said.

* * *

Gwilym Thomas came into my room as I put the receiver down.

'Well,' he said, 'the postponed committee and remaining stages of the Larna bill are safely down in the Commons business statement for next Tuesday, at any rate.' Then he noticed my expression. 'Something wrong, Chief Whip?'

I told him about the change in the Larna opinion poll.

'I shouldn't worry,' he said, 'these things can fluctuate considerably. And your opposite number in the Commons isn't having things too easy either. Ancillary Services is rearing its ugly head again.'

'What's happened now?'

'Well, when the standing committee met at ten this morning, the government hadn't been able to provide some assurances that the Labour members had been asking for but said that they wanted to maintain progress and would provide the information at some later stage.'

'Yes, Henry Chanter thought that might happen.'

'Well, Tug Wilson and his boys refused to accept this and bullied their whip on the bill into going to see his chief who in turn took it up with Mr Chanter. He maintained that the proceedings in a committee are a matter for the committee itself which should be allowed to make its own decisions. The Labour Chief Whip reported this back to his members on the committee – all very convoluted, I'm afraid – who said that this was totally unacceptable and formally announced that they would disrupt proceedings after ten pm and again prevent any further progress being made on the bill. In the meantime, apparently, they've gone over the head of their own Chief Whip and demanded a meeting with the Leader of the Opposition. And that's where the matter stands at the moment . . . watch this space.'

*　　*　　*

The week's postponement of the Independence of Larna Bill in the Commons had one advantage as far as I was concerned in that it had enabled me to catch up to a large extent on my paperwork as newly appointed acting Chief Whip. There was a considerable amount of this in any case, and as a lot of it was new to me, the following week seemed likely to be even more time-consuming and demanding. Taking all this into consideration, it was late into Friday afternoon before I managed to leave Westminster and drive down to Thyrde for the weekend.

When I reached Swiss Cottage, an *Evening Standard* placard on the pavement caught my eye: CARIBBEAN LEADER ASSASSINATED.

I knew instinctively, with a totally numbing certainty, that there was only one person that that could refer to. Somehow I pulled the car into the side of the road and went over and bought a copy. The lead story was short but devastating.

The much-loved first minister of Larna, the honourable Zechariah Hall, was shot and killed today by an unknown gunman, who later made his escape. This tragic event took place during the colony's annual National Day celebrations, held in some form of native meeting-place, the site of age-old tribal rites and still preserved in the very heart of the island's modern capital, Kilpatrick Town. The grand old man breathed his last on the sacred Otter Stone, a quaint survival from Larna's historic past.

I drove the rest of the way back to Thyrde House in a sense of total personal bereavement for the loss of someone who had instantly endeared himself to me, not only as a statesman but even more so as a man.

Tribal rites, sacred 'otter stone', quaint survival! How like the press to get it all wrong. And then I thought . . . perhaps they hadn't got it so very wrong after all.

*　　*　　*

I didn't manage to get through to Larna on the telephone until late on Saturday afternoon.

'Yes, Catriona Campbell, here. Who is it?'

She sounded totally devastated.

'Derek,' I said. 'I'm so terribly sorry. Would you rather not talk about it?'

'Bless you, no I'd like to. It was all so sudden and I was two or three feet away from him when it happened. The governor was absolutely splendid for once. ZH died in his arms.'

'Have they got the chap who did it?'

'No, and they probably never will. The police think it was a contract killing, Mafia probably. But we all know who's responsible.'

I heard her draw her breath in sharply. And then she went on.

'The leading members of the People's Progressive Movement were invited on to the terrace as usual and this time they all turned up. Septicus and four others.'

'Establishing their alibis?'

'That's right. And Septicus is making the most of it already. Do you know what the little toad's done today? Called publicly for a day of national mourning for "his dear friend and colleague, ZH", just as he knew we were about to announce one; it makes me want to vomit,' she said.

'What about the Larna National Party,' I said gently, 'when are you going to choose your new leader?'

'We've already done so.'

'Quick work!'

'Not really. We couldn't afford to hang about, in the circumstances. And, in any case, ZH nominated his successor in the moments before he died.'

'Who's he going to be?'

'It isn't a "he", it's a "she".' For the first time, I could detect in her voice just a suspicion of that throaty giggle of hers.

'Who, then?'

'Me,' Catriona said.

*　　*　　*

The content of the leading articles in the Sunday papers the next morning, while couched in their various distinctive styles, were otherwise almost identical.

They expressed horror at the manner of the killing and their praise for ZH as a statesman and regret for his loss at this of all times were unstinted. They showed surprised at the youth and relative obscurity of the woman who had been chosen to replace him and their good wishes as she embarked on such a mammoth task were genuine. They applauded Dr Septimus Baker for his magnanimity in taking the lead in giving due praise and honour to his fallen opponent.

Of this last, that under the byline of the editor of the *Sunday Times* was a representative specimen.

> Of course [he wrote] we would rather have seen Larna, with all her traditional ties with this country, remain as an independent monarchy, but, if this is not to be, which of us would not in his heart have a feeling of satisfaction and even pride that we had been able to pass on one of the best aspects of our own parliamentary democracy, that of respect and friendship between factions, even to an emerging leader determined to take his colony out of the Commonwealth fold.

On Monday the sixth of December there was a dramatic scene in the chamber of the House of Commons when, at half-past three in the afternoon, Albert Wainwright, the leader of Her Majesty's Opposition raised a point of order at the dispatch box. He called the attention of the House to the government's intransigence over its handling of the Ancillary Services Bill in standing committee upstairs. In this situation, he said, he was not prepared to continue with the 'usual channels' and wished to give notice that they would be broken off forthwith.

'Bit drastic, isn't it?' I said to Gwilym Thomas who was my informant. 'What's made him do that?'

I had the unworthy suspicion that he was getting some form of perverse pleasure out of the misfortunes that were being visited on his own opposite number in the Commons.

'Well, you remember the to-ing and fro-ing on Thursday? The shadow cabinet elections are due shortly and this is a time when all Labour front-bench spokesmen feel the need to demonstrate their muscle power. The Trade and Industry man's no exception and it seems he went with Tug Wilson to see the Leader of the Opposition this morning.'

'But I wouldn't have thought that Albert Wainright was the sort of chap to be jockeyed into panic action.'

'True enough,' Gwilym said, 'but remember the entire Labour Party regard the Ancillary Services Bill with particular loathing. They genuinely believe that they're suffering under an injustice in this particular case. And a move like this will be popular with the unions and the party as a whole and draw attention to the policy divide between the government and the opposition.'

'Well thank goodness it didn't happen over the Larna bill,' I said.

*   *   *

Tuesday morning. The seventh of December. Three days left.

Henry Chanter put his head round the door. It was his turn to come and see me at six that evening. I looked at my watch.

'Hey, you're seven hours early,' I said. 'Come in and sit down. And let me give you a drink, anyway.'

'Yes, I think I'd better. And give yourself one as well, while you're about it. You're going to need it,' he said.

'Whisky?'

I poured one out for each of us.

'Tell me the worst,' I said.

'Right then. Albert Wainwright went and saw Charles Fortescue this morning. The price set by the opposition for restoring the "usual channels" is a further delay in the Independence of Larna Bill.'

'Just like that?'

'No,' Henry said, 'not *just* like that. What they'd really like is for us to negotiate a far more leisurely timetable with them for the Ancillary Services Bill. But they realise that it may be difficult for us to give them that so what they're prepared to accept instead is enough of a delay in the Independence of Larna Bill *to write in safeguards over the right of access to this country for Larnacans after independence.*'

'In other words, you give in to us over Ancillary Services or we'll bugger up Larna. But that's blackmail,' I said.

'Not really, Derek. Look at from their point of view. It's mid-term between elections and they badly need a victory of some sort. You know what they think of the Ancillary Services Bill, they genuinely hate any form of immigration control and furthermore they refuse to believe that the Larna People's Progressive Movement are the out-and-out baddies that we know them to be.'

'I suppose so,' I said. 'Anyway, the Prime Minister turned Albert Wainwright's proposition down flat, of course?'

Henry said nothing. Then he slowly shook his head. I leapt to my feet.

'Now calm down, Derek. Ancillary Services *is* our flagship bill for the session and it's mid-term for us too, remember. If Charles Fortescue hadn't been prepared to negotiate, we'd in all probability have lost out not only over Larna but over Ancillary Services as well.'

'That's all very well,' I said. 'But I was persuaded into it against my better judgement, didn't even know where Larna was when this whole thing started, and now, having been sweating my guts out over it all these weeks, it suddenly seems to have paled into insignificance compared to some piffling little privatisation measure. I wish to God that Tom Lavenham was still around.'

Henry Chanter shook his head again.

'I doubt if even Tom would have been able to turn things round now,' he said.

I subsided slowly into my chair again.

'Something has just occurred to my nasty suspicious little mind,' I said. 'Do you think that this whole row over Ancillary Services might be nothing but a ploy on Tug Wilson's part, prompted by Malcolm MacRodrick of course, with the sole purpose of delaying the Independence of Larna Bill?'

Henry sat in silence, considering the matter for quite some time.

Then, 'You know . . . you might just be right at that.'

I stood up again, more slowly. Henry followed my example.

'Even so,' he said, 'I doubt if there's anything that can be done about it now. You're welcome to try, of course; it's too late to change back the business in the Commons this afternoon, but there's still Wednesday and Thursday left. I wish you luck,' he said.

*　　*　　*

There was still Wednesday and Thursday left and I had a two-pronged attack open to me. Charles Fortescue, the Prime Minister, through Tony Dysart, my own boss as Leader of the House of Lords who had already offered to do everything he could, and Albert Wainwright, Leader of the Opposition, through Geoffrey Robertson. I sought out Geoffrey first who showed cautious optimism.

'Aye,' he said, 'maybe what influence I have could just sway things and now if ever's the time to try it. Albert's not the man to be unreasonable over things that really matter. I'll sound him out this afternoon.'

Tony Dysart was not so hopeful.

'I'll do what I can, of course. But Charles is in a difficult position at the moment, remember. Don't expect too much,' he said.

Geoffrey came to the House of Lords that afternoon. I saw him standing at the bar of the house as question time was drawing to a close and went out to meet him. As I came up to him it was clear from his whole demeanour that he had not been successful.

'I'm very sorry,' he said. 'Albert would have liked to have helped but the whole party is in such a state at the moment that he just didn't dare to. He's a good man, so are most of our people, but they're all under the spell of Mr Malcolm MacRodrick; they *need* to believe in him and I just can't shake them.' He paused. 'I'll tell you one thing, though, Derek. The word is that our Malcolm's now committed himself to such an extent financially, not only on himself becoming clan chief but also on the PPM gaining power in Larna, that if either one of them should go sour on him, he's a ruined man,' he said.

It was some consolation, I supposed, but in the circumstances not much of one.

I had a message later in the afternoon to go to the Lord Privy Seal's room.

Tony Dysart look worried but, with him, that was nothing to go by.

'I did my best, but he feels he can't go back on his agreement with the opposition now. Apparently it was Percival Strickland who blew it and it's him we have to blame for the PM's original decision.'

Very little said or done by that odious little man could have surprised me by this time, but I found it hard to credit even him with such monumental irresponsibility.

'How so?'

'Well, Charles consulted him before replying to Albert Wainwright and it seems Percy gave it as his considered opinion that with the death of its leader, Zechariah Hall, the advantages to us of the Larna National Party over the People's Progressive Movement had largely disappeared and that the result of the elections had lost their significance.'

'Stupid, pompous little prat!' I said.

'I'm inclined to agree with you, but that's how it is, I'm afraid.'

'Look, Tony,' I said, 'I remember Tom telling me that, as Chief Whip of the Lords, he had the right of instant access to the Prime Minister. Do you think that that applies to me too, now that I'm acting for him?'

'I'm sure it does.'

'Well, I don't want you to think I'm going over your head, but would you have any objection if I were to invoke it now?'

'Not the slightest. And the best of luck to you,' he said.

*   *   *

The Prime Minister listened patiently and with the rapt attention that had made him universally and rightly popular.

Then, 'I'm sorry, Derek, I really am. But it's just too late,' Charles Fortescue said.

*   *   *

Coming out of the Prime Minister's room, and turning to the right for the quickest way back to the House of Lords, the one man of all people I ran into was Malcolm MacRodrick. He glanced down the corridor from which I was emerging. It was all too obvious where I had been. He looked back at my face. My lack of success was all too obvious from my expression.

'Hard luck, old boy. Can't win 'em all,' he said.

I stormed off back to my room in a state of cold fury and rang Jack Singleton. There was nothing I could do to get back at Malcolm, but I could at least take it out on Her Majesty's Principal Secretary of State for Foreign and Commonwealth Affairs, bloody Percy Strickland, who had been his unwitting tool. It wouldn't do any good but it would go a certain way towards relieving my own feelings.

Jack answered the telephone himself and I told him what I wanted.

His voice was grim.

'I'll fix that, be glad to,' he said. 'I happen to know that he's got a slot first thing after cabinet tomorrow. Only wish I could be there to see it myself.'

'Won't you? Why not?'

'Sent in my resignation this morning. And I made it clear that I won't be persuaded out of it. Only reason you've caught me now is I've come in to pick up my things,' he said.

*   *   *

Percy Strickland looked up from his desk coldly.

'Well?' he said.

The coldness in his voice as well as his whole manner suggested that it was an impertinence of someone as insignificant as myself to take up the valuable time of a senior cabinet minister and, in particular, one of such eminence as himself.

'It's good of you to spare the time to see me, Foreign Secretary,' I said. 'I wanted to have a word about the Independence of Larna Bill.'

'What of it?'

'I understand that the advice you gave to the Prime Minister earlier in the week was this. That since the assassination of Zechariah Hall, there was no longer much to choose between the Larna National Party and the People's Progressive Movement and that effectively the urgency for the passage of the Larna bill no longer existed. Is this true?'

'I may have said something to that effect . . . if it's any business of yours.'

'My taking an interest myself in the situation in Larna in the first place was at the personal request of the Prime Minister,' I said.

'Oh.' He subsided slightly. 'Well, be that as it may. What chance would a slip of a girl have against a hardened political campaigner like Dr Septimus Baker?'

'Have you met Miss Campbell?'

'No.'

'Well, I have,' I said. 'And do you realise that in the few moments between being hit by the assassin's bullet and actually dying, ZH took it on himself to name Catriona Campbell to the Governor of Larna as his chosen successor.'

'The ramblings of a dying man.' Percy was starting to bluster now.

'And do you realise that, purely as a result of the advice that you took it on yourself to give to the Prime Minister, the elections in Larna will now not take place until March, by which time Rodrick MacRodrick will almost certainly be dead, his brother Malcolm will be chief and owing to his influence the PPM will sweep in at the polls, take Larna out of the Commonwealth and use the island for their own personal gain, with drug-running, money-laundering and every other kind of undesirable practice, and three hundred years of outstanding colonial rule will have been thrown away merely for the sake of appeasing the opposition?'

I realised as I said it that I was shamefully plagiarising Tom Lavenham, but I *was*, after all, acting in his place.

'I owed a duty to my cabinet colleagues.'

'But what about the duty you owed to the people of Larna?'

Percy Strickland made a last effort. He visibly puffed up like a pregnant toad.

'And who do you think you are, young man, to lecture me about my duty?'

He had a point there. My coming to see him at all was pure self-indulgence on my part. But that did nothing to excuse his own behaviour.

'Somebody had to,' I said.

*   *   *

I rang up Catriona in Larna and confessed to her the full awful sequence of disasters. She listened without a word. Then . . .

'Don't blame yourself, Derek,' she gave that delightful throaty little giggle, 'because that makes the pair of us. The latest opinion poll was published out here this morning. We're down to forty-five per cent to the PPM's forty-seven, a swing of fourteen per cent since June that comes to, for the first time they're ahead – by two points.'

*   *   *

There was only one possible course of action left to me. If, even at this late hour, I could persuade Black Rod and he in turn could persuade Rodrick to name him as his successor, with his influence as clan chief behind Catriona she might just make it. It was still far from certain as to the side on which his loyalty lay but he couldn't be worse than Malcolm and, with his position in the Royal Household, he was someone on whom a certain amount of pressure could be brought to bear. And he *had* been born out in the Caribbean Larna.

In the event my interview with Alastair MacRodrick was all too short.

'I'm afraid I must stop you there, Derek. I appreciate everything you've been saying, but the answer's still "no". And, in any case, it's too late. I've just had a telephone call from the castle to say that Rodrick's dying. I think you and I should fly up there tonight.'

CHAPTER TWELVE

My first impression of the laird's bedroom was of dim standard lamps and huge mahogany furniture. Gusts of rain were slapping the window panes in great gobs from the blackness of the world outside. Dougal MacRodrick, immaculate in doublet and kilt, stood protectively on one side of the great white-covered bedstead; Amanda the whippet, bolt upright in her tartan dog-bed, her eyes fixed on her master, sat on the other – she as aware as I that a great spirit was in the process of leaving the world.

Dougalina, massive in streaming yellow oilskins and matching sou'wester on the quayside, had met Black Rod and myself off the laird's own boat which had been sent to collect us from Oban. His decline, she told us, had started to accelerate from the moment that he had been told of the assassination of his old friend, ZH. Coming on top of the deaths of his wife and Ranald, their only child, it had been just one thing too many for him to bear.

I had rung up Catriona from the airport to tell her about Rodrick and she had sounded every bit as devastated as I.

The MacRodrick's skin was stretched tautly over his gaunt cheekbones and had a strange, almost translucent, quality to it. He was lying back in a long-sleeved white nightgown, his frail hands, on which the blue veins stood out, above the covers, one clutching a much thumbed Bible bound in tattered black leather. I went over and gently took the other in my own.

The whippet beside me gave a low warning growl.

The laird opened his eyes.

'Steady . . . Amanda . . . old girl.'

It was barely audible.

Then he looked at me. 'Good of you . . . to come . . . Derek,' he said. 'I'd like you to have Amanda . . . when I'm gone . . . will you take her?'

'I'd like that quite enormously,' I said.

I had for long had a deep feeling of guilt over having deceived my way into the friendship of this good old man and I was suddenly struck with the conviction that, unless I confessed to him and sought what absolution might be forthcoming before it was too late, I would never forgive myself for the rest of my life.

'Look,' I said, 'there's something I've got to tell you, sir.'

A ghost of the old twinkle came into his sunken eyes and he shook his head.

'Don't worry, Derek, I know what you're going to say.' His voice too was marginally stronger now. 'What sort of a fool do you take me for? You're just like your father, old Derry Mallicent was never much good at any kind of conspiracy either. Harumph! Trouble is, you're too darned honest, the pair of you. After all, you were out to help my Larna . . . and I can't object to that.'

The relief was almost overwhelming.

'Thank you,' I said.

After a bit . . .

'It will be all right, you know . . . about the succession . . . and Larna.'

His voice had sunk again to little more than a whisper.

'I'm sure it will.'

I knew of course that the poor old boy had got it wrong, but it would be pointless, not to mention unkind, to disillusion him now.

'I'll be able to give news of you to old Derry . . . he'll be proud of you.'

There was another pause, very long this time.

Then suddenly The MacRodrick's head fell to one side. Dougal reached forward and put a hand to his wrist.

He turned to me.

'Aye,' he said. 'That's him, m'lord.'

And, at the same moment, the whippet put her nose up in the air and emitted a long, low, heart-rending howl.

I stroked her poor sad head, went round and put a hand on the head stalker's shoulder . . . and left them to mourn their dead.

Some time later, I was sitting in the library with the door open, staring at the fire. Almost subconsciously, I became aware of a soft pattering sound coming down the passage. Then I felt a cold damp nose insinuating itself into my hand.

*   *   *

Monday the thirteenth of December, the day fixed at remarkably short notice for the installation of the new clan chief, was clear, bright and chilly. Thursday night's storm had kept up throughout the rest of the weekend, as though even the elements were determined to join in the universal mourning for The Laird of Larna. Today, however, there was that marvellous light that very often follows particularly foul weather conditions, every detail and colour variation in the far distant hills of the mainland on the one side and the nearer summit of *Ben na h Iolaire*, the hill of the eagle, on the other being etched out sharply against the cold pale blue of the sky.

The clan-gathering ground itself presented a sight only to be seen once in a generation but one that must have remained virtually unchanged over many centuries. From a very early hour, all the men of the island had been converging on the castle in full highland dress. Caledonian Macbrayne had laid on a special boat from Oban that had arrived at Kilpatrick Quay at ten o'clock that morning.

I had been found a place on a platform erected for the press and television crews at the far end of the arena, probably the only innovation of recent times. To my right front immediately below the terrace and lining that side of the low wall beyond which lay the sheer drop to the sea, was a high dais on which, in three tiers of gilded chairs, sat those senior members of the Clan MacRodrick who had no active part in the ceremony. At the far end of the front tier, the only man not in highland dress and there no doubt as the personal guest of the clan chief elect, I could see Dr Septimus Baker, wearing the same paramilitary-type grey tunic and trousers that he had worn at that traumatic dinner on the second night of my last visit to the castle. Next to him sat the president of the American Clan Society, John J. MacRodrick Junior, at this distance his rather bilious version of the clan tartan being indistinguishable from that of his neighbours, and on my side of him, giggling and making little pushing movements at each other, Roddy and Rannie, a single eagle feather in the bonnet of each.

In the body of the gathering ground, every inch of the rest of the space encircled by the low wall and the terrace below the south face of the castle was packed with the lesser members of the clan, standing shoulder to shoulder, each dressed in the MacRoderick tartan, predominately green in colour but which I by now knew to be surmounted with the odd blue square enclosed by bars of black, the whole interlaced both horizontally and vertically with thin white single lines alternating with double lines of red. Every man of them had a bunch of the grey-green grasslike leaves of the clan badge in his bonnet which, as sea-buckthorn is deciduous, I reckoned must have been dried and carefully preserved for any major clan occasion such as this that might happen to take place in the winter months. The entire gathering ground was alive with a medley of excited, laughing, chattering voices and gesticulating hands and arms for, in spite of the inherent sadness of the occasion, the late chief having been loved as much, and perhaps more than many of his predecessors, this was something to be remembered, cherished and passed on to child and grandchild by each of those present, for the rest of their lives.

Above and beyond the still empty terrace the flag at half-mast billowed in the stiff breeze around its pole, sunlit on the topmost pinnacle. Ten foot square, Dougal had told me, it was the personal banner of The MacRodrick, now lying in state in the great hall of the castle. Six lymphads, ancient boats, in black silhouetted on gold, sails furled, oars in action, arranged in two vertical columns of three, each pair rowing away from each other to the west and to the east respectively, to symbolise the sea traffic between this and the other Larna.

Rather to my surprise, and search though I might, I found that the imposing figure of the head stalker, Dougal MacRodrick, was nowhere to be seen.

Suddenly, there was a stirring among the crowd, a lowering of voices and a shift of the general attention towards one particular point. I looked in that direction myself and saw that a door in the castle wall that I had not noticed before, to the seaward end of the terrace, had opened and a figure emerged. It was Malcolm MacRodrick, magnificent in doublet, plaid, kilt and sporran, with lace at throat and wrists and three eagle feathers sprouting from the sea buckthorn on the bonnet that dangled from his left hand.

The ceremonial broadsword had yet to be added but, apart from that, he presented an identical image to that in the portrait of Ranald, Rodrick's great-grandfather, Dougal's great-great-grandfather, that hung in the castle hall.

He strutted over to the front of the terrace and stooped to give a proprietorial pat to the Otter Stone.

Then he straightened up to his full height again, put the bonnet on his head and stood there, hands on hips, surveying the crowd. The little doctor, Septimus Baker, was clapping his hands above his head. Malcolm waved at him and sporadic cheering broke out among the rest of the dignitaries on the dais but I noticed that it was not taken up in the body of the gathering ground.

At that moment, Malcolm caught sight of me over the heads of his fellow clansmen and with a sweep of his feathered bonnet gave me a low derisive bow. I looked away quickly only to have my gaze fall on John J. MacRodrick and Septicus, leaning towards each other and pointing in my direction – I couldn't hear them, of course, but it was easy enough to conjure up in my imagination the amplified boom of the one's laughter and the infuriating high-pitched little giggle of the other. It was silly of me, I suppose, but, with all Malcolm's other iniquities, I found this final act of gloating on the very threshold of his triumph hardest of all to bear.

I glanced down at my watch. It was twenty to twelve. The installation ceremony was timed to start sharp at noon.

Then, as though prompted by the same thought, I saw Malcolm MacRodrick turn and walk back to his little door and through it into the castle again.

Malcolm had won, damn him, every step of the way.

To be fair to him, he had also gambled quite a lot too. He had risked the loss of what promised to be an outstanding political career, but that would have been the least of his worries. He would have faced financial ruin certainly, imprisonment even, for whatever complicity he might have had in the murder of his nephew and possibly that of ZH as well. Whether he won or lost the gamble, all hung on whether or not he was successful in acquiring the chiefship – the People's Progressive Movement consequently gaining power out in Larna, everything that he might expect to gain in reward from the new regime, not least his own immunity from prosecution – and it was the culmination of all this that he had been striving for that we were about to witness now.

At five minutes to twelve there was another stirring of interest among the crowd, another silencing of chatter and shift of attention. Again I followed the line of the general gaze and this time a figure came through the small archway to my left front that led from the castle courtyard and again it was Malcolm. But not the Malcolm of a quarter of an hour ago.

He had lost all his air of self assurance, his doublet and kilt seemed to hang about him, his bonnet awry on his head had lost two of its eagle feathers. He shambled across to the dais and gestured to Septicus and John J. to shift up and make room for him in the line of chairs. They and his two boys leant anxiously towards him and seemed to be asking him questions which he waved impatiently away.

In a state of total perplexity, shared I was certain by every other man present, I stood and watched.

At twelve noon to the second, a single trumpeter appeared at the foot of the flagpole, raised his horn to his lips and blew. The clan dignitaries on the dais rose to their feet. The clansmen massed in the body of the gathering ground drew themselves up and stood rock still. Then, softly at first from the direction of the castle courtyard, and swelling as it drew nearer, came the sound of an air from the bagpipes that I recognised, having heard it twice before, as 'The MacRodricks' Salute to Larna', the march of the Clan MacRodrick. In a moment or two, the three pipers themselves, in single file and some five paces apart, appeared one after another through the small archway, the one in the lead having the unmistakeable rolling lope of Dougal MacRodrick. Once through, they turned left and up the flight of stone steps that led to the terrace.

These were followed, again some five paces behind, by the standard bearer, his standard appearing first, dipped so as to clear the archway, and once raised again on the near side proving to be a scaled-down replica of that which was still fluttering at half-mast on the castle top, with its six black lymphads standing out in the sunshine against their ground of sea blue.

The next to appear bore a large parchment scroll in his right hand, he no doubt being the clan bard as I remembered from Malcolm's vivid description from some seven weeks before of the ceremony which was being enacted before me now.

Dougal and his two fellow pipers, once having reached the centre of the castle wall, had halted, turned with their backs to it and were still beating time with their feet as the procession continued to appear.

The tension which had been building up since Malcolm MacRodrick's hasty reappearance was almost unbearable now. All eyes were on the small archway. This time it was the Gentleman Usher of the Black Rod who appeared, no stranger to ceremonial he, but in full highland dress more imposing than I had ever seen him before, bearing in his right hand a long white-painted wooden staff, in his left a belt holding its sheathed claymore.

There was an audible release of breath from all around me; he was clearly well known to every clansmen there. Then I noticed, probably at the same time as everyone else present, that his bonnet held only two eagle's feathers and his role must be that of the senior elder of the clan. The new chief was yet to come.

Alastair MacRodrick had reached the Otter Stone in the centre of the terrace and he too turned and stood behind it with the standard bearer on one side of him and the clan bard on the other.

As the pipe music continued, the attention of the entire gathering ground was again rivetted on the small archway.

Then, in an atmosphere charged as with static electricity, we watched as the new Chief of the Clan MacRodrick came through it, turned to the left and, in perfect time with the beat, ascended the flight of steps, marched along the terrace and came to a halt directly across the Otter Stone from Alastair MacRodrick.

Catriona Campbell! Apart from the three eagle feathers rising proudly from the badge of sea-buckthorn on her bonnet, she had on what looked like a short velvet jacket over a white polo-neck sweater with a skirt of MacRodrick tartan that came down just below her knees and a pair of black stockings or tights. Yet, in spite of what had clearly been a hurried improvisation and in sharp contrast to the former gorgeousness of Malcolm, her sheer presence was such that she seemed to dominate the entire arena.

Then, as the pipe music ceased, with an inclination of her neck she bowed her head to the distinguished elder of her clan.

Every person present, even the members of the press beside me, was transfixed as though cast in bronze.

Still we watched, as Black Rod handed the white wand that he had been holding to the clan bard beside him. Reaching forward with both hands, he buckled the belt, hung with the ceremonial broadsword in its scabbard, round Catriona's slim waist. Then he took her left hand, received the wand back from the clan bard and placing its butt on the ground by her feet, arranged her fingers gently around it at a point two-thirds of the way up.

Finally, he took her right hand in his, held it high in the air, and turning towards the main body of the gathering ground, spoke in a strong clear voice, while far above him the single trumpeter, silhouetted against the brilliant blue of the sky, began to raise the chief's personal standard slowly and steadily to the top of its mast.

'Clan MacRodrick, I here present unto you Catriona MacRodrick of MacRodrick, the undoubted Chief of this Clan,' there was an infinitesimal pause as he turned in the direction of the dais in order to address the next words specifically to the senior members of the clan, 'inheritor thereof by the Laws of God and Man,' again a pause and back to the main body again, 'who is willing to accept the chiefship.'

There followed an unquantifiable interval of utter silence. Looking back on it, it seems to me now that just for those few brief moments hushed too were the sound of the waves crashing on the rocks below on the one side of us and the roar of the river in full spate on the other. Even time held its breath.

Then, starting deepthroated among the dignitaries on the dais, taken up by the massed clansmen in the body of the gathering ground, rising to a crescendo, rolling and reverberating throughout that historic amphitheatre, ascending finally the hills of the island until it reached the very peak of Ben na h Iolaire there to rouse wonderment in the brain of the eagle himself, came Clan MacRodrick's reply.

'GOD BLESS OUR CHIEF AND US FOR HER CAUSE.'

EPILOGUE

Late that night, lying in my usual room at the castle with the lights out, I thought through the events of the remainder of the day.

The rest of the installation ceremony I found more difficult to follow. But it had ended with an address from Catriona, in which she pledged herself to take her duties as Chief of the Clan seriously and, by returning to Scotland as often as her political duties allowed, seek to reinforce the already strong ties between the two Larnas. And when she finished with a passage of what I was later assured to be near-perfect Gaelic, the roar of approbation showed that she had won over the hearts of her fellow clansmen completely.

Malcolm, Septicus, John J. and the two boys, Roddy and Rannie, had sat through it all as though they were in a daze.

Later in the day, Black Rod had sought me out in the library.

'I think that you, of all people, deserve an explanation, Derek.'

'Well, I must confess, I had been wondering,' I said.

Alastair MacRodrick smiled.

'It all goes back quite some time. Devoted as my cousin Rodrick and his wife were to one another, she never seemed to be comfortable in the Caribbean. Perhaps she had some premonition that something was going to happen to her adored son on the island but, whatever it was, after the first few years of their marriage on his frequent visits he always went out to Larna alone.'

'Yes, I think I've heard that before somewhere,' I said.

'He had a very beautiful Larnacan housekeeper out there, called Rebecca Campbell, and in due course the inevitable happened and Catriona was born. Well, when his son, Ranald, was killed in that motor crash, Rodrick never had any doubt that it was murder and he was determined that whoever was responsible shouldn't profit by it. And, when Rodrick's wife died soon after the funeral, the means became available to him. After a decent interval, just after you first came up here in fact, he went out to Larna and, with Dougal and ZH as the sole witnesses, married Rebecca Campbell. That was the real reason for his last visit to the island.'

185

'Thereby legitimising Catriona and, under Scottish Law, making her the natural heir to the chiefship? But . . . hey, wait a minute . . . Rodrick was long married at the time Catriona was born!'

Alastair shook his head.

'That doesn't matter. As you say, the Common Law of Scotland has always allowed those legitimated by subsequent marriage to succeed to dignities, titles of honour and armorial bearings. This was widened by the Legitimation (Scotland) Act, 1968, to include all legitimised persons, "whether the illegitimacy resulted from adulterine or non-adulterine bastardy", and the chiefship of a clan comes under "armorial bearings".'

'I see.'

'And you already know the effect that just *being* the Chief of the Clan MacRodrick has out on the island; imagine the combination of that with being the leader of the still highly respected ruling party. The elections will be a foregone conclusion. I doubt if Septimus Baker and the PPM will even try.'

I nodded.

I knew from my own experience that of that there could be no doubt at all.

'But the absolutely vital thing was that nobody should know about Rodrick's remarriage and Catriona's consequent legitimation. Otherwise, with two murders having taken place already, she herself would have been in the greatest of danger. We didn't think it safe even to tell her about that, although she's always known she was Rodrick's daughter, of course.'

'But won't she be in just as much danger now?' I said.

'No. At my suggestion, Catriona has written to Lord Lyon, King of Arms, naming me as her successor in the event of her early death, and failing me, my two sons, thereby bypassing Malcolm and giving her reasons for doing so. So, if anything were to happen to her, it would only serve to add credence to those reasons.'

'And does Malcolm know that?'

Alastair MacRodrick's face took on an air of total contentment.

'He does since this morning. I took great pleasure in telling him that myself,' he said.

Catriona had been so tied up with clan business all day that I had only seen her once, briefly, in a passage; she had taken my hand, kissed me on the cheek and thanked me, before being bustled away.

Thanked me!

Whatever for, I thought rather bitterly. Rodrick and his cousin Alastair had already had the whole thing sewn up between them, just as they'd always assured me they had, and my own efforts had achieved nothing – unless you count making things a little bit more difficult for Malcolm MacRodrick, which I supposed could be regarded as an end in itself. And then I was cheered up by the recollection that it was just as well because, if it *had* been left to me, Malcolm would have had it all his own way.

Perhaps, I thought, I'd get another chance of seeing Catriona tomorrow. The trouble was, I had to leave immediately after Rodrick's funeral. And that was at eleven o'clock in the morning!

Patches of moonlight came and went on the walls of my room as the clouds scudded by in the sky outside.

All this time, the whippet, Amanda, had been curled up in a tight ball in her tartan-covered dog-basket between my bed and the window and suddenly I heard her rouse herself and sit bolt upright, tense and alert, listening to something.

Then I too heard it, the sound of footsteps approaching along the corridor outside. There was a gentle tap on the door. The handle turned and the door opened almost imperceptibly.

'Derek . . .' a tentative whisper, '. . . are you awake? It's me, Catriona. Can I come in?'

The door opened more widely and then shut again.

A slim shape was just discernable as the footsteps approached the bed.

A slight shiver.

'It's cold out here.'

I folded the edge of the bedclothes back invitingly.

There was a pause.

Then the sound of a garment slipping to the floor.

The figure, more defined now, leaned over me. I could feel the warmth of her soft breath as she lowered her face to mine. Then . . .

'Move over, you selfish old racist,' she said.

And after that we neither of us had time to say anything very much.

The MacRodrick put her cool slim arms round my neck and, as she hugged herself up to me, I could feel her firm, lithe body start to shiver within the velvet of her skin. The next twenty minutes produced versatility such as I had never yet even dreamed of. It bore some affinity to the solving of a Chinese puzzle, but with the difference that the achieving of more entanglement and convolution rather than less was the object of this particular exercise. The changing patterns in black and white caused by the clouds moving against the moon outside on the walls of the bedroom, were finding their reflection between the sheets that surrounded us. And all the desires that had been building up in me over the weeks became magnified and reduplicated until, with a total cohesion and final unimprovable culmination, they found their expression at last.

For a long time we lay together in contented silence.

Then, 'Mac Ruaraidh Mor,' I murmured softly.

Catriona sprang apart from me as though the words had deafened her.

'Come off it, Derek. I've been having trouble enough getting used to that all day, without you starting.'

'That's all very well,' I said, 'but Catriona's a bit of a mouthful to have to use at moments like this.'

'Well . . . I have got another name. It's my first actually, the one I used all the time I was growing up. But I don't know whether you'd get on with that any better.'

'Try me.'

A stray moonbeam caught the glint of white in the grin on Catriona's adorable, dark honey-coloured, face.

'Rodrickina. After my father. My friends call me Rod,' she said.